EVA CHASE

Wanton Wonderland

The Looking-Glass Curse
Book 3

Wanton Wonderland

Book 3 in the Looking-Glass Curse trilogy

First Digital Edition, 2019

Cover design: Sly Fox Cover Designs

Ebook ISBN: 978-1-989096-32-1

Paperback ISBN: 978-1-989096-33-8

 Created with Vellum

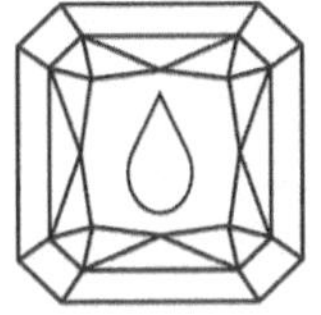

Lyssa

My eyes fluttered open to bright lights and white walls, and my first thought was that I'd somehow fallen asleep in the White Knight's office in his high Tower apartment. The smells weren't right, though: crisp and plastic-y with a hint of chemical cleaner. Neither were the sounds: a steady electronic beeping filtering through a wall and the murmur of the TV set mounted across from me.

I shifted to sit up on the padded surface I'd been lying on, and a thin blanket slipped down my chest. Over the coarse blue fabric of a hospital gown. An IV line slid against my arm. A dull ache spread through my torso and limbs and up the back of my neck to gnaw at my skull.

"Lyssa!" my mother said with a sharp intake of breath. She tipped forward in her chair where she'd been sitting next to my bed to grab my hand. "Honey, are you really awake? Can you answer me?"

"Mom?" I said, bewildered. Her graying blonde hair hung limp around her thin face as if she hadn't washed it in a few days, and her light brown eyes glinted with a liquid shine that was more than just the reflection on her glasses. "Of course I'm awake. What's going on?"

I was in a hospital room, obviously. My pulse stuttered with the memory of the dark wet night I'd fallen into when Theo had sent me through the mirror from Wonderland, the horn and the glare of headlights bearing down on me. I couldn't remember anything after that. How far from my Otherland home had I landed?

"Oh, sweetheart." Mom gave me a careful hug, as if she was afraid the embrace might hurt me. "You were hit by a truck on the highway just a couple miles outside the city. Thankfully the driver called in the accident, and the paramedics rushed you to the hospital right away."

This was my local hospital then. Even though I hadn't been thinking about any specific place in this world when I'd come through the mirror, I'd managed to end up close to familiar ground.

I let out a breath, and my ribs twinged. For being hit by a truck, I didn't feel *that* bad. My arms looked pale but unmarked other than a few pink splotches and the IV. My legs moved beneath the blanket when I tested them. A brace was wrapped around my left wrist, but otherwise I didn't seem to have any bandages. It was actually kind of weird.

"I guess I got really lucky," I said.

"You did," Mom agreed. "Not that I could tell when they first called me in. You were bruised and scraped all over, and they were sure something had to be broken… The doctor said it's incredible you survived. They think that strange shirt you had on must have protected most of the critical areas."

She gestured toward the other side of the room. My vest of armor, made of flexible strands of Wonderland metal woven together with an arc of five rubies beneath the neckline, rested against the bedside table. The impact of the accident hadn't even bent it out of shape or cracked any of the gems. Relief washed over me, followed by a smack of cold as the rest of what Mom had said sunk in.

"When they called you in," I repeated. I couldn't see anything more than a hint of bruises and scrapes on me now. "How long have I been here? I don't remember anything."

"You've been going in and out of consciousness," Mom said, a tremor running through her voice. "And even when you seemed awake before, you were so dazed you couldn't say anything or really do anything. You took a blow to the head—they fixed everything they could, but with the possible brain injury, they weren't completely sure you'd be yourself again—"

She cut herself off with a swallowed sob. "I was so scared for you, Lyssa. I've been here every day, talking to you, trying to help bring you back…"

A lump rose in my throat at her distress. The time she was talking about was a total blank for me. She must have been so freaked out. Even when my life was going well, Mom fussed over the possible catastrophes I might encounter all the time—now she was *never* going to believe me when I told her she didn't have to worry about me.

At the same time, panic dug even deeper. "How many days? How long has it been?"

"Almost four weeks," Mom said hoarsely.

Four weeks. Oh, God. I didn't know how much time had passed in Wonderland while I was laid up here, but that was definitely longer than I'd wanted to be gone.

I hadn't wanted to leave at all. Theo had brought me to the mirror to try to save me, but I'd rather have stayed and kept fighting, however I could. We'd only just freed the Queen of Hearts' prisoners. Who knew what she'd have done to Wonderland's people next?

Theo had revealed himself as her son, Prince Jack, assumed murdered for decades. He'd said he was going to challenge her, force her to change or give up her rule—clear a path for *my* rule as the Red Queen and the rightful heir to the throne. He'd said he would come for me when he succeeded. Maybe he had.

The only way he could have found his way to me here was by using the sketch of Aunt Alicia's house that Hatter had. But I wouldn't have been at the house or anywhere nearby. He'd have had to return to Wonderland empty-handed, not knowing where I'd gone or why.

Either everyone I cared about back in Wonderland was struggling to survive the Queen's fury without me, or they'd been left with an empty throne. They'd think I'd abandoned them. I had to get back soon—now.

"I had a ring," I said tentatively. "I was wearing it like a pendant. Do you know what happened to that?"

Had the vest managed to protect my proof that I was the Red Queen's heir too?

"Oh. Yes. They gave that to me. I think I have it…" Mom dug into her purse with her free hand and produced a plastic baggy that held the chain with the gold ring, its large ruby setting still encased in a shell of filigree. I had to restrain myself from snatching it from her.

"Was it your grand-aunt's?" she asked. "I've never seen it before."

"Yeah," I said. "Aunt Alicia left it for me. Can I…?"

I reached out, and she gave the baggy to me. Her fingers tightened around my other hand. "Do you remember what you were doing out there by the highway, sweetheart?" she asked. "It was an empty stretch—no stores or houses nearby, and it was pretty late at night."

Even if there had been buildings nearby or it'd been earlier in the day, I shouldn't have gone wandering right onto the highway on foot. Clutching my ring, I groped for a reasonable explanation to give her that wouldn't freak her out even more. The ache was still creeping through my head, making it hard to think. Not that I would have had an easy answer ready clear-headed either.

"I stayed up organizing the house and realized I didn't have much food around, so I looked up a late-night place to have dinner and figured I'd walk there," I said, hoping my tone was convincing enough. "It looked closer on the map. Or maybe I got turned around. It was really dark on that stretch, and the rain started—I would have called for a cab, but my phone died on me. Just a really bad situation all around. I must have tripped over something to end up on the road. I don't remember that part."

Mom didn't look any less worried with that explanation, but she must have decided any further questions could wait a little longer. "Oh!" she said. "I have to let the nurses and the doctor know you're awake. And Melody—she'll be so relieved. Your brother, too. He came to see you a few times, you know."

She got up and hustled into the hall, pulling her phone from her purse as she went. My stomach knotted as she went.

How much longer was I going to have to stay here recovering? More and more days while Wonderland's people—my people—might assume I'd abandoned them like Aunt Alicia had before?

The doctor hustled in, a tall woman in a white lab coat that set off her dark brown skin. She eyed me and the equipment around me, and for a second I thought she looked puzzled. She came over to the side of the bed.

"Miss Tenniel," she said. "I'm glad to see you've rejoined us."

"So am I," I said in a weak attempt at humor.

It did earn me a small smile. "I'm Dr. Nicholson," she said. "How are you feeling?"

"Kind of achy," I said honestly. "But… not really that bad. My mom said I've been here for four *weeks*?"

She couldn't somehow have accidentally said "weeks" when she'd meant "days," right?

"Twenty-six days," Dr. Nicholson said. "But you've proven very resilient." Her gaze twitched toward the metal vest for a second before she caught it. "I'll need to give you a quick exam now that you're back with us."

"Of course."

She shone a light in my eyes and had me test my grip and my range of motion. I was definitely weak from all the lying around I'd been doing. Just lifting my legs up and down a few times was tiring me out. The doctor looked pleased with what she saw, though. Well, pleased and a little puzzled.

"Am I going to be okay?" I asked when she was finished.

"As far as I can tell," she said. "I have to admit, Miss Tenniel, yours has been a rather unusual case. But I see every reason for optimism."

Maybe the vest had protected me with its magic as well as its armor. I wet my lips. "Now that I'm awake, can I go home?"

"With the amount of time you've been unconscious, we'll want to monitor you for at least another day," Dr. Nicholson said. "And even once you're discharged, you'll need to take it easy for a while as you recover your strength. There's also…"

She sank into the chair where Mom had been sitting before and fixed me with a firm but compassionate look. "I haven't mentioned this to your family, but I think it's important I bring it up with you. When you arrived at the hospital, you had a number of small but deep cuts around your lower legs and your hands. They didn't match your injuries from the accident. In fact, I can't think of any sort of accident that could have caused them. Did you want to talk about how you got those?"

Ah, that would be a "No." I'd gotten those cuts freeing the Queen's prisoners and fending off her guards while mushroom-drugged to ten times my regular size. The guards' swords had cut into me like little knives. If I told the doctor that, she'd send me to the psychiatric ward.

"My memory around the accident is pretty fuzzy," I said. "I'm really not sure."

Dr. Nicholson didn't look as if she believed me. "Have you been under a lot of stress recently, Miss Tenniel? We have counsellors here you can speak with if you have any difficult emotions you need to work through in a productive way."

Oh. *Oh.* Understanding hit me like a smack to the head. She thought I'd cut myself out of some kind of self-harming urge. I guessed that wasn't too much of a stretch when by all appearances I'd also walked straight into traffic. Shit.

Hasty denial would probably just make me look even more unstable. I smiled instead. "I really appreciate the offer. I'll let you know if I think I need that. For now I'd just like to rest some more."

"Of course," Dr. Nicholson said. "That'll be good for you."

As she got up, my best friend appeared in the doorway. Melody gave a little cry and rushed over to me. "Lyss! Oh my God. I'm so glad you're okay." She shot the doctor a pointed glance. "She is okay, right?"

"It appears she'll make a full recovery—and a rather speedy one," Dr. Nicholson said. "Go easy on her for now!"

"'Go easy on her'," Melody muttered to herself as the doctor ducked out. She raked a hand through her fine black hair and brandished a patchwork tote bag. "I had stuff packed for as soon as you pulled through. Because I knew of course you were going to pull through. Lyssa Tenniel wasn't going to let some truck get the better of her."

I had to laugh. "What did you pack me?"

"Jeans and one of your favorite T-shirts, all other clothing essentials, and a book I think you'll like in case they aren't ready to let you leave quite yet. *Are* they letting you leave?"

"The doctor said they need to monitor me for a little while longer," I said, my gut tightening all over again. "It sounds like it shouldn't take too long if they think I'm doing that well." If they didn't decide I needed to be carted off to the psychiatric ward after all, for my own protection. "Did you see my mom when you came in?"

"Yeah, she's sorting something out with the nurses about your insurance or I don't know what." Melody sighed and then grinned. She grasped my hand like Mom had. "Do you really feel okay? You know you can tell me if you don't. How you ended up out by the highway—it didn't have anything to do with that asshole, did it?"

"No," I said quickly. I'd given Melody a story about a neighbor I'd been planning to hit up for a booty call as a roundabout way of talking about visiting Wonderland. That lie spiraled a little out of control when she'd found me after my return the last time bleeding all over Aunt Alicia's house. Now she thought some psycho guy lived in the area and might come after me again. "I'm really okay. I mean, not perfect, but if Mom hadn't told me I was hit by a truck, I wouldn't believe it."

Melody kept smiling, but her brow furrowed. When Melody let herself look worried, you knew she was really freaking out. "I want you to know I've got your back, whatever you need, here and once you're back home. I'll grab groceries for the apartment and air everything out, and—"

"The apartment?" I interrupted. "When I get out, I'm going back to the house. I left a bunch of stuff there—I'm still sorting through everything."

Melody's mouth flattened. "Lyss… I don't think that's such a good idea—you being on your own out there after everything. That place seems like it's getting to you somehow. I've never had to visit you at the hospital in the entire ten years I've known you, and within a few days of you inheriting that place, you're in here *twice*?"

Okay, so maybe Wonderland hadn't turned out to be the best for my health, but that was the Queen of Hearts' fault, not anyone else's. And a whole lot more people could be getting hurt because of her right now. If Melody could have understood…

But she wouldn't. No one would. How could I ever explain to anyone what I'd found there, why it was important to me? *I'd* thought I was hallucinating the first few hours I'd spent in Wonderland, with the actual reality of it all around me.

That fact hit me with a punch of queasiness. I cared about Mom—of course I did—and I didn't want to worry her more. I loved Melody like a sister. But I couldn't share anything with either of them about the people and the place I'd fallen in love with.

"Country living comes with unexpected dangers?" I said with an attempt at a wry smile. "It's just a coincidence. You've been through the house—you didn't see anything all that weird there, did you?"

"No. But still. Your mom and I were talking while you were out of it…" Melody looked away and then pulled her gaze back to mine. "We're taking care of it for you, okay, Lyss? It's all still yours; we're just getting it sorted out so you can move on."

I blinked at her. "What do you mean, you're taking care of it?"

She sucked in a breath through her teeth. "We hired movers to come and pack up the place, bring all the furniture and the rest to an auction site. Anything that looked like it was a real heirloom or had sentimental value we already set aside in a storage locker. They should be in there to grab it all today, and then—"

My heart stopped. My voice crackled as it came out, but I couldn't hold it steady. "Mel, that stuff is mine. You can't just—"

"We're looking out for you," Melody said, squeezing my hand. "I promise, you'll be relieved when it's all taken care of. You just have to—"

She kept talking, but I could hardly hear her over the renewed thumping of my heart. It pounded at a panicked rhythm behind my ears. Fuck. Fuck, fuck, fuck. That was about all the coherent thought I was capable for forming for the first few seconds.

Then my practical side, the side that had held me together through Dad's long illness and death, through Mom's depression and my other brother's acting out—the side that had held our whole little family together when I'd been just eight year old—kicked in.

She'd said they were packing up the house today. It was only about an hour's drive from here. I could still catch them before they took away the mirror. If I was fast.

I had to leave. To manage that, I had to get rid of Melody.

"Okay, Mel, maybe you're right," I said when she paused in her explaining. "Sorry. It freaked me out a little, having it sprung on me like that."

"I know," Melody said. "I'm sorry."

"Could you—would you mind—" I touched my belly. "I'm actually feeling kind of hungry. Would you check with the nurse if I'm allowed to eat anything, and if I am, grab me something you know I'll like from a vending machine or whatever? That would be so awesome."

"Of course." My best friend sprang up, not a hint of suspicion on her face. Because even after my various injuries, she couldn't believe responsible, play-by-the-rules Lyssa Tenniel would ever do something as drastic as break out of a hospital against doctor's orders.

She slipped out of the room. I listened to her heels tapping away, and then I tugged the IV free from my arm with a wince, pressing the tape over the puncture point like a Band-aid.

Melody had left her tote bag on the chair. My head spun as I tugged on the clothes, but I didn't have time to take it easy. When I knew where my mirror to Wonderland was—then I'd rest some more.

I fastened the chain around my neck and tucked the ruby ring under my shirt again. My armored vest would look way too weird in here, so I stuffed it in the tote bag for now. Discarding the hospital gown on the bed, I wobbled over to the doorway. A glance outside showed no one I recognized in view—no one who was likely to realize I wasn't supposed to be walking around. I summoned all my strength, and then I set off on my escape.

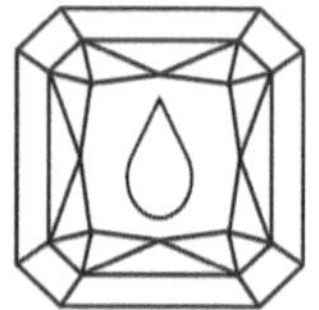

CHAPTER TWO

Lyssa

The elevator door stood right ahead of me at the other end of the hall. I walked slowly so I could keep my balance, aiming to look leisurely rather than on the verge of collapsing. When a sharper tremor ran up my legs, I braced myself with my hand against the wall, clutching my tote bag against my side.

Pushing myself onward, I dodged a metal cart and dragged in a ragged breath. Ten more steps. Nine. Eight…

I was at five when a familiar voice carried down the hall. *Two* familiar voices. Mom and Melody were chatting with each other as they came toward me, presumably on their way back to my room.

With a lurch of my heart, I threw myself toward the elevator. My thumb jabbed on the button, that hand holding me upright while my legs trembled. I managed to straighten up just as the car arrived with a *ding!*

A couple of nurses hurried out. I darted past them and

jammed my finger on the button for the ground level. The door was just sliding closed when a yell reached my ears.

"Lyssa!"

The elevator was already dropping. I sagged against the wall, gripping the railing. *Come on, muscles. You've had almost four weeks of relaxing. Time to get with the program.*

I had to push my posture a little straighter and paste a smile on my face when a couple who must have just been visiting someone got on at the second floor. Sweat started to trickle down my back. The elevator whirred down one more level. I darted out the instant the door whispered to the side.

The main lobby—I had to find it. I had no idea where my car was, but there'd have to be taxis outside. I had to get out of this building before anyone figured out how far I'd gone. I—

I nearly barreled right into a slouched figure ambling toward the elevator. My shoulder bumped his arm, and his "Whoa!" set every nerve on high alert before he even glanced down and said, "Lyssa?"

My older brother Cameron was staring down at me. I hadn't seen him since our family dinner last Christmas, which he'd showed up late for and left from early after a poke through Mom's wallet.

As kids, we'd had the same white-blond hair, but unlike mine, Cam's had darkened to a shade closer to brown. A new scar flecked his right cheekbone, and his lips automatically curled into a sneer. I wasn't sure his mouth had known how to make any other expression since he was twelve.

"What the hell are you doing down *here*, sis?" he said.

I could have asked him the same thing. Yes, he must be here to see me—Mom must have called him like she'd said she would—but I didn't know why he'd bothered. It wasn't as if he'd cared about anything other than what I could give him in ages. But in that moment my mind latched onto one small but vital fact.

Cam liked cars. He always had a clunker he was driving around while he waited for the funds to "fix it up."

"I'm leaving," I said. "You drove here?"

His sneer wavered. "Uh, yeah. But what—"

I grabbed his elbow and pushed him back the way he'd come. "You're my ride. Let's get going. There's someplace I need to be, fast."

"Are you sure it's a good idea for you to be going anywhere, Lyssa?" he said, peering down at me as I hustled him onward.

Old Lyssa would have tried to appeal to his better nature, or, failing that, to bargain with him. I discovered that Lyssa who was heir to the throne of Wonderland, on the other hand, had exactly zero fucks to give for my brother's shit.

"*I'll* worry about whether it's a good idea or not," I said, my voice coming out with a strident, authoritative tone that was new too. "I need to get somewhere. You wanted to see me. Easy solution for both of us."

Cam's eyebrows jumped up, but to my relief he didn't argue. "All right, all right," he said. "The parking lot is this way. I'll just warn you, you'll have to clear the junk off the passenger seat."

The junk was about a dozen McDonalds food

wrappers, a broken pair of headphones, and a crumpled, empty box of cigarettes. I swept everything onto the floor and climbed in, my nose wrinkling at the greasy nicotine smell that permeated the whole car. But beggars couldn't be choosers. I didn't know where my purse was. Now that my whole attention wasn't focused on staying upright, it occurred to me that I didn't have any way of *paying* a taxi for an hour-long ride.

Cam started the engine with a couple of sputters leading into a low growl. I glanced behind us as he pulled out of the parking lot, but I didn't see any sign of pursuit. With luck, Mom and Melody and whatever nurses they alerted would spend a while checking around the hospital before deciding I must have left.

I had the feeling that, especially after my brief outburst when Melody had told me about sending away the house's contents, Aunt Alicia's property was the first place they'd check when they realized I'd fled the coop.

"Take a left," I said. "We're going to want to get on the highway heading north. I'll tell you when we need to get off again."

Cam looked at me sideways. "You're heading back to her house—Aunt Alicia's."

"Yep."

I didn't figure I owed him more answer than that. As he drove, cursing at a pedestrian who was taking too long to cross the street, I fiddled with the brace on my wrist. The bones mustn't be broken, or I'd have gotten a full cast. When I flexed the muscles there, they didn't ache any worse than the rest of me did. I wasn't sure I needed the brace anymore, but what if I hurt myself all over again by taking it off?

After another bout of swearing at the driver in front of him who he felt was taking a turn too cautiously, Cam aimed the car down the highway and hit the gas. My shoulders jolted against the worn seat.

"So," my brother said after a short silence, with a wheedling note in his voice that I could recognize in an instant. My back tensed. He'd only agreed to drive me without complaint because this ride came with strings attached. "Aunt Alicia left her entire property to you, huh. I hear it's quite the place."

"It's a nice old house," I said cautiously. "But kind of in the middle of nowhere."

He nodded. "You're unloading it and all her stuff, then?"

I guessed Mom hadn't mentioned her plan with Melody to him. Not surprising.

"I haven't totally decided yet," I said. "I only had it for a few days before…" I gestured to myself to indicate the accident.

"It seems pretty unbalanced, don't you think, that she gave all that stuff just to you—and, I mean, it used to be Dad's house too. We should both have some say what happens to it."

He couldn't have been more predictable. I'd be willing to bet this was the whole reason he'd hurried over to the hospital when he'd found out I was awake. He'd probably hoped I'd be more suggestable in my weakened state. He hadn't even asked me how I was feeling after I'd just woken up from an awful accident, and he was already angling for a cut of the money from selling the house, or for me to pay him off to keep the peace if I didn't sell.

Which, yeah, maybe would have been more "balanced"—if our family had ever been balanced. If he'd ever done more than take, take, take, when he wasn't breaking other people's things and leaving me and Mom to pick up the pieces, both figuratively and sometimes literally.

The last time Aunt Alicia had visited us, he'd dented her car jumping around on the hood and then cursed her out for telling him to get off. He hadn't exactly been on his best behavior most of the visits before then either. Why the hell did he think he deserved one cent from her?

"Aunt Alicia left it to me," I said, still trying to be diplomatic. "I haven't seen much of anything around that would have been Dad's except some old toys and books, if you're interested in those. If I find anything else, something it'd make sense for you to have, I'll let you know."

Cam scoffed at the idea of taking childhood bits and pieces. It wasn't memories he wanted; it was only cash. "There've got to be a few pieces you could sell off quickly. You can see this car needs work. I'm living paycheck to paycheck here. We're family. You're not going to give me a hand when you got this huge gift dropped into your lap?"

"Cam, I just got out of the hospital. You want to give me a break?"

"Well, when am I going to get to ask you again? You hardly talk to me anymore. Like you're so much better than me."

A flare of anger went off in my chest. I didn't have the

energy to put up with his bullshit right now on top of everything else. Why did I even bother trying to keep the peace anymore? My brother had shown time and time again that he couldn't care less about Mom or me.

"I don't talk to you because every time I do, you're either insulting me or looking to get something out of me, like right now," I said. "Since when have *you* ever cared about family? When you were getting yourself suspended from school and nearly sent to juvie, while Mom was working her ass off just to put food on the table? When you wrecked *her* car driving around high? When she had to empty her savings account bailing you out for the fifteenth time last year?"

Cam's face flushed red. "If you don't think I'm worth being around, I can let you out right now. Find some other schmuck to drive you." He craned his neck, looking for the next turn-off.

My hands balled into fists in my lap. The authoritative energy that had filled me earlier rose up again.

A queen's blood ran through my veins. I'd freed all of Time and challenged a mad tyrant to her face. If Cam thought I was still the same old careful, dependable Lyssa, he was in for a big fucking surprise.

"No," I said, my voice ringing from my throat. "You are going to keep driving, and we'll talk about balance. For the ten years from when Dad died to when I left for college, I was the one holding the family together, making sure Mom didn't go off the deep end, doing everything I could to see that we kept the house and had something to eat, while you ran around acting like an asshole."

Cam sucked in his breath to speak, but I cut him off.

"I know. You lost your dad. Guess what—so did I. I was freaked out too. But I didn't get to go crazy, not even a little, because you took up all the space for that. So I think you owe me a hell of a lot more than I owe you. All I'm asking is for you to drive me an hour outside of town. You can do that, or you can forget it if you think we're *ever* talking again."

For a few minutes, Cam couldn't seem to speak. We drove past an exit, but he stayed in his lane. Finally, he swallowed audibly and gave a little cough as if to find his voice.

"What the hell happened to you in that coma, Lyssa? You don't sound like… you."

"It wasn't the coma," I said. "I've been figuring out a lot of things lately."

He hesitated a little longer. Then he said, "You did take care of a lot when we were kids. I was doing my best too, you know."

Because of the acknowledgment and because he was still on the highway, I didn't argue with that statement. I wasn't going to praise his efforts either, though. "Okay," I said.

"It's just easier for you," he went on. "You always seem to know what you're doing and how you're going to do it, where you're supposed to be. I… don't really ever feel that way." His voice dropped with the last sentence as if he didn't totally want to say it.

I almost laughed. Easier? But I could see how my life might have looked that way to him. He had no idea.

Maybe I hadn't really had a clue either. As I gazed at the regular fields dappled with regular trees along the side of the highway, an uncomfortable pressure wound around my heart. Had I really known where I was supposed to be any time since I was a kid? I'd spent so much time in Wonderland thinking about how I had to get back here, but what did I *have* here, really?

I had Mom and Melody, sure. But they were other people with their own lives. Beyond that… How much had I really been living, and how much had I been waiting for things to fall into place? For this boyfriend or that job to turn into the one I really wanted?

When had I let myself dream about anything other than just having a regular existence? What would I dream about if I did?

The answer was obvious now. I'd felt more alive in Wonderland than I ever had here. I wanted to see just how wonderful it could be without the Hearts crushing everyone's spirits. Wonderland needed me more than anyone in the Otherland ever had… and I needed it more than I'd ever needed anything here. *That* was where I was supposed to be. I felt it with every fiber of my being.

"I didn't really feel like I knew what I was doing either," I admitted. "I just kept going, kept following the path I thought I was supposed to, because I was too scared of what would happen if I didn't."

Cam sat with that comment for a while. I didn't expect him to apologize for anything from our past or even the conversation that had just happened, but at least he didn't snark about it.

"Are you going to be okay?" he asked, like maybe he actually wanted to know.

The start of a smile touched my lips despite the knot of tension inside me. "I think so."

We didn't talk much after that other than me giving directions when it was time to get off the highway, but the air in the car tasted at least a little clearer. To give Cam credit, he didn't bring up his interest in the inheritance again. My nerves had almost settled when Aunt Alicia's house came into view up ahead—with a big white moving truck parked out front.

I jerked forward in my seat as if that motion would propel the car faster. "Come on," I said. A couple of guys were walking from the house to the truck carrying what looked like the dining room table. Fuck. How much had they already packed up?

"What's going on?" Cam said, but he revved the engine at the same time. We sped down the driveway and jolted to a halt beside the truck. I opened the door the second the wheels stopped moving, slinging Melody's tote bag with the armored vest over my shoulder.

"Stop!" I shouted at the movers. "This is my house. I didn't give permission for anyone to move this stuff. You've got to put it all back."

The guys with the table paused and set it down on the pavement. The one with the bushy beard gave me a puzzled frown. "Look, we've got clear instructions—there was a woman here earlier who opened up the house for us—"

"She went behind my back while I was in the hospital," I said. "It's *my* house. Isn't it?"

I glanced at Cam for back-up where he was stepping

out of the car. He looked a little bewildered, but he nodded automatically. The movers glanced at each other.

"Just—don't take anything else until we get it all sorted out," I said. "I have to see what's already gone."

I'd recovered a little strength during the drive, but my legs were trembling again by the time I reached the front door. I soldiered on, gripping the railing tight as I hauled myself up the stairs, freezing through a wave of nausea on the third floor, wobbling up the spiral staircase to the attic.

My head emerged into the little room at the top of the house, and my whole body stiffened.

It was empty. Everything was gone—the bookcases, the chest… My mirror to Wonderland.

I scrambled back to the ground floor as quickly as I could. I'd just reached the doorway when a car engine thrummed in the distance. When I stumbled out, Melody's bright blue Nissan raced into view along the country road heading toward us.

My stomach flipped over. After the stunt I'd just pulled running away from the hospital, she and Mom might have grounds to get me committed. They sure as hell weren't going to stand around while I had the movers haul all Aunt Alicia's stuff back into the house.

There was only one way out of this mess. And it was the way I wanted to go anyway.

One of the movers let out a shout as I dashed past him toward the open back of the truck. My legs swayed, but adrenaline carried me up the ramp and into the dark interior. Tables, chairs, and bookcases were tightly packed all around me.

A prickling pull ran over my skin and down into my chest, tugging me forward. Around a stack of boxes. Over a bedframe.

There. The mirror's glossy surface glinted faintly near the back of the truck. I gasped in relief—and heard the thump of car doors slamming outside.

No time to think. No time for doubt. I leapt at the mirror with arms outstretched.

With a hitch of my lungs, it yanked me through its cool surface and sucked me down.

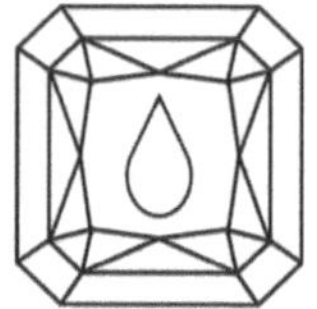

Chess

A person could move across the city of Wonderland far above the streets simply enough with the right companions. I was plenty spry on my feet, and Dum could jump from one side of an intersection to another without breaking a sweat. Here and there, Dee would vault me over with his springy arms, and I'd attach a rope for him to swing across on.

We mostly stuck to the middle of the roofs, away from any eyes on the roads below. Our destination, the Tower, gleamed silver against the sky up ahead. We didn't need any maps or signs to figure out where to go. Every time we had to cross to a new block of buildings, we scanned the street for members of the Hearts' Guard first. Their scarlet helms made them easy to pick out even amid the revelers dancing on the sidewalks.

I tugged the scarf wrapped across my lower face

tighter at the sight of a heap of roses on the pavement. The palace workers had been coming through the city every morning tossing fresh blooms here and there throughout the city. Their cloying scent prickled faintly through the fabric even this far up. Down there, it seeped around door frames and down chimneys. The Clubbers couldn't escape it.

And so the whole city had become a vast version of Caterpillar's Club.

The thump of bass and a tinkling of strings carried from one of the speakers on the corners as we hurried on across the next roof. My steps fell into the beat of their own accord. The epic dance party going on all through the city would have been a welcome celebration if it'd been happening because those people *wanted* to party and not because the Queen was pulling out all the stops to keep them distracted and sedated.

At the club, at least we'd been able to choose whether we went and how long we danced, even if that choice had sometimes felt inevitable.

"It just never wears off, does it?" Dee said through his own scarf with a muffled laugh, peering over the edge. "That guy there fell asleep right in the middle of the street! Never tell a Wonderlander it's time to go to bed, right?"

He winked at me, but his cheer sounded a tad forced. The last couple weeks had been a strain on us all.

"I guess it'd be too much to wish for a blight on all the roses in the land," Dum muttered. His demeanor hadn't changed much in recent times, but then, he'd always been more on the gloomy side.

"Oh, she'd cook up some other way to screw us over."

Dee shook his head. "Whatever I might say about the Queen of Hearts, she is resourceful."

"If I didn't know better, I'd say she's already lost her head," I said, matching his light-hearted tone. "A pity that isn't the case."

Dum snorted. "In every way that makes things worse for us, she has. I wonder—"

He stopped himself with a furtive glance my way. I suspected I knew what he'd been thinking of. Or rather, who. Grinning fiercely behind my scarf, more for myself than anyone else, I leapt from one set of slanted yellow singles to another of mint-green tiles veering in the opposite direction.

I wondered too. What had happened to Lyssa after she'd disappeared into the Hearts' palace those weeks ago? How long had she lived before the Queen had tired of the game of questioning her and—?

No, I wouldn't think about that part.

Mostly I wondered what Wonderland would look like right now if our lovely Otherlander had been sitting on that palace's throne. The thought stuck with me like an ache in my bones, easily forgotten if I was focused on other things, but always there if my mind wandered.

If we'd fought a little harder— If I'd gotten to her faster in the fray—

"Chess!" Dum called, as loud as he dared, and I realized the twins had gotten quite the lead on me. I picked up my pace to catch up.

The silver spire of the Tower loomed over us. We stopped on top of the building across the street from it and considered the challenges ahead.

Two guards were stationed directly outside the Tower door. The roses pinned to the collars of their pleated uniforms contained some sort of antidote to the drug the others were laced with, so that they could keep their wits, such as any of them had, while keeping an eye on the city.

A couple more guards with similar blooms beneath their chins marched by as we watched, but after a minute they passed out of view amid the dancers around the corner. I tipped my head toward the twins.

"Ready?"

"Piece of cake," Dee announced, and tied a rope around a jutting weather vane so he and his brother could scramble down into the alley on the other side of the building. I fixed one of my ropes to the random railing at the Tower side. I couldn't drop it yet, or the guards might notice it. For now, I reached toward the in-between space where I could move without being seen. The music below dulled.

The twins had to work fast once they hit the ground. Roses scattered the streets here too, more than our scarves could hope to protect us from for long up close. With a faint thump, they set their feet on the wall and skidded down one right after the other. Then they dashed through the scattered revelers toward the Tower.

Dee aimed a punch at one shop window. Dum aimed a kick at another. The guards shouted, and the twins took off—in opposite directions. The guards charged after them, giving me my opening.

I tossed the rope and threw myself after it, only gripping it to slow my fall. The second my feet touched the ground, I sprang toward the Tower. The music and the aimless chatter farther down the street completely muted the sound of my steps. The guards hollered somewhere farther off, and I hoped the twins made it to the Spades waiting for them before the toxins in the air took over. All I could concentrate on right now was in and up.

I slipped past the Tower door—by the lands, let none of the Clubbers catch its brief swing—and hurtled into the elevator shaft.

"Twenty-seventh floor, Chess coming calling. The White Knight gives his blessing," I said quickly.

The cushion of air propelled me upward. Thank the lands the White Knight had thought to include that failsafe for his closest associates so we could still access his apartment if he wasn't in it.

Although, how close to him could I really say I'd been, current revelations taken into account?

The whisper of the elevator door closing behind me was so familiar, the gleam of the pale walls on the other side so familiar, I could almost have believed I'd find him sitting behind his big white desk in that big white room. But the White Knight's office stood empty, as did the rest of his apartment.

Would he ever come back here? I'd thought I'd seen a true joy in his expression when he'd fit the pieces of one gadget or another together to make it something real, but maybe that had all been pretense, like so much else.

For now, *we* needed those gadgets. He'd had a few days in here planning for our next efforts after Time had been freed—he'd talked about preparing equipment. Let's hope he'd prepared something that we could benefit from in our present time of need.

I started with the built-in shelves along the walls, picking up various devices and eyeballing them to determine whether they were finished or only works in progress. Ah, here was that extendable metal rope and the spinning cutting tool he'd put great use to on the Checkerboard Plains. I stuffed those into the sack slung over my shoulder and moved on.

The drawers in the worktables offered up a few more goodies. One held a contraption in the shape of a gun that he'd assembled before, during the freeze. It could melt metal in a matter of minutes. Here was the funnel that could throw one's voice up, down, or around corners. Here some treads that could be fixed to our shoes to allow us to climb almost any surface.

None of it was exactly what I'd come for, though. But then, his most useful inventions were also the ones that would have looked too suspicious if left easily accessible. Where would he have hidden those away?

I poked around his desk feeling for secret compartments, but none revealed themselves. Perhaps not in his office at all? I prowled farther into the apartment.

I'd been in the more private areas of the White Knight's home plenty of times. When a woman at the club or in the park had particularly caught my fancy, unless I'd already had company with me I was pleased to share with, I'd generally brought her over here to "meet" the Inventor. More often than not, if he was in, he'd been game. Those might have been the only times he'd indulged himself in that side of life in general. I'd never seen him making moves on anyone on his own, although who knew how various private meetings with the other Spades might have ended, without me there to witness?

He'd been discrete, and he hadn't pursued anything continuous. Until Lyssa. How much had he already known, before the Red Knight had even laid out the Hearts' torrid history? He must have known something, mustn't he?

Because he wasn't really the White Knight or the Inventor. He was Jack, Prince of Hearts.

Even now, trying to connect the man I'd known as the White Knight to the boy I'd caught glimpses of around the palace, I couldn't quite make the pieces fit. But I *hadn't* ever seen more than occasional glimpses of Prince Jack, after all. The Queen had kept her youngest son apart from the Diamonds' leisure activities as if he were her most prized possession. Actually, not just as if. He had been. I'd seen the way the sheen in her eyes would almost glow when she so much as mentioned his name.

She's fucking obsessed with that kid, I'd murmured to the Duchess once. The Duchess had laughed and not argued even a little.

I definitely didn't want to think about either of those women. I narrowed my attention down to the task at hand, rifling through the White Knight's closets and wardrobes and cabinets, checking under the sofas and the bed. My mind did enjoy a good wander, though. Thankfully it managed to wander in a more useful direction this time. I stepped back into the hall, and my gaze came to rest on the door to the games room.

The White Knight would want to hide incriminating

inventions somewhere no one would think to look for the instruments of rebellion. Like in a room devoted to play.

I didn't go much for Inventor-style games, so I hadn't spent much time in that space. I nudged open the door and considered the gray shelving units that lined one wall. The other three walls were the same blank white as in his office. All the better to not intrude on the fantasy challenges the gaming gear could invoke.

Any of the tools lying on those shelves could call up a host of translucent images at a touch. The White Knight had once told me that the White Knight before him had said this space had once been more of a training room to help people learn new skills. The younger Spades had come up with systems of ranking and points that I didn't know much about. But…

These egg-shaped devices tucked away on the back of one shelf looked familiar. I picked one up and sniffed it. Yes, that was the burnt smell of singe powder, all right. These were the White Knight's smoke bombs, which had served us well on more than one mission. I'd take all of those, thank you very much.

If any of the Queen's people had come sniffing around here themselves, he could have explained it away as part of one of the games. Very clever.

I scanned the other shelves and pocketed a few more things, my stomach starting to sink until I crouched down by the far end of the room. A real grin leapt to my face. I picked up the heavy cloth the White Knight had wrapped across his face on our mission into the palace grounds last month.

He'd said it was to filter out the smell of the roses. As far as I knew, Prince Jack hadn't been allergic, so this might not serve our purpose after all, but it was worth a try.

There were two more of the masks folded just behind the one I'd spotted. That was a start. With a flash of victory in my chest, I dropped them into the sack with the rest of my loot.

I hurried back to the office. Leaving would be much easier than entering had been, since as soon as I was out, I could just run, and the guards wouldn't know where I'd gone. But someone might decide to come up and check on the apartment, and it wouldn't do to be caught here. The Knave had ways of making the elevator do his bidding, proper commands or no.

Stopping there by the elevator door, my momentary good mood deflated. I'd stood right here with Lyssa when I'd first brought her to meet the White Knight. *I'd* taken her to him. It'd been Hatter's suggestion, yes, but I'd gone along with it without a second thought...

How much of this catastrophe was my fault for not looking harder, not paying more attention? For having spent all those years visiting the palace lolling around and thinking only of self-satisfaction, not bothering to think much about anyone who might matter later?

How much were a few masks and other tools going to change anything now? She was *gone*. The lovely woman whose smile had lit me up inside was—

I gritted my teeth and brought back the fierce grin that had steadied me on the rooftop. Maybe this expedition would get us nowhere. Maybe it'd been pointless. But whatever had happened to Lyssa, she hadn't let us down, not one bit. I wouldn't let her down either. We'd fight until we couldn't anymore. That was the only path I cared to follow now.

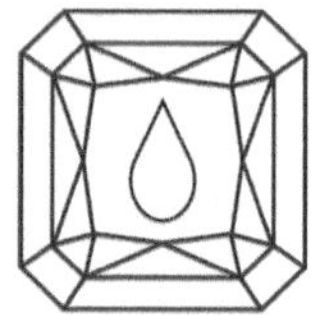

CHAPTER FOUR

Lyssa

My body spun through the vast shifting tunnel that would spit me out into Wonderland, and I clutched the tote bag with my metal vest tight to my chest. The fall was long enough for a few pangs of guilt to find me—what would Mom and Melody think, with me fleeing the hospital and then somehow disappearing on the moving truck? How were they going to cope, not knowing what the hell had happened to me?

I'd come back. When things in Wonderland were settled and safe, when I knew I wasn't leaving everyone there in the lurch, I could hop back through the mirror and clean up the mess I'd left behind as well as I could.

Right now I had to be ready for the mess that might be waiting on Wonderland's side. I dragged in a deep breath and braced myself for the smack of the pond's salty water.

The cool liquid shot over me, and like every time before, I found myself abruptly floating upward rather than tumbling down. The muted light playing across the shifting surface above me suggested it was daytime. Harder to hide.

I spread one arm to slow my ascent and kicked toward the edge of the pond so I'd be close to the shelter of the vegetation when I emerged. The strain trembled through my weakened muscles.

Fucking truck. Fucking Wonderland mirror that had decided to drop me in the middle of the highway just because I hadn't pictured a place to arrive. Maybe a little of the Queen of Hearts' hostility had rubbed off on it.

I managed to reach the dark rocks with their glittering specks of mica before my lungs demanded air *now*. As quietly as I could, I lifted my head from the water and sucked in the tang of salt and ferns.

A figure was moving through the brush along the other side of the pond. I froze, gripping the gritty-slick side of the rock. A flash of a red helm showed between the fern fronds. It eased away farther away from the bank, out of view. I didn't see any other guards around at the moment. This might be the best chance I got.

Clenching my jaw against the protests of my limbs, I hauled myself out of the water with as careful a balance between haste and quiet as possible. After a few stumbling steps, the ferns had closed around me. I sank down on the damp soil and gave myself a moment to rest and take stock.

The vest would do me a lot more good on me rather than in this bag. I squeezed as much water as I could out of my drenched T-shirt and pulled the flexible armored bodice over my head. It was a bit of a struggle working my arm through with the brace around my wrist. I considered the padded gray fabric for a moment and decided I'd risk removing it. It would make me stand out more as someone not of this world than even the armor would, and I might need that extra bit of mobility.

I eased the brace off and tucked it into Melody's tote bag. That bag might draw attention too… After a moment's indecision, I hid it under a fallen frond.

Tentatively, I crept through the densely clustered ferns. The fronds tickled over my bare arms. My feet only made a faint murmur on the ground between them. I kept my ears perked and my body tensed to run if I had to.

Hopefully I wouldn't have to. I wasn't sure how far these legs would carry me.

Maybe I was being over-cautious. If Theo had gotten through to his mother, that guard might have been ambling around waiting to see if I'd appear so he could help me back to the city. But after everything I'd seen of the Queen of Hearts and her court, I didn't want to take any chances.

The ferns gave way to the forest of trees with jade and emerald-brilliant leaves. As I slunk on, a rustling reached my ears from up ahead. I stopped, gripping a nearby branch, every nerve on high alert.

A pale figure moved into view between the trees. I stiffened when I recognized her.

It was Mirabel, the woman the Spades had called the White Queen. She was wearing one of her typical woolly white dresses, but the fabric had grayed, patchy with smudges of dirt and other stains. Her golden curls spilled over her shoulders in disarray, only a few coils still pinned on top of her head. The curls almost hid the dark pink ridge of the scar that peaked from her hairline at her temple.

I hadn't seen Mirabel since I'd found out the truth of her identity. She was the Queen's daughter, a Princess of Hearts. It was the Queen who'd struck her and left her with that scar—and with her thoughts even more addled than they'd been already, with her ability to look both forward and backward through time.

Theo had said Mirabel wanted to see the Queen displaced as much as everyone, that she'd fled the palace and helped the rebels ever since then. I wasn't totally sure I could trust Theo's assessment of his own sister, though, especially since I still wasn't totally sure how much I could trust Theo.

He'd been trying to protect me when he'd nudged me through the mirror back to my world. He'd sworn to face his mother and fight for Wonderland head on. But he'd also spent who knew how many years hiding who he was and orchestrating the Spades' battles mostly in the background, where it was safer. He'd lied to them, and to me, more times than I could count.

Mirabel was heading straight toward me, though. Her glimpses of the future could very well have told her I was here. And *she'd* never given me any reason to distrust her. I couldn't judge her based on who her mother or her brother was.

I eased away from the tree. Mirabel's pale eyes brightened when she saw me.

"There you are!" she said, speaking in a whisper. "We only came a short way, but it seemed like a long time."

As usual, it wasn't super easy figuring out what Mirabel was talking about in her disjointed way. At least she looked happy to see me. I found myself smiling back at her.

"What are you doing out here?" I asked, matching her volume. "Why did you leave the Tower?"

Her body swayed for a second, and she wrapped her arms around herself. "They all left. And they came. The roses, everywhere—I had to find my way here. I had to find my way to you. We've already gone and come."

My throat tightened with sympathy. She sounded even more loopy than usual. How long had she been wandering around in the forest alone? I couldn't ask her and expect anything close to a straight answer.

She might be able to get us to someplace better, though. I touched the side of her arm lightly. "Do you remember where we came from? Is there somewhere we should be?"

"I—" Mirabel blinked hard. She rubbed her temple, and her mouth twisted with effort. "There is light, but I don't know how far away. The music and the stink—I didn't like it. But that's where you were needed. They always needed you. We can go, I think. We met her. She knew the way."

Okaaaay. I let the White Queen take the lead, walking half a step behind her as we wove through the woods. Mirabel's hands moved in furtive gestures by her waist. After a few minutes, I realized she was going through the motions of knitting without her needles or yarn.

Any doubts I'd had about her seemed ridiculous, watching her now. This woman wasn't *capable* of scheming or duplicity. She could barely keep track of herself in the present, let alone juggle all kinds of lies. I sure as hell couldn't blame her for not wanting to broadcast her heritage.

Maybe I couldn't blame Theo for that either. He still shouldn't have hidden so much else from me, though. He'd realized who I was, how I'd fit into Wonderland's history, long before I had, but he'd kept all that to himself for his own reasons.

"Have you seen—" I started to ask, and Mirabel raised her hand in a wave. For a second I thought she was hallucinating a friend up ahead. Then a slight figure rose from behind a bush where it'd been crouched in hiding.

The skinny woman in front of us was one of the Spades, but not one I'd really have wanted to run into. The second I looked into her pointed face with its beady, ferret-like eyes, I remembered her skeptical look at the meeting where she'd suggested I had no place in Wonderland at all. That my being there had made it worse for all of them.

None of us had known then that I had Wonderlander blood running through my veins. Unless the handful of people who'd made that discovery with me had spilled the beans since I'd been gone, she *still* didn't know. It was still hard to forget how unwelcome she'd made me feel with a few quick words. The same sensation prickled over me now as her eyes widened with what looked like horror.

"The Otherlander," she said quietly, blinking hard. "Where did you—How—Where have you *been*?"

My stomach clenched into a ball. I'd obviously been gone long enough for the Spades to assume I'd abandoned them—just like Hatter had predicted I would, back when we'd first been getting to know each other. I'd led them to that huge battle at the palace and then I'd just disappeared.

Well, I was going to have to face the rest of the Spades sometime. When I explained, when they realized I'd come as soon as I could, they'd understand, right? It was just the initial questions and hurt that I was queasily anticipating.

"I'm here now," I said. "I'm sorry."

"You take us to the others," Mirabel informed the ferrety woman in a brisk tone as if she should already have known that.

The woman left off staring with a jerky bob of her head. "Yes. All right. Yes. We have a little time before the next patrol comes around. Quickly."

She motioned to us with a twitch of her hand. I peered through the woods around us as we followed her on toward the city. From that comment about the guards, clearly the Queen was still in command and out to crush the Spades. How much more had the people of Wonderland been through while I'd been lying in a daze in that hospital bed?

The vivid walls and roofs of the buildings at the edge of the city came into view through the trees. A faint smell, sickly sweet like fresh roses dipped in corn syrup, reached my nose. The ferrety woman knelt by a boulder at the foot of a tree and heaved it up to reveal a trap door and a passage underneath. She pointed for us to head down.

Metal rungs formed a sort of ladder down into a

damp tunnel. My feet hit the ground on rocky earth at the edge of an underground stream. It flowed on through a passage that was only about a foot taller than I was, the flickering blue glow of the water lighting up the rough stone walls. Where we stood, the stream stretched only a few feet across, but farther down, it doubled and then tripled in size to brush the passage walls.

The ferrety woman came down after us, closing the trap door over her head. She ushered us in the other direction, which I thought was leading us under the city. We had to leap the stream a few times when it branched with the caves, and at one wider spot we hopped across a makeshift bridge of stones. The ceiling slanted a little higher. The rose smell had faded the second we'd come underground, replaced by a crisp mineral scent.

Voices reached my ears over the hiss of the passing water. My pulse stuttered. The ferrety woman led us around a bend to an alcove at the edge of the stream, where a few of the collapsible cabins Theo had brought for our trip across the Checkerboard Plains had been set up around a heap of supplies.

One of the redheaded twins was leaning against that stack peering at a creased piece of paper. Doria and a couple other Spades I vaguely recognized were slicing bread and fruit on a makeshift table. And farther over by the cave wall, the other twin was standing with Chess in huddled conversation, Hatter listening in from where he was poised by a cabin doorway with a furrowed brow.

With the blank gap in my memory, to my mind it could have been only a day ago I'd last seen my two lovers, but my chest wrenched as if it'd been a year. The last time

I'd seen them, they'd been pinned to the ground by the Queen's guards. But they were here, alive and looking reasonably well, although Hatter was going sans hat. I guessed he hadn't been able to make it back to his shop.

I wanted to fling myself at them, but my uncertainty about their reaction locked my legs. In that instant, Chess glanced up.

"Look what I found," the ferrety woman said, jabbing her thumb toward both of us. Before the words had even left her mouth, Chess bounded forward, the widest grin I'd ever seen splitting his handsome angular face. He threw his brawny arms around me and spun me around in a powerful embrace.

"Lyssa," he murmured. "My lovely." He sounded so choked up that a lump filled my throat in turn. I had to clutch the front of his shirt to keep my balance when he set me down. Then he was kissing me, and if my legs wobbled with the rush of heat from his arms and his mouth, oh well.

He eased back, still beaming, and managed to tear his gaze from me long enough to dip his head toward Mirabel. "White Queen. It's good to see you too."

Hatter had stepped toward us. He was staring, his green eyes searching my face as if for confirmation that I really was me. How long *had* I been gone?

"Hatter," I said, my voice rough, and that snapped him into action. He tugged me into his arms, his embrace as tight as Chess's had been, his head tipping next to mine. The lime-and-wood-smoke smell of him filled my nose, and tears sprang into my eyes.

They weren't angry at all. Nothing but happy to see me, just as overjoyed as I was to see them.

Still, an apology tumbled from my mouth the second Hatter released me. "I'm sorry. I came as soon as I could. There was an accident, in the Otherland—"

"You were in the Otherland?" Chess let out a breathless chuckle.

"You've got nothing to apologize for, Lyssa," Hatter said, his hand sliding down my arm to clasp my fingers. "Hearts take me, we thought you were *dead*."

Oh, God. That was why the ferrety woman had looked so unnerved by the sight of me. "I—I don't know how long it's been here—I don't know what's going on— didn't Theo manage to pass on some kind of word?"

Chess's expression turned puzzled and sad. "None of us has heard a thing from Theo—Prince Jack, I suppose we should call him now—or seen him since he walked into the palace with you two weeks ago."

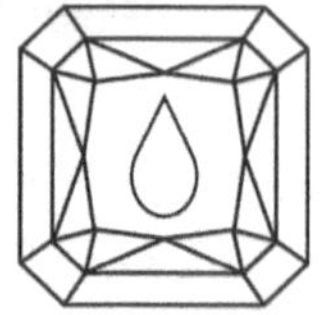

CHAPTER FIVE

Lyssa

"Two weeks?" I said, repeating Chess's words. "And there's been no sign of Theo at all? Has the Queen even mentioned him?"

"Not where we've been able to hear," Dum muttered.

"Then…" The words stuck in my throat like a jagged rock. It hurt forcing them out. "Are you sure *he's* still alive?"

"It put the Queen over the moon to find out her precious prince wasn't murdered after all," Hatter said. "I can't imagine she'd decide to reverse that revelation."

"He made her believe he was on her side," I said. "I don't know how happy she'd have been when she found out he wasn't. He helped me escape—he took me to the mirror to the Otherland that she keeps in her chambers. He said he was going to challenge her and set things right."

But he hadn't succeeded. I'd been frustrated with him

for deciding it wasn't safe for me to stay and fight alongside the Spades, but he'd probably saved my life. If the Queen hadn't shown even him any mercy…

Theo had been afraid of her rage. Afraid of what she'd do if she found out he'd left her purposely and worked with the Spades against her for years. But in the end he'd stood up to her anyway, to save *me*. To try to clear the way for me to the throne. And maybe he'd died taking that stand.

A wave of nausea rolled over me. My legs wobbled, both from that and the trek here. Chess caught my other arm.

"You look like you could stand to get off your feet for a minute or two, lovely," he said gently.

"That might be a good idea," I admitted. "I just got out of a hospital, actually. And I wasn't really supposed to leave."

"*What?*" Hatter said. He grabbed a box and helped me ease down onto it. "Were you and the prince attacked on the way to the looking-glass?"

"No," I said. "I just—I wasn't focused enough when I went through. I landed in kind of a dangerous spot, and a car hit me. I was really out of it for almost a month, Otherland time. Technically I wasn't even supposed to be up and walking around yet, but I found out my mom and my best friend had arranged to take all the furniture out of Aunt Alicia's house, and I was afraid I'd lose the mirror that could get me back here."

Chess's bright blue eyes widened a little. "As much as that devotion speaks in your favor, I'd like to speak up for self-preservation. Yours, of yourself." He motioned to the other Spades. "Bring some food over—and some of the drinking water."

With my queasiness, I wasn't sure how much food I'd be able to get down, but as soon as the plate of fresh bread and sliced fruit was in front of me, hunger gnawed right through my nausea. I hadn't had a proper meal since the last time I'd been in Wonderland. I had to restrain myself from shoving it all in my mouth, taking small slow bites instead, watching my responses to make sure I wasn't overwhelming my recently out-of-commission body.

Between the nourishment and the seat, a deeper sense of steadiness spread through me. I swallowed a mouthful of pear and glanced around at the Spades. "What else has been happening in the last two weeks? Why are you down here? This isn't all that's left of the Spades, is it?"

Hatter shook his head where he'd propped himself against the cave wall beside me. "There are a few other pockets scattered along the River Down. We thought it'd be wiser to spread ourselves out so we can't all be caught at once."

"One thing's for sure: the Queen was pretty shaken up by the way you barged in there and freed all those prisoners," the twin I thought I could now identify as Dee said, with a rough laugh. "She has guards patrolling everywhere up there, and they're bringing out fresh roses laced with the kinds of drugs the Clubbers liked to smoke at Caterpillar's—everyone's partying up there. They can't think straight enough to do anything else."

"Down here is the only place we can avoid getting caught in that high too," Dum put in. "It's made it hard to get anything done, even to follow what she's up to.

Chess just picked up some equipment that'll help a little, but… we haven't been much of a rebellion since then."

"But you're here now," Dee said, smiling wide. The eager glint in his eyes looked a little desperate. "You can figure out how to topple her."

I knew why he was saying that, but a few of the people around me didn't. I glanced over at Mirabel, who'd sat herself down on the stone floor beside one of the cabins. Did she even know who I really was and what I represented to her family?

When I'd first found out, when we'd made it back to the city with the Red Knight and his revelations, I'd asked the small group who'd been with me not to say anything to anyone else. I'd needed time to figure out whether I was ready for the responsibilities that came with being the Red Queen's heir—whether I *wanted* to accept them.

Those responsibilities didn't feel like a burden now, though, not even with the news I'd just heard. There was no reason to keep the truth of my heritage quiet. After the stunt I'd pulled, growing to ten times my size to barge into the Queen of Hearts' gardens and crash her mock trial, I couldn't possibly be in any more danger from her than I already was.

"That's why I came back as quickly as I could," I said. "It might have been risky, but—I realized something that day when we freed all those people. This is my home. I belong in Wonderland. I don't want to leave my old life behind completely, but what I have here, what I need to do here, that comes first. I'm the however-many-greats granddaughter of the rightful rulers of Wonderland, and I'm going to take the throne back as the Red Queen."

After I had my bearings back, anyway. The second I finished speaking, a tremor tickled through me. I had to grip the side of the box for balance.

"Hold on, what's this about?" one of the other Spades said. Dee bounded over to exalt in a hushed voice about our adventures and discoveries on the Checkerboard Plains, and I was more than happy to let him convey that information.

Chess squeezed my shoulder. "And we need to look after our true queen. We have many fine abodes if you'd like to rest your head as well." He swept his arm toward the cabins.

"No," I said automatically. I'd spent most of the last four weeks in some sort of sleep. I wasn't in any hurry to return to that state. "I think I just…" I tugged my hair back behind my ears and grimaced at the feel of it. The brief dunk in the Pond of Tears hadn't made up for nearly four weeks with no showers. "Is there anywhere I can wash here? I think I'll feel better if I can clean myself up."

The corner of Hatter's mouth quirked up. "One thing we have plenty of down here is water."

Chess glanced from him to me and gave us a smile that looked a little sly. "Why doesn't Hatter get you where you'd like to go? I'll slip upside with our new equipment and see if I can't get a clearer answer of what happened to our White Knight turned Prince of Hearts."

My heart squeezed. It wasn't as if Chess hadn't spied on the Hearts' people plenty in the past, and I did want answers about Theo, but I'd only just gotten back here. Only just found him again. I grasped his hand for a second. "Be careful, okay?"

"I have every intention of making it back to you now that you've made it back to us," he said with a grin.

Hatter held my elbow as I got up, not insistently but just firmly enough that I knew I could lean on him if I needed to. His gaze slid to Doria, who'd come over to join the cluster around me.

"You know I'll be fine without you watching over my every move," she said, wrinkling her nose at him but smiling at the same time.

"Of course," Hatter said. He'd loosened up on his daughter as he'd become more active in the rebellion again himself, but I could imagine their current precarious situation had woken those protective parental urges right back up.

We left the camp behind, following the stream around a couple of bends in the caves and past another split.

"Here we are," Hatter said.

I stared for a moment, taking in the scene up ahead. The current of glowing blue water veered to the side, hitting the wall and then… flowing right up it. The stream coursed on in a diagonal line that reached right up to the ceiling and spiraled around back to the ground farther down the passage. Where the water crossed the cave ceiling, some of it rained down toward the floor into a pool that had formed there. But some of it defied gravity completely.

It wasn't the weirdest thing I'd seen in Wonderland. This was a place where unicorns walked around on two legs and talked, where feathered dragons might belch fire in your face, and where mirrors could transport you to other realities. But still, it was pretty freaking weird.

"That'll work," I said, already imagining the water rushing over me and washing all the lingering grime away.

"One of the few perks of our current living situation," Hatter said dryly. He started to peel off his maroon suit jacket. "It's a little slippery under the downpour. I think I'd better go with you to make sure you don't need a return trip to that hospital, so I suppose I'm getting a wash too."

Oh. Heat unfurled from low in my belly as I watched him shed his shirt and unbutton his slacks. Hatter wasn't as buff as Chess or Theo, but there was still plenty to admire about his broad-shouldered but otherwise lean form. Plenty of taut muscles I'd enjoyed running my hands over and feeling against me more than once. Um. Right. I was supposed to be getting ready to wash too.

I tugged off my woven metal vest with a twinge in my wrist when I bent it at a slightly odd angle. Note to self: Be especially careful with that arm. I set it down next to Hatter's steadily growing pile of folded clothing and reached for the hem of my shirt.

Now Hatter was watching me, everything off except for his silk boxers. A flush spread over my skin at his approving attention, especially when my small breasts jumped with the yank of my shirt over them. It wasn't as if he hadn't seen me naked before, but then it'd been in the heat of the moment. This intimacy felt much more deliberate.

When I'd stripped completely, he dropped his boxers too. He picked up a bar of what I guessed was soap, deep fuchsia in color, and guided me over to the stream's natural shower.

The first spray of the water was warmer than I expected—not as hot as I'd have usually liked to shower, but pleasantly refreshing. For the first several moments with it rushing over me like a gentle waterfall, any self-consciousness I'd been feeling was swept away with the rivulets that trickled across the rocky floor into the pool.

Hatter rubbed the soap over his dark blond hair, the pink bar's essence mingling with the blue-tinted water to create a lilac foam. He handed it to me, and I worked it all through my own much longer hair. God, that felt good. I scrubbed away every bit of oil and grease, leaving the pale strands squeaky clean.

When I'd washed my hair and face to my satisfaction, I moved to offer the soap back to Hatter, and paused with a playful spark of an idea. Instead I rubbed the bar over his chest myself.

Hatter set his hand over mine, but he didn't stop me. He just leaned close enough to speak without water streaming down between us. "Thought I could use a little help, did you?"

"Not so much that you *needed* it as that you might enjoy it," I said with a smile. "Or I will, in any case."

He made a humming sound that turned more ragged as I eased the bar of soap lower, across the flat planes of his belly. His hand came up to slide over my wet hair. I tipped my head to meet his kiss.

Hatter's mouth was hot and sweet with a hint of the water that had turned our lips slick. From the first instant of the kiss, I didn't want to stop. I didn't just belong in Wonderland. I belonged with this man.

Somewhere in the middle of that, I lost my grip on

the soap. Hatter traced it over my curves as we kept kissing, teasing it under my breasts and gliding it over my nipples until I whimpered. He kissed me harder. His rigid cock brushed my belly, and a giddy tingle ran through me. I reached down to give that part of him a good rubbing too. He groaned and tugged me closer.

"I don't want you to think I'm glad to have you here just for this," he murmured by my ear in a voice full of promise. "But I did miss having you like this too. Are you sure it's not too much?"

"We'll just—take it easy," I said, with a hitch of my breath as his deft fingers grazed my clit. Fuck, none of me wanted easy right now. I wanted hard and fast and everything he had in him. Whether my body was up for that in my current state of health was another matter.

Hatter walked us to the edge of the pool where the stream's shower eased off. When he sat me on the stone ledge while he stayed in the water, he stood at the perfect height for his hips to fit between my splayed legs.

Need burned from my core, but Hatter wasn't the type to rush. He drew me into another kiss, his talented hands massaging my breasts, my ass, until my nerves were trembling for reasons that had nothing to do with any injury.

"Please," I mumbled against his mouth. My hand closed around his cock, reveling in the soft skin over that solid length before I urged it toward me. Hatter's breath stuttered.

"Here?" he said with an arch of his eyebrow. His fingers trailed down my stomach to my sex. I scooted closer with a gasp as his tip brushed my opening. Then he was pressing inside, and everything narrowed down to the hot taut slide of him filling me completely.

"Lyssa," he murmured between kisses, as if confirming to himself that I was here. "Lyssa."

"Hatter. So good." I let out a little cry as he plunged even deeper, pleasure sparking up from my core, and he paused with a look of concern so heartfelt it made my pulse skip a beat.

"I'm fine," I reassured him.

"Let's make sure you stay that way while I'm taking you someplace so much better than fine," he said, his lips grazing my cheek.

He started to move again, steady rolls of his hips, sending bliss shooting through me with each thrust. One hand slipped down between us so his thumb could settle on my clit. As I whimpered and arched against him, he braced his other arm behind me. His fingers dipped around my ass to probe my other opening where he'd filled me once before. I was held completely, penetrated in every way.

I made an inarticulate sound, overwhelmed by the sensations he was stirring all through my body. Pleasure blazed up inside me. Just like that, I was a goner. His thumb flicked over my clit, his cock plunged into me at the perfect angle, his fingers teased my ass, and I came apart in his arms.

Hatter groaned as I clenched around him. Ecstasy rippled through my body, and he propelled it higher with a few quick jerks of his hips. Then he flooded me with even more heat.

His breath seared over my chest as he held me, his

head bowed, catching his breath. I clutched him in return. I was here. Maybe up there outside these caves everything was wrong, but this moment was nothing but right.

Hatter kissed me again, so tenderly it brought an ache into my chest. He stroked his hand over my back.

"You asked me some questions, that last night you were here," he said in a low voice. "I'm not sure I answered them adequately."

"Questions?" I said, searching my memory. We'd talked about an awful lot of things in the time we'd spent together here.

He pulled back far enough to meet my eyes. "Watching someone walk away from you to what you think will be their death has a way of clarifying things," he said. "And I want to say it now while I can. I love you, Lyssa."

My arms tightened around him. A smile stretched my lips. It was suddenly far easier than I'd expected to say, "I love you too."

"I don't know how this will end up, with you the Red Queen and all—"

"I'm pretty sure a queen can decide to be with whatever man she wants," I said firmly.

The corner of his mouth twitched upward. "And however many she wants?" he suggested.

"I don't think you have to worry about me bringing in *too* many others," I muttered. My thoughts leapt to Chess, and then to Theo… How could I even know what to feel about him when maybe I should be grieving him right now?

"Either way, it'll be up to you." Hatter touched his

nose to mine. "I'll be here helping you make your way to that throne however I can. That's all that matters."

I hugged him to me, and we stayed locked in that embrace until my damp skin started to cool in the open air. My legs didn't wobble too much when I pulled myself back onto them.

Our little interlude must have taken longer than it'd felt like, because by the time we'd dressed and made it back to the camp, Chess was standing amid the others. I couldn't tell from his expression what he'd found, but he didn't look upset, which at least suggested it wasn't anything tragic. My spirits lifted.

"How did your expedition go?" I asked, hurrying over.

"In some ways better than others," Chess said. "I couldn't find a reasonable place to cross the palace wall. But I *did* determine that one old 'pal' of ours is still going back and forth between the city and the palace." He grinned wide enough to show his fangs. "We'll get in there and get our answers about the prince. Rabbit can be our key."

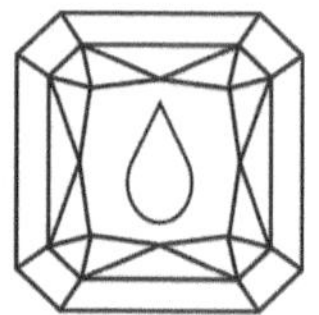

CHAPTER SIX

Theo

The smell of roses permeated the entire palace, but it hung particularly thick in the inner quarters. It practically colored the air in the hall the guard was hustling me down. Even when I breathed through my mouth, the odor seeped up into my nose. The sensation of fluttering petals and prickling thorns clouded my mind.

I sank as deep into my head as I could, holding onto the one thought that really mattered. The one goal I had to see through. No matter what my mother did to me, no matter what else her underlings flashed in front of my eyes or whispered in my ears or pricked my skin with, I wouldn't let myself be a victim. I'd come to the palace with a purpose, and I'd see it through. One step at a time, one piece at a time.

Lyssa was waiting for me. She and all the rest of Wonderland were counting on me.

My knees ached as we drew up in front of the door to the Queen's private chambers. They seemed to be the favorite spot of the tormentors my mother called her "doctors." Tiny pins jabbed under the knee cap. They made a lot of use of the spaces between my wrist bones and along the line of my jaw as well. Just remembering those moments brought back shards of pain.

"Come in," the Queen of Hearts commanded in her cutting voice. The guards around the door eased it open, and the one escorting me hustled me inside.

My mother was sitting on the throne of her private audience room, this seat a more subdued affair than the immensely grand throne in the public hall near the front of the palace—or even the portable one she had her attendants heft her along on when she left the palace grounds. A studied eye could tell it had been even simpler before. The Hearts' craftspeople had fixed golden panels etched with roses and vines over to the elegant lines of the cherry wood frame. No doubt the gold brocade on the velvet padding was our family's own addition too. All of it holding the throne's power in check so it couldn't burn this wrongful ruler like Lyssa's sword had rejected my hand.

The vast mauve skirts of the Queen of Hearts' dress nearly overwhelmed the throne's base. She leaned forward as I trudged along the velvet carpet toward her. The guard's grip on my arm tightened. He was nervous of her response. Even though he'd had no more to do with my "treatment" than the guards at the door had, my mother might very well take out any disappointment on him.

And disappointed I expected she'd be, once I'd seen my mission through and could speak freely.

We stopped a few feet from the throne. The Queen stayed seated, peering down at us with her coolly glinting eyes, her lips pursed. The coils of her copper hair framed the edge of her crown like foam escaping from beneath it. Her breath released with a faint hiss.

I looked back at her, keeping my expression slack. My right arm, the one the guard wasn't holding, shifted against my side. Nudging the bit of machinery I'd hidden in the loose sleeve of my shirt a little closer to the fitted cuff.

"How are you doing today, Jack?" my mother said in a tone that could have been taken as gentle if you missed the barbed edge underneath. I wasn't sure the Queen of Hearts' had the ability to be truly gentle after all these years of brutality.

Theo, I thought. *My name is Theo now.* But that detail wasn't worth arguing over, not when it would ruin the rest. I had to choose my battles wisely. And for now, I had to play to what little sympathies she possessed to get this job done.

"Rather sore," I said. "And regretful that I've caused you so much distress."

"Oh?" A gleam of hope lit in her light brown eyes.

I took a step forward, and the guard released his hold. *He* didn't want to get any closer. Which served my purposes just fine.

"I was so young, and I acted too hastily, doing what I thought I needed to do," I said. "I didn't give enough consideration to the pain my disappearance would cause you. If I could only show you how sorry I am for what I put you through…"

I took another step and knelt by the folds of her skirts. The rose scent clogged my nose as I leaned my forehead beseechingly against them. I spread my arms wide as if offering myself up to her mercy—and my right hand came to rest on the side of the throne.

There, that was the edge of the largest panel. I'd noted how the slabs of gold fit together when I'd come before the Queen in days past. Just as I'd observed the way the golden sheen in my mother's eyes shone brighter when she was sitting on this seat, the way that glow shivered over her body in fits and starts the longer she stayed there.

I'd been around the artifacts of the Red royal rule enough in recent weeks to recognize another one when I saw it now. This throne had once been the throne of the Red Queen, co-opted by the supposed Queens of Hearts for their own purposes. They had no royal magic of their own, but our history provided a clear testament that they took no concern in stealing the power of others.

With a subtle flick of my wrist, I palmed the device from my sleeve and jammed it into the small gap beside the panel as quickly as I could. I'd built the small but powerful contraption with every care I could in the spaces between the doctors' attentions, out of little offerings from my older siblings, several of whom had stopped by to ingratiate themselves with our mother's named heir. Each material on its own wouldn't have raised any suspicions. Even if they'd consulted with each other, which wasn't like the Hearts at all, I doubted they'd have the inventive instincts to guess what I'd put together.

"Enough of that, now," my mother said, urging me up with a ruffling of her skirts, but her tone was partly approving. Subservience from any quarter never failed to appeal to her. "No son of mine should lower himself to groveling. What do you have to say about this foolery you mentioned before, about letting our subjects run wild?"

Only my mother could have seen easing up on executions and offering some basic freedoms as encouraging people to "run wild." I straightened up, my mouth tightening. I'd accomplished the one small task I'd needed to carry out today. There was no need to pretend anymore, even if I'd lost any hope that my words would sway her.

The trouble was that the "treatments" she'd had her "doctors" inflict on me hadn't been entirely unsuccessful, even if they weren't curing me of the disease she thought I had. A stabbing pain ran up the fronts of my thighs and the sides of my forearms when I even thought the words I wanted to say. Sharp splinters of pain radiated from my jaw right up to my scalp, muddling my head even more than the rose smell did.

My mother thought the Spades had brainwashed me somehow. She'd ordered her doctors to wipe the rebellion's influence from mind. But I'd built that rebellion. Those principles and desires were a part of me, running right down to the core. They couldn't root them out. Their efforts only fractured who I was.

"Not run wild," I managed to say. A thudding ache spread across the back of my skull. I could have pretended to agree, but I would *not* lie simply to protect my own skin, not a single time more. If I acted the part she wanted, if I supported the horrors she'd carried out, she'd only feel more certain in them. "I merely wish to see them live under a more even hand. I've spent a lot of time among them, Mother—I know they don't wish to defy you. If you would just listen to me while I explain—"

The Queen jerked to her feet with a swish of her skirts. "Enough," she snapped. Her face had flushed crimson. "This is more of the same twaddle you spewed when you first came before me." She whipped around to aim her glare at the guard who'd brought me. "What did the doctors say of his progress? Why haven't they cleared the awful taint from my son yet?"

The guard stiffened. His face turned as white as hers had red. "I—I believe they thought they had reduced the effect, Your Highness," he stammered. "They said they'd bled out the worst of it and that he responded well to their re-education."

I'd had to play along with them before they'd willingly send me before the Queen for her consideration. A head or two might roll today. After all the bleeding and the rest, I couldn't find it in me to care very much.

"Please, Mother," I said despite the growing headache and the pains clamoring for attention all through my body. "All I want is to see Wonderland be as wondrous as it can be—as it once was. We could be the ones to bring glory and joy to the entire realm. Don't you want that?"

I didn't expect her to listen, not after everything I'd already been through, but even this one guard seeing my attempt might tip someone in the right direction. All I could do was keep trying.

The Queen of Hearts let out a ragged laugh. "Glory

and joy? The only glory this place is capable of happens right here. You're still sick, Jack. I won't hear any more of this raving. Get him out of here—and tell the doctors I want them here to account for their failure immediately."

"Yes, Your Highness. Of course, Your Highness," the guard said with a frantic bob of his head. He tugged me toward the door. I stumbled as I went, a wave of dizziness throwing off my balance.

I was heading back to more of that. They'd cut deeper, bombard me harder with images and words of the rule I was supposed to believe in. The guards we passed in the hall didn't show the slightest sign of sympathy or concern. I couldn't rely on anyone but myself here.

I had to hold on. I had to fend off the worst the doctors inflicted on me and keep as much of my head as I could. My mother still maintained enough hope that I could be the son she wanted to keep me alive, and so I had to hope that I could make some difference here.

All of Wonderland was counting on me, and I'd see my neck severed before I let them down again.

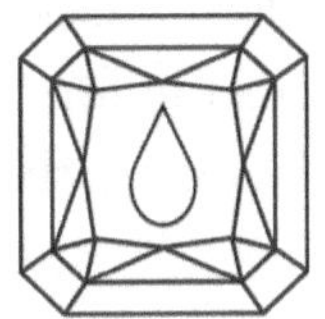

CHAPTER SEVEN

Lyssa

Wonderland's glowing underground river didn't extend beyond the city's limits in the direction of Caterpillar's club. I slunk along the darkened streets behind my sense of Chess's invisible form, my breath warm and humid inside the cloth mask he'd given me to cover the lower part of my face. A hint of the rose scent trickled in, but not enough to affect our minds—or Hatter's, beside me. Which was a good thing, because the guards had laid out heaps of their drugged flowers all along the borders of the city to ensure no one snuck out to the clearer air beyond.

There wasn't much dancing on these outer streets, but we did pass a couple slumped together next to the road with their clothes in disarray, as if they'd fallen asleep halfway to having sex. Someone was singing a tuneless, wordless song that filtered through an upper window into the cool night air.

The Queen of Hearts might not have chopped off these people's heads, but her latest tactic of control had left them pretty much out of their minds.

Chess turned visible just long enough to motion us down an alley. The tap of a guard's footsteps marched past us on the road we'd just left. We skirted the direct route to the club and slipped into the forest of starkly green trees that sprawled around it. After the few days I'd had to continue recuperating while the Spades made their observations to construct our plan, barely any lingering pain from the accident remained in my body. I felt almost like my normal self again.

After we'd walked several minutes, even the wisp of rose that had reached my nose faded away. Hatter tugged his mask down and dragged in a deep breath, and I did the same, welcoming the rush of the crisp forest smells.

"Chess?" I murmured.

Our fanged companion shimmered into view with a brush of his hand over my shoulder. "Almost there."

"You're sure he won't have guards with him?" Hatter said under his breath.

"He hasn't the times I've watched so far," Chess said. "You'll just have to keep those hat pins of yours ready in case he's switched up his routine." His grin glinted in the dim moonlight that penetrated the leaves overhead.

Hatter made a slightly disgruntled sound, but he adjusted the sleeves of his suit jacket—an unusually subdued navy blue—where I knew he had at least a couple of those pins at the ready. We stalked on through the forest, Chess leading the way. My heart thumped louder with each rustle of the branches above us.

"Do you think the Queen took Unicorn's head for helping us?" I asked finally. The question had been rattling around my brain since Chess had said he hadn't been able to set eyes on our recent ally since the horned fighter had helped us break into the palace grounds.

"Could be," Chess said softly. "Could be she took both him and Lion, not knowing who to blame. Or they could be laying low with all appendages intact. Not many of the Diamonds are venturing far beyond the palace lately. We shook them up well, and they needed a good shaking."

Unicorn hadn't done anything all that obvious, his bashing into the gate set up to look like an accident, but the Queen had executed people for a lot less. She often executed people for nothing at all, from what I'd seen. Him simply being in the area when I'd burst into the palace grounds might have raised her suspicions.

Whether he was alive or dead, he hadn't shown any sign of being able to help more. Which was why we were on our way to chat with an even more uncertain ally.

Chess held up his hand for us to stop. I made out a narrow path of flattened grass that wove through the trees to a gnarled old oak. Its branches crisscrossed each other and wove together like a latticework, and between its arched roots lay a round mahogany door so polished you could hardly believe it had spent any time outside. I eyed it for a moment.

"Rabbit lives in an actual rabbit hole?" I said.

"I had tea with him once," Chess said with an enigmatic air. "It's rather nicer on the inside than the outside, as holes go. Which is not very far, in his case. He wants to stay put, not find himself elsewhere."

Hatter shot his friend a bemused look. Giving straight-forward answers wasn't exactly Chess's forte. But after everything I'd seen of Wonderland, I knew that hole could as easily open up into the fanciest ballroom I'd ever seen as the earthen room I'd expect.

You couldn't really expect anything to be as you'd think in Wonderland—not even when you'd seen the thing in question before.

I tugged off the blouse I'd wore to hide my armored vest and slid the ruby necklace out to rest on the interlaced metal. For this conversation, I wanted to look every bit the queen.

We stood in the shelter of the trees a few paces from the path, all of us staying silent after that. The breeze whispered through the leaves, and small creatures scampered through the brush. The buzz of a fly zipping past my ear made me flinch. Out on the Checkerboard Plains, we'd encountered some giant insects more massive than I hoped to ever have anywhere near me again. Especially since those insects had seemed to be as interested in removing our heads as the Queen was.

A chill was starting to seep through my clothes when a faint pattering reached my ears. I tensed, holding my body even more still than before.

Rabbit's white-furred form came into view down the path. Just as his home appeared to be an actual rabbit hole, he looked like an actual rabbit—one about as tall as I was, half-walking half-hopping in a trim pinstriped waistcoat. He was muttering quietly to himself. It reminded me of the one time I'd seen him before, when I'd had to dodge him in the passages beneath the club on my way to the now-broken mirror there. He'd been fussing about how Caterpillar's demands always made him late, no matter how hard he tried to keep up with them.

He hadn't sounded all that happy with his boss. There had to be something we could offer him—something I could offer him—that would sway his loyalties. Chess believed there was, anyway.

Rabbit tugged a watch out of his waistcoat pocket, glanced at it, and flattened his long furry ears closer to his head. He hop-walked a little faster. As he tucked the watch back into his pocket, Hatter and Chess stepped out onto the path to intercept him, Chess in front and Hatter behind.

Rabbit startled, his ears springing straight up. He hopped back a step and spun to see that way was blocked too. "Well, I—" he started. His voice started to rise. "It really is quite rude to hold up a person on their way. I must protest that—"

Chess held up his hand. "Before you do too much protesting, Rabbit, consider who you'd be calling for help too. The ones who've left the entire city in a daze? The ones who'd take *your* head the second you seem like a problem? Do you really think we're more dangerous than them?"

Rabbit sputtered a bit, but he didn't appear to have a coherent answer. He thumped one long foot on the ground. "Well, what do you want, then?" he asked, his dark eyes twitching from Chess to Hatter and back again.

I eased forward then, right in front of him. "We want

information from the palace," I said. "And possibly a way to get in and out for that building. I'll repay you, of course."

Rabbit stared at me for a moment, his posture going rigid. He had to recognize me from the day weeks ago when I'd stomped into the palace gardens at ten times my usual height. He knew I was the "Alice" the Queen of Hearts was after.

"What makes you think I could offer you any of that?" he said tightly.

"You're the only one making his way to and fro from the palace," Chess said. "Besides the guards. All the Diamonds are staying in and all the Clubbers are staying out. You have to go right to the Queen's private chambers to get to her mirror, from what I hear. *You* must hear plenty along the way."

"I keep to my own business." Rabbit's nose twitched. "It won't do me any good to be mixed up in yours."

"It might, though," I said. "She isn't going to be queen forever. I'm the Red Queen, and I will take back the throne the Hearts stole from my family. If you help me, I'll be able to offer you an awful lot."

"And if I don't?"

I gazed back at him evenly. "I won't take your head. I won't hurt one whisker on your face. Did I hurt anyone when I came to free her prisoners, even when they were jabbing at me?"

His expression relaxed slightly. I hadn't. I'd made a point of showing how different my methods were from the Queen of Hearts'. I wasn't sure I could keep up that peacefulness through the battles ahead of us, but I'd spill as little blood as I could manage.

"The Queen of Hearts would take your head," Hatter said. "For looking at her wrong. For saying the wrong word."

"For being a tiny bit late," I added.

"Or possibly even early," Chess threw in. "It's only a matter of time now that you're brushing up so close to her, you know, Rabbit. We're trying to *save* you from the trap you're stuck in."

"It's not a trap," Rabbit said with a sniff. "It's a job. *I've* done my part for Wonderland. I've helped keep people happy and entertained."

Hatter raised his eyebrows. "Do you really think they're all that happy now?"

"The Queen is distressed. We can return to our regular club activities when she's calmed down."

"And are you treated all that well in the club either?" I said. "Caterpillar is constantly bossing you around and running you ragged. Aren't you tired of living under his thumb? Isn't there somewhere else you'd rather be?"

Rabbit bristled so quickly I could tell I'd hit a nerve—but not the way I'd wanted to. "I'm *exactly* where I want to be," he said. "I've worked within the club from the day it opened, and I've made it as good a place as any in Wonderland. Leave it to Caterpillar?" He scoffed.

The glint in his eyes and the passion in his voice lit an answering spark in me. It reminded me of how I'd felt when I'd declared that I was taking back the throne.

He'd just handed me what I'd needed—the key to his desires.

"What if we left Caterpillar out of it completely?" I said, raising my chin as if I had no doubt at all that I could fulfill the offer I was making. "What if, once I'm on that throne, the club passes into your hands as the new owner? You can run it any way you like—within reason, of course. You can make it better than he ever let you."

Rabbit's mouth opened and closed and opened again without a sound. An eager quiver ran through him. But he was hesitating.

I drew on every ounce of longing I'd felt since I'd found my way into Wonderland. "It's what you've dreamed of, isn't it? It could be yours. Don't pass up that chance. I *want* to hand you your dream on a platter. What has the Queen of Hearts ever given you except terror?"

Rabbit only wavered another half a second. "What do you want to know about the palace?" he asked in a hushed voice.

I restrained the grin that tried to spring across my face. "What have you heard about Jack, the Queen's son— the one everyone thought was dead, who was living as the Inventor? Is he in the palace?"

Is he alive? That part of the question was enough to make my urge to grin fade completely.

Rabbit rubbed his small white chin. "That matter has been kept very quiet, but I have caught a thing or two. I believe she's attempting to cure him of the Spades' influence. Has him shut away somewhere with doctors attending to him in the inner quarters of the palace."

A wave of relief rushed through me. Chess smiled wide. Hatter didn't look quite as pleased, but he didn't look upset either, which I guessed was about as good a reaction as I could have hoped for given his fraught history with Theo.

"All right," I said. "Then we're going to need you to get us into the palace and as close to where they're keeping the prince as you can without drawing too much suspicion. You're supposed to go back tomorrow, aren't you?"

The night felt even thicker as we made our way back to the entrance to the caves, but my spirits were light despite the darkness. We had a plan; we had an ally even if he was a bought one. With Theo by our side, with everything he knew about his mother, we'd be ready to topple the Queen of Hearts once and for all.

We were just slinking around the side of a building when Chess's invisible arm held me back. I froze.

A squad of the Queen's guards burst into the street out of one of the buildings, what looked like a tavern. They were herding several men and women, all of them young to middle-aged and reasonably fit, their eyes glazed with that drugged haze.

"Where are they taking them?" I murmured. An uneasy prickling filled my stomach. I couldn't see how it could be for anything *good*.

"Looks like to the palace," Chess said as the guards hustled the small crowd on past our shadowed hiding spot.

One of the guards turned his head our way, and I stiffened even more. But beneath his dented red helm, his face had almost the same vague expression as the drugged city people. His eyes slid over the street and the buildings lining on it without pausing for a second. He snapped his head back to the route ahead with the same blank expression.

Hatter must have noticed my confusion. "That's a pearl-headed one," he said softly as the guards marched out of view.

"Pearl-headed?" I repeated.

He nodded. "When the Queen beheads people, if they were reasonably physically capable, she sends them out to the sea. That's the work my 'friend' Carpenter is doing now. They have a process where they can grow a new head in the old one's place, like a pearl in a shell. They're never like they once were, though. The new person is nearly mindless."

"But he's out there with the rest of the guards," I said.

"The Queen imprints them in some way to make them see her as their one leader, and any orders she gives them, they'll follow as well as they can," Hatter said. "They have no thoughts of their own, as far as anyone's been able to tell. Mostly she uses them for servants doing menial tasks around the palace, but she's supplemented the Hearts' Guard with them too."

I hugged myself, holding back a shudder. The prickling that had filled my stomach earlier seeped through the rest of my body with a chill.

We needed to get Theo *soon*. Every moment the Queen of Hearts stayed on that throne, who knew what new horror she might commit? I just hoped we'd be in time to save those people from whatever fate she had planned for them.

"Let's go," I said. "We have preparations to make for tomorrow."

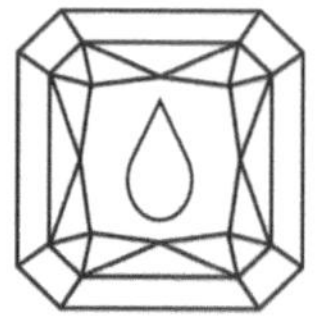

Lyssa

Rabbit's ears flattened to his head when he saw the four of us waiting in the spot just off the road to the palace where he'd told us to wait. "The more I'm bringing, the more likely they are to get suspicious," he said, shifting his weight from one foot to the other.

"It'll only look like three," Chess said brightly. He faded away to his grin, and then that blinked out of sight too. "I find our way, Hatter opens it up, and Dee can shove away any who try to block us."

"And the Otherlander?" Rabbit muttered.

Chess reappeared in a flash, his grin gone sharp with the glint of his fangs. "The Otherlander is more a Wonderlander than even we can claim, and it's her palace we're storming."

I touched his brawny arm to reassure him that I didn't need further defending. "I'm not sure Theo—Jack—will leave unless I can talk to him," I said. Theo had come to the palace with plans of his own that obviously hadn't worked out, but I wasn't sure whether he'd be willing to let go of them without a lot of convincing. And from what he'd said, he'd made those plans for me, so the convincing might need to come from me too.

Rabbit let out a huff of breath and gestured for us to follow him. "Get on your disguises now. You never know when the guards will wander."

Chess vanished. Hatter, Dee, and I pulled on the white hoodies one of the Spades had quickly sewn together for us. We tied the filtration masks over our faces and tugged the hoods tight over our hair so no one could see much but our eyes. If anyone at the palace recognized us, especially me, it was game over.

But Rabbit had clearly earned a lot of the Queen's trust. The mark of her seal still stood out starkly crimson against the thin white fur of his palm. He'd told us that she'd imbued it with enough power that it only faded once a week, to save her the hassle of approving his entrance every night.

I couldn't enjoy the warm afternoon air or the bright sun overhead. The thump of our feet against the cobblestones echoed the thudding of my pulse. We were walking right into the lion's den, and we weren't ready to fight the lion yet. But we had to get Theo out.

His mother had been trying to "cure" him, Rabbit had said, but he hadn't known more than that. What had the Queen been doing to her favorite son who'd then betrayed her?

He might be alive, but after all this time, was he okay?

We slowed as we approached the gate to the palace gardens. The gate I'd barged through like a giant a few weeks ago, as it happened. I resisted the urge to hunch my shoulders under the guards' stares. One of them frowned.

"Who's all this?" he asked Rabbit.

"With the increased demand, I'm running through my usual supply too quickly," Rabbit said. His cheek twitched, making his whiskers jitter nervously, but his voice held steady. "I need assistants to ensure I can gather the necessary ingredients in time."

"What's with their clothing?"

"To mark them quickly as my assistants, and to ensure the toxins of the Otherland don't affect them, since they haven't my experience there," Rabbit said.

The guard's frown didn't budge. "I don't know... *They* don't have the mark of the seal."

Rabbit's whiskers quivered again, but this time he managed to make them look indignant. "Shall I tell the Queen it is your fault when the club is unable to produce enough of her concoction to dose even half of the needed roses?"

The guard blanched, and the other one waved us toward the gate. "Get on with it, then."

As we passed through and the bars clanked shut behind us, I heard one murmur to the other, "I'll be glad when this whole to-do in the city is done with, won't you?"

The guards were getting frustrated with the Queen's tactics too. That was good. Every bit of leverage we had on our side was a step in the right direction.

Rabbit took us on a swift journey along the garden

paths to a side door in the palace. The flowers blooming all around us formed a sickeningly sweet bouquet of scents that the mask couldn't totally shield us from.

At the door, our escort had to go through a similar song and dance about why we were with him, but shorter. I guessed these guards figured if the gate sentries had let us through, who were they to argue?

Inside, Chess brushed his fingers over my arm in a gentle gesture to let me know he was slipping ahead. The rest of us treaded carefully across the velvet-carpeted halls, past ornate tapestries and paintings with gold frames. The arched ceiling loomed high above our heads. No one much was around along the route Rabbit took. We didn't hear a sound other than the whisper of our steps.

We went up a flight of stairs and down another hall. Where it branched, Rabbit held up his hand. He'd told us last night that we'd need to part ways before we reached the Queen's private quarters—the rooms I'd been in once before, where she kept the mirror to the Otherland. Theo wasn't in her own chambers but, Rabbit suspected, somewhere not too far away.

I tipped my head in acknowledgment and thanks. Rabbit gave me a pained smile and headed onward at his halting gait. Hatter leaned against the wall, his eyes wary as he scanned our surroundings. Dee stretched his arms in front of him as if readying himself for a fight. I hoped we wouldn't end up needing his skills for that purpose, only to speed our escape.

Chess had known we'd wait for him here. He should be scouting out the halls around here invisibly, watching for a hint of Theo's location. If any guards wandered by while we were waiting for him, we'd just have to hope the excuses we could come up with worked as well as Rabbit's had.

The seconds ticked by, seeming to crawl over my skin. I crossed my arms over my chest. Hatter set a reassuring hand on my side, and I shot him a grateful glance. Dee bobbed on his feet impatiently.

Then Chess spoke out of nowhere, his playful voice right by my ear. "I've determined where we are going, so let us go forward. Straight ahead, the second left, and then a right. There's a door with two guards outside. Dee and I can deal with them."

The creeping feeling intensified with his casual acceptance of the violence he expected to come. "We don't *kill* anyone," I reminded them. "Not if we can help it."

"Of course not, lovely," Chess said. I could almost hear his smile. "I'm not partial to permanent endings myself anyway."

"Are you sure Theo is in that room?" I asked as we started down the hall. My gaze darted back and forth, every nerve on edge.

"I can't think of what else they'd be guarding there," Chess said. "And I watched for long enough to see a couple of those doctors the Queen must have working on his 'cure' emerge. I suspect we'd be better off getting to him before they get around to coming back."

We walked a little faster. The velvet carpet absorbed most of the sound of our feet. Hatter brought his hat pins into one hand, spinning them between his nimble fingers. I'd have admired his dexterity, as familiar as it was becoming, if I hadn't been so nervous.

Where we would take the right turn Chess had mentioned, we stopped. "Dee," Chess murmured. "Ready?"

The redheaded twin nodded, his eyes glinting eagerly. His spirits had seemed dampened since I'd found the Spades in their underground hideout, almost as subdued as his serious brother, but this mission had perked him up.

The air shifted as Chess sprinted down the hall. At a thump and a groan, the rest of us dashed after him.

The two guards had sprawled next to each other, pressing their hands to their foreheads. Chess must have slammed their heads together. Before they could gather their wits enough to fight back, Dee's elastic arms were jerking their uniforms up over their faces. He yanked their arms from the sleeves, knotted those and tugged them tight as a straitjacket, and tossed the guards into another room Chess had just opened the door to. Their muffled shouts fell away completely with the click of the door closing.

Hatter had already knelt by the other door, the one they'd been guarding. His fingers tensed and flexed as he worked his pins in the keyhole. The process seemed to be taking him longer than usual. He knit his brow, a curse slipping from his lips under his breath.

Voices carried from down one of the nearby halls. My pulse lurched—and the lock released with a metallic hiss. Hatter straightened up, met my eyes for just a second, and turned the knob.

The door swung open into a small room with rosy pink walls. We all darted inside to avoid notice. Then my gaze caught on the seat in the middle of the room and the figure sitting in it, and my throat constricted.

Theo was wearing clothes that presumably befitted a prince—crimson trousers and jacket over a pale pink shirt, gold detailing around the cuffs and collar—but I recognized his well-muscled body even without his usual white dress shirt and gray slacks. I *had* to recognize him from his body, which was tied to an ornate wooden chair with ropes around his wrists and ankles, because a metal helm sat over his head, completely hiding his face.

Tinny sounds seeped out of the helm. His arms and back were tensed against the chair, his hands balled into fists. A dribble of... was that blood? ...streaked through the sweat beading on his throat.

Oh God. What the hell were they doing to him?

I sprang forward and grasped the helm. Dee's face had paled, but he leapt in just as quickly to fumble with ropes. Hatter hustled around to the other side of the chair.

I yanked on the helm, but it was so heavy it didn't budge, even as my muscles strained. Then Chess was beside me, a solid presence even if I still couldn't see him, setting his broad hands next to mine.

"One, two, three," he murmured, and we heaved on the helm at the same time.

With a clacking sound, it lifted up, revealing Theo's rumpled curls—the golden shade that was his natural color, not the dark brown I'd been used to—and his sweat dampened face. His cocoa-dark eyes stared at us for a few seconds as if still seeing something that was no longer there before they focused on me. He blinked, and his lips parted.

"Lyssa," he said hoarsely. "You—You were supposed to *wait*—"

A horrified laugh sputtered out of me. I tossed the helm to the side. "It's a good thing I didn't. We're getting you out of here. Can you stand?"

Hatter and Dee had snapped the ropes. Theo pushed himself to his feet and took a couple of steps. His legs held his weight steadily enough, but his head listed a little from one side to the other in a way that made me queasy, watching.

Dee grasped Theo's arm, joy shining in his face even as concern flashed through his expression. Theo had taken him in when the twins' mother had been afraid the Queen would conscript them as guards because of their valuable talents. They'd lived and breathed the Spades since they were kids—and Theo, as the White Knight, had been their sort-of king. Only right now, seeing the play of emotions on his face, did I realize how wrenching the last couple weeks without their leader must have been for all his people.

Theo had lied, yes. He'd hidden things from me and from the Spades—from everyone. But he'd meant a lot to people in spite of that. Maybe he'd been honest with them in the ways that mattered most.

We could work through the ways that mattered most to me some time when we weren't in the middle of the palace of our greatest enemy.

"You'll be all right once you're done with this place," Dee said, as if to convince himself and Theo. "We've got you."

"You do," Theo said, with a little more confidence. "You do."

"Here, you'll want to wear these. They'll help us get you out." Dee handed over a white hoodie and a strip of cloth that was a pretty close match for our masks.

Theo pulled them on, his legs swaying slightly under him. His head jerked around abruptly. He reached toward me. I grabbed his hand, he tugged me closer, and in the rush of my relief, nothing that had happened before the last five minutes seemed to matter very much at all.

I threw my arms around him and hugged him tight. Theo returned my embrace with a rasp of breath that sounded both startled and pleased. His lips brushed my cheek. His voice spilled out warm and urgent.

"I did what I could. I got it ready for you."

"What?" I said, confused, as I forced myself to pull back.

A flicker of a smile crossed his lips. "Your throne," he said. "I swore I'd see you on it. I've cleared the last part of your way there."

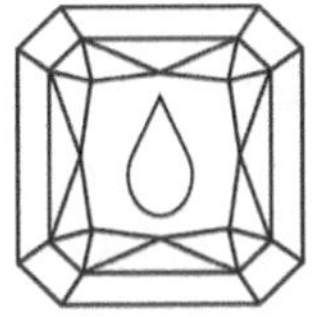

CHAPTER NINE

Hatter

"Does he seem quite like he did to you?" Dee asked me under his breath where we were leaning against the wall of the cave. On the other side of the alcove where we'd set up our bunch of foldable cabins, the former White Knight, now Prince of Hearts, was sitting with a plate of food one of the other Spades had brought him.

There'd been cheers and exclamations all around when we'd arrived with our supposed leader in tow. Theo—Jack? —had immediately grabbed Mirabel in a grateful hug. He'd asked for a couple of hours to recover himself before we assembled the Spades who still remained down here to hear what he had to say.

So far, that recovery had involved a shower and a change of clothes, rinsing dye powder through his hair to turn his curls back to the chestnut brown they'd been as long as I'd known him, a brief interlude in one of the cabins looking over the loot Chess had brought back from his office, and now a meal.

I supposed I couldn't fault him for needing to get his bearings after the situation we'd found him in, but there were plenty of other offences I wasn't ready to absolve him of yet.

"Whatever the Queen of Hearts had her doctors doing to him, it shook him up some," I said. Theo still held himself with the same confident posture he'd always had, but his gaze flickered more than I remembered. Sometimes he tensed for no apparent reason, as if he were controlling an impulse he didn't want to give in to.

Our White Knight had always given the impression of being perfectly in control, to the point that it'd annoyed the shit out of me. This Prince of Hearts appeared to be wavering on the edge of losing himself.

"He's only been back a little while. He'll get back to his old self soon enough," Dee said, with characteristic optimism. He couldn't quite summon a smile, though.

I wasn't sure I totally believed what he'd said either. The Theo we'd known had been the man he'd constructed for us to see, as much an invention as his various devices. Now that façade was broken. How could he ever be the exact same person he had been, when that person had always been at least in part an act?

Word had spread to the other pods of Spades in the underground caves despite Theo's request that we hold off on a real assembly. A few people drifted into our alcove, and then a few more. Doria came out of one of the cabins and lingered there, watching. Seeing my daughter hesitate to approach the man she'd followed without question just a few weeks ago set my teeth on edge.

Theo raised his head and seemed to take note of the new arrivals. His shoulders stiffened for just a second in the pale green shirt someone had lent him—even that hint of tension not quite how he'd usually have presented himself. Then he drew himself up with that assured air I now knew was a princely one.

The Queen of Hearts' fucking *son*. It was right there in the authority of his stance, the boldness of that square jaw. The youngest descendent of a line that came and took what rightfully belonged to others while squashing every sign of dissent.

Oh, yes, he had plenty of offences to account for yet.

"Spades," the prince said in his familiar rolling baritone. It filled the alcove and the passage beyond. Most of us looked sallow in the eerie glow given off by the stream, but somehow it lit him up like a supernatural aura of power. "I'm so glad to have come back to you. I wish I could take longer to relish my freedom, but we have far too pressing concerns we must address as quickly as possible."

All the Spades emerged from the cabins or turned from what they were doing to listen. Dum and Mallo left off the game of cards they'd been playing to pass the time. Lyssa looked up from where she'd been sitting with Chess.

The tension in her expression made my heart squeeze. I loved that woman, I did, with every fiber of my being, and I knew how much Theo had hurt her beyond anyone else. He'd played her like a fool, taking her on that ramble through the Checkerboard Plains as if he had no idea that the artifacts might be meant specifically for her, why she could slow the train or calm a jabberwock.

No matter what his reasons had been, my arm itched with the urge to pay him back for that pain with a punch or two where he'd hurt too. But Lyssa wouldn't like that. He was hers to deal with as she saw fit—and as queen, what she wanted to deal with, she did.

"You'll have heard a lot of things in the last few weeks," Theo went on. "I want to lay the facts as bare as possible. I *am* the son of the Queen of Hearts—I once went by the name Jack, and I faked my own murder so that I could escape from under her thumb and try to set things right on the other side of the palace walls. I kept my original identity a secret to avoid discovery that might have led to the end of the work I was doing, but I hate that I've needed to lie to you."

Murmurs carried around the camp. Everyone had heard the gist of the story by now, but some might still have hesitated to believe it until hearing it from the man's own lips.

Theo's gaze roved over the gathered rebels, as dark and steady in this moment as it had ever been. "This is the truth: I am Theo now, not Jack. I am the man you called your White Knight and your Inventor. I'm not a prince— and I never was. The Hearts stole Wonderland's throne from the queens and kings you should have had. But the Red royal family has returned to us. You can still come to me for guidance, and I hope I can offer much that is useful. When it comes to who leads us, I defer to Lyssa, the descendant of the Red Queen and the rightful ruler of Wonderland, as should all of you."

Lyssa's pose stiffened. She'd acknowledged the story of her origins with the rest of the Spades, but she hadn't tried to lord it over anyone. She obviously hadn't expected Theo to highlight her role quite that directly or emphatically. Even as I bristled on her behalf, though, I felt the rightness of his words.

Maybe he could have warned her he'd be pointing a spotlight on her, but we *should* place her word above his. He should renounce all claim on the palace or the throne in deference to her. That was the least she deserved.

Theo made a beckoning gesture, his expression softening as he met Lyssa's eyes, and Hearts take me if I couldn't see an affection and admiration there not so different from what stirred so often in my chest in her presence. Lyssa stood and took his hand to let him present her to the Spades. Despite her earlier surprise, a pleased flush had colored her cheeks. I didn't think the affection went only one way.

Well, she had always been fond of him too. If he redeemed himself, all the better for all of us. When we'd won her proper place back for her, there wasn't any doubt which of us was best suited to stand beside her at that throne, was there?

The thought niggled down my spine until I clamped my jaw and shoved it away.

"We will take back the throne," Lyssa said, her clear voice filling the room as powerfully as Theo's had. The rubies on her woven vest gleamed, but not quite as bright as those brilliant blue eyes. What a woman she was, my looking-glass girl. "We will end this reign of terror. I know I haven't been with you for very long, but I feel like I belong here. I feel connected to all of you, and there's nothing I'd like more than to see all of Wonderland as joyful as it seemed to be when I first got here—but for real this time."

A cheer rose up through the gathering. I raised my voice and clapped my hands to add to it, and so did Dee, with a hint of a furrow in his brow. He and his brother had admired the White Knight so much, I couldn't imagine how this mess had affected him.

"I believe the first step we must take toward seeing our queen to her rightful place is to take back the artifacts of the Red's rule," Theo said, his hand coming to rest tentatively on Lyssa's waist. "The ruby-marked sword and scepter are hidden away in the home belonging to our own Hatter." He tipped his head toward me with a familiarity I couldn't stop from rankling me. "I understand the Queen of Hearts has instructed her guards to keep a close watch on the premises, but I believe I have a plan that can get us to those treasures. Hatter, will you assist?"

Did he honestly expect me to refuse? "Of course," I said automatically. Perhaps I should have waited to hear his plan first, but with the way Lyssa beamed at me, it was hard to have any regrets. That was, until Theo's gaze flickered again, his mouth flattening against an involuntary twitch of his muscles.

My stomach knotted. Our Inventor had always been quick with his plans. Was the man who'd come back to us really ready to take on the Hearts' Guard already—or was he going to lead us straight back into the Queen of Hearts' clutches?

"That one?" Lyssa murmured beside me, pointing to one of the guards ambling down the street past my hat shop, keeping his distance from the wandering revelers.

Theo peered over her shoulder. All three of us were outfitted with the masks that filtered out the Queen's drug, but even with the lower half of his face covered, his gaze was penetrating.

I wished I could feel totally secure it'd stay that way. Even though his plan had made a reasonable amount of sense, we were still depending on him to pull the first part of it off.

"Yes," he said to Lyssa. "That's one. You can always tell from the slightly unnatural stiffness to the way they move. I'll take him."

He slipped away through the shadows along the street, after the pearl-headed guard. His plan required a guard's uniform, and he'd suggested we find a pearled one if we could, to make the taking easier. I couldn't deny the wisdom there.

Our White Knight had more combat skills than I'd have suspected given his tendency to hang back behind the scenes. He whipped out a cord he'd brought with him and used it to yank the guard to him. The slam of his hand to the man's forehead left the figure slumped. He dragged the guard into an alley and returned a few minutes later in the traditional red-and-pink pleated tunic and red pants, the heart-shaped helm perched on his head and the antidote rose tucked into his collar. He'd kept his mask up as we'd discussed.

"Wish me luck," he said under his breath as he passed us. He strode into the hat shop.

Lyssa grasped my hand as we waited. The thrumming rhythm of the music playing down the street vibrated over my skin.

"Do you think we should have made him wait, or let someone else do this part?" Lyssa whispered to me. So, she'd noticed he wasn't exactly in tiptop shape too.

"He does know what demeanor the guards will respond to better than anyone else in the Spades," I said. "And he can pull off that authoritative presence. I think we should keep an eye on him, be ready to step in if he falters, but I wouldn't have agreed to go along with this plan if I'd been *that* worried."

Lyssa nodded, and I took a small particle of satisfaction from having reassured her. We braced ourselves, our eyes fixed on the doorway. Theo was meant to go in and announce to the guards that the roses just dropped on this street had been laced far too heavily with the drug, more than the antidote they all wore could stave off. They were to retreat a few blocks for an hour until it dissipated. The story would also explain the mask he was wearing, which would also stop them from identifying him.

I'd tried to find a loophole, a reason to question his judgment, but I hadn't seen one. And we hadn't been able to come up with a better plan for retrieving her sword and scepter on our own. Lyssa had been right when she'd said we needed him here, at and on our side.

At the sound of raised voices, my pulse hiccupped. It was only a stream of guards from inside the building emptying into the street. Seven of them in total, with Theo at their heels. "Three streets to the north and one west, and wait there for further instructions," he said, as if him giving commands were perfectly natural—which in a way it was. "I've got to clear everyone else out of the area."

The guards made a few puzzled sounding noises, but they headed off down the street in the direction he'd indicated. I let out my breath, but my body stayed tensed. We weren't in the clear yet.

Theo strode in the opposite direction, past us, peering through the shop windows as if looking for other comrades. Every now and then he took a quick glance over his shoulder. After the fourth of those, he glanced our way and motioned quickly to the shop.

The guards had moved out of sight. This was our chance.

Lyssa and I dashed together for the hat shop doorway. The sight of my merchandise strewn across the floor and counters made my chest twist. Ignoring that pang of discomfort, I snatched up a simple top hat as we hustled on to the stairs and set it on my head in a way that immediately set me more at ease.

I could rearrange my hats. I could make new ones. The guards hadn't hurt anything permanently.

As long as Lyssa's artifacts remained in their hiding place undiscovered.

I must have been spending too much time lurking around in the underground passages in the last few weeks and not enough getting my exercise. By the time we reached the fourth floor, I was winded. Lyssa stopped with a gasp of breath that comforted my ego a little, and we hurried down the hall to the upper apartment's master bedroom.

I sprang into the lead. The wardrobe had been my design; I knew exactly where to press the second I'd whipped the door open, exactly how much pressure to apply for the panel to swing around. Lyssa let out a sigh of relief when the gleaming sword and scepter came into view.

She lifted the scepter first, her pale fingers curling around the dark cherry wood staff. The massive ruby in its frame of gold glittered as she shoved it into the sack she'd brought. She slung the bag over her shoulder and reached for the sword. The ruby embedded in its hilt flashed as if in welcome.

Then a shout carried from the street below.

My back went rigid. Lyssa snapped up the sword and swung around. My hatpins all but leapt into my hand. Someone thumped along the street's cobblestones, raising his voice in a bellow.

"Hey! You there! What's this story you're telling? What unit are you meant to be with? Our orders were to never leave this building unguarded."

He had to be talking to Theo. Theo could flee underground, but that man stood between us and escape. I wasn't sure our former White Knight had the wherewithal to do more than save himself right now.

I looked at Lyssa—her wide eyes, her determined expression, so beautiful and so fierce at the same time— and my mouth and my body moved before I'd even really thought about it.

"I'll go down," I said, stepping toward the hall. "I'll lead him off, and you can get back to the trap door."

Before I'd even finished speaking, more footsteps thundered on the road outside. I was going to have more than one guard to distract. My gut clenched, but a surge of adrenaline overwhelmed it. I was about to race toward the stairs when Lyssa caught my arm.

"No!" she said. "Hatter—you don't need to throw yourself into the line of fire for me. We'll get out of this together. There has to be a way. We can—we can go across the rooftops."

She tugged me toward the window. I started to balk, the layout of this block unfurling in my head. Then a single sharp thought pierced the mad haze that had been rising through me.

We *could* take the roofs close enough to the underground entrance to be pretty sure of making it. All the city folk were either sleeping or reveling in their drugged state. We could slip through the window of another building farther along and go straight through a house without anyone likely to complain.

Lyssa shoved the window open just as a door banged open downstairs. I boosted her onto the shingles and scrambled out myself. The cold night air filtered through my mask, waking me up even more.

"This way," I said, grabbing her hand and trying not to think about the hasty way I'd almost run straight into danger on her behalf. "Follow me."

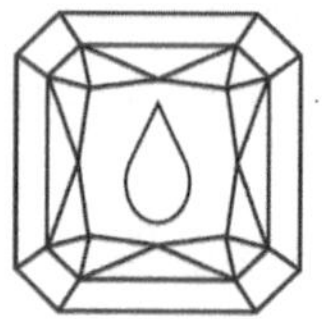

CHAPTER TEN

Lyssa

It felt strange just leaving the magical sword and scepter of the Red royal line sitting out in the cabin I was now sharing with Doria and the ferret-faced woman—whose name, Mallo, I'd finally gotten—but it would have felt even stranger carrying them both around in the caves. I still didn't even know how to use their magic. After the disarray when we'd fled Hatter's house last night, Theo had suggested he could help me work with them, but I wasn't sure when that would happen with so much else up in the air.

The images from the city above, the people so loopy, had haunted my dreams. They'd kept my sleep restless and short. My cabin-mates were still sleeping under their blanket, their breaths rasping faintly, as I tugged my clothes into something resembling neatness as quietly as I could.

Most of the camp was still sleeping. I knew a couple

of the Spades would be standing guard farther down the caves near the closest entrances, but the only other person up near the alcove was Theo, sitting a little ways off by the edge of the stream. His head bent low as he twisted a bit of metal onto a thin black device he was holding. Still the Inventor, even now. I guessed old habits died hard.

He was so absorbed in his work that he didn't notice me coming over until I'd almost reached him. His head jerked up, and his fingers clenched around the device as if he was afraid he'd drop it. The second he saw me, the tension fled from his expression. He smiled at me, warmly but maybe not as confidently as he might have a few weeks ago.

"Couldn't sleep?" he said.

"I seem to have gotten more rest than you did." I sat down at the edge of the stream next to him, leaning to let my fingers ripple the lukewarm water. Its blue glow sharpened the angles around Theo's square jaw, the slightly crooked nose he'd purposely let heal wrong after his mentor, the previous White Knight, had broken it for him.

Even with that minor imperfection, he was handsome as a prince. Honestly, the flaw made him even more so— more real and less like a work of fiction.

But so much of our time together had been fictional. Just the story he'd wanted to tell me and not all the darker and more fraught pieces he'd wanted to keep hidden.

"I've got a lot of work to do," Theo said. He set the device down on the smooth rock beside him. "If I'm going to see you on that throne, we've got to determine a way to get more than a handful of us into the palace. Or a way to make the guards stand down no matter what my mother says. Neither is going to be easy."

"You know, you can take a little longer to recover from what she put you through," I said. "She had you trapped in there for weeks, messing with your head, hurting you…" My gaze fell on the thin pink lines of healing cuts at the corners of his jaw. I suspected there were more beneath his clothes. "No one will blame you for taking it easy for a day or two."

"I'd blame me," Theo said firmly. "I promised you I'd clear the way for you—that I'd make it safe for you to come back. But it isn't at all, and she's destroying everything that matters about this land." He rubbed his hand over his face. "I know her. I matter to her. I should be able to work out a way to turn things around."

"She has powerful magic and hundreds of people on her side, too afraid to do anything but follow her orders." Or incapable of even considering it, in the case of the "pearl-heads" Hatter had told me about. I restrained a shiver at that memory. "But I'm here now, and we've got you back, and we've managed to get the artifacts. We're already turning things around."

Theo looked at me for a long moment. The intentness of his dark brown eyes sent a tingle over my skin. My body remembered all too well what it was like to be wrapped in those strong arms, to meet the heat of his kiss with my mouth.

"I owe you so much more than this," he said. "Maybe we would have overcome her already if I hadn't let my ego and my ambitions sway my thinking. I'm not even sure how many of my decisions were practical and how many I simply convinced myself were. The only thing I do know for sure is that I haven't made up for any of it until the Queen of Hearts has fallen and you're safe in the palace that should have been yours all along."

His hand edged forward as if to take mine, but he hesitated just shy of contact. We hadn't touched since that quick hug when we'd found him in the palace. My emotions jumbled in my chest, but whatever I was feeling, however I decided our relationship played out from here, I didn't want to push him away completely.

I slid my hand the last half an inch to brush his. He wrapped his fingers around mine immediately with the same solid, comforting grasp he'd always had. A rush of warmth shot through my veins, and a large part of me wanted to scoot a little closer, to melt into his embrace like I had in the past. I held myself back.

"I think you're being too hard on yourself, like you always have," I said. "I'm still upset about the way you lied to me, but I *understand*. You were right that you weren't ready to take on the Queen of Hearts to get my throne back—no one here was. I certainly wasn't. I wish you'd trusted me with the whole truth of who I was, at least, sooner, but… You'd only known me a couple weeks. You'd seen yourself as the heir to that throne for decades. It's— it's a mess. Maybe I'm still confused and I'm going to need some time to sort out my feelings, but I know for sure that you've always truly wanted what's best for Wonderland. You don't need to prove that to me."

Theo's smile came back with a quirk of his lips. "And that generosity," he said, his gaze still holding mine, "is one of the many reasons I love you. I meant that when I said it before. I might not have proven my devotion yet, but I will. Whether you ever find you can return those feelings or not. You haven't been here long, but you've already shown me things about what a ruler should be that I'd let myself forget. I'll fight to the end, and it'll be for you as much as for Wonderland."

My breath caught. I squeezed his hand harder. Before I'd found out about his lies, I'd been falling for Theo. The qualities that had drawn me to him were still there. I wasn't ready to say the words back to him, and I didn't know when or if I would be, but hearing him talk like that made my heart sing.

"Theo," I said, not sure what to add.

He shifted a smidge closer, his other hand rising to brush over my hair. "That's all I ask for," he said. "For you to know who I am, who I'll continue being from this day forward. I'm so sorry for how I deceived you before. You have my word that I'm committed to being nothing but open with you now, and we'll just see where that takes us. You're my queen."

He said the last words so fervently I couldn't help myself. I tipped toward him, seeking out his lips. He returned my kiss in an instant, his hand coming to rest on the side of my neck, his thumb tracing a line of sparks over my cheek. His mouth moved against mine sure and eager but restrained, not the headlong passion with which we'd come together the last time we'd had sex. Still letting me lead the way.

The rose and raspberry smell of him filled my nose. I should have wondered before about that faint flowery scent that clung to him as if it were part of his essence.

But it tasted sweeter on his lips than anything I'd encountered in the Queen's palace.

He wasn't his mother. He wasn't his family. That was enough for me to share this moment with him.

I curled my fingers into the fabric of his shirt, pulling myself even closer. In the back of my mind, I was conscious of the cabins in the alcove just a few steps away and of all the walls around my heart that I wasn't ready to let down.

I could still have this. Just a kiss, or maybe two, with the man who'd first made me feel like I deserved every joy Wonderland could offer.

Footsteps rapped over the stone, echoing against the cave ceiling. I drew back from Theo, and we both turned as one of the Spades from the other camps jogged into view. His expression was tight, his hands fisted. Theo sprang to his feet, and I followed.

"Whi—White Knight," the man said, coming to a stop, stumbling a bit over the title Theo had admitted wasn't entirely rightfully his. "I was scouting out around the edges of the city, like we've been doing regularly since we came under to the River Down."

The other members of our camp started to emerge from the cabins at the sound of louder voices. Theo started to speak and then looked to me. A prickling ran over my skin. I needed to lead these people now. If I told him to handle this, he would, but I had to get used to the role I was reaching for, didn't I?

"What happened?" I said, keeping my voice even but attentive. "What did you see?"

"The guards were bringing more of the Clubbers off to

the palace," the sentry said. His gaze flicked between me and Theo. "A couple dozen of them this time. I don't like the looks of it at all."

"Did they say anything about what they were doing with them?" Dum asked. He and his twin had come out of the nearest cabin to join us. "Has the Queen announced anything?"

The sentry shook his head. "Not that we've heard. And the guards weren't saying anything other than to keep the Clubbers walking. They were all still drugged out of their heads—they'd just left the city."

Dee turned to Theo with a hopeful expression. "Did you hear anything about her planning a round-up while you were in the palace, boss?"

Theo's shoulders had tensed. "No," he said. "No, I—"

He flinched and clapped a hand over his eyes, hunching over for a second. My heart lurched.

"Sorry," he said quickly, jerking himself straight. His hand hadn't left his eyes, and his mouth pressed in a thin line before he went on. "Just an after-effect—the treatments—I've got it. I'll be fine in a moment."

His voice had gone ragged. I touched his arm tentatively and then more firmly when he didn't retreat. He let out a stuttered breath and raised his head with a sheepish smile. The twins smiled back at him, but Dee's lips wavered. He looked more frightened than reassured.

"We have to assume whatever the Queen wants with those people, it isn't good," I said, pitching my voice a little higher to bring everyone's attention back to me. To get us back on track to solving this problem rather than focusing on Theo's momentary lapse. "Is there any way to fend off the guards, to stop them from taking more people?"

The sentry sputtered a laugh. "If we could do that, we could take the whole palace."

Fair enough. "And the city people couldn't fight back even if they were willing to now, thanks to the drugs. Okay." I squared my shoulders as the idea came to me. I didn't know how well it would work, but it felt right, and that was the best we could go by. The people in the city had been trapped just as much as Theo had, and like him, they couldn't help us unless we helped them first.

"We have the three masks. I want us going out in shifts and bringing two or three people back to the caves each time. We'll set up another camp where they can rest while the drug leaves their system. And then they can decide whether they want to stay with us and fight for their freedom, or head back into that stupor again."

Mallo frowned where she'd come up by the twins. "If they go back up, they might tell the guards where we've taken shelter."

"I think we've got to take that chance," I said. "We've got to believe in the people of Wonderland. The Queen has shown how far she's willing to go. Once they're here, and they see how much safer they are than they were up there… I think it'll turn out we have a lot more allies than we did before."

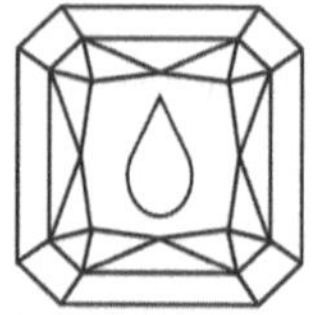

CHAPTER ELEVEN

Chess

I'd had conflicted feelings about using my ability to disappear in the past, but only when it was for self-serving reasons. Prowling around the walls to the palace gardens, watching the guards' eyes slip right over my invisible form, I got nothing but satisfaction.

The knowledge of how my special powers could be of use was why I'd gone to Hatter, out of everyone, when I'd needed shelter and security after my torture at the Duchess's hand. It was why I'd asked him to introduce me to the White Knight when I was sure my head was going to stay on my shoulders, and why I'd put myself at the disposal of the leader of the Spades ever since. The Queen of Hearts and the people who carried out her will had been a poison in Wonderland long before she'd sent her guards to strew drugged roses in the city streets. In this one way, I could provide a bit of help no one else could.

It was the least and the most I could do.

There hadn't been much activity in the gardens earlier this morning, but as I passed the west gate, the whir of what sounded like an air trolley caught my ears through the muffled atmosphere of the in-between. It came from farther along, by the north gate. I hustled along the grassy hill, glancing toward the wall to see if I could catch any glimpse of the vehicle from my slightly elevated position.

Its hunched, plated roof, like the silvered shell of an immense beetle, glinted beyond the hedges. I reached the road that stretched out from the gate just as the iron-barred door swung open. The air trolley hissed out, hovering half a foot over the ground, bits of dirt flying up in its wake.

The things could hold about fifty people if they packed in tight. This one today held maybe thirty. Several of them stood by the openings that let in the air between the silver posts, all in the uniforms of the Hearts' Guard. The others, sitting on the benches, wore garish Clubber clothes, their eyes pinkish and expressions vague enough to convince me they were still at least a little drugged.

My gaze stopped on a figure just straightening up near the back of the trolley, which the guards had otherwise kept clear. I'd never talked to Carpenter, but I recognized him from his rounded gut encased in those canvas overalls, his jowly face partly hidden by a grizzled brown beard. A chill whispered over my skin.

What was *he* doing with this crowd? And why were they heading along the road that led to the sea?

My mind was quick enough to put together the obvious answer, but the rest of me balked at accepting it. Carpenter had been looking at something at the back of the trolley. I couldn't make out what from here. That might be proof in one direction or the other.

I set off after the trolley, speeding from a jog to a lope to a sprint. I wasn't as fast on my feet as Hatter, but I could cover ground in a good amount of time when I needed to—and the trolleys didn't move all that fast anyway.

I caught up with it still in sight of the palace. Carpenter had gone to sit on a bench just behind the city folk. I pushed myself a little faster to come up beside the trolley, and then slowed to gracefully catch a bar at the back. With a hop, I swung myself onto the step at the back of the trolley without more than a slight hitch to the vehicle's constant hiss. No one looked my way.

A salty, watery, near-rotten odor reached my nose before I'd even leaned over the back wall. I braced myself.

Between the back benches lay heaps of a ridged greenish-black material. Empty oyster casings, heaped on top of one another. At least enough for every Clubber on that trolley, I'd estimate.

My stomach turned over. That was the proof I'd expected but hoped to find false. I leapt off the back of the trolley before it could carry me any farther from home and watched it whir off toward the Oyster Cove, my legs unwilling to move.

The Queen was turning all her captured city folk into pearl-heads. Fresh as possible, I guessed—their heads to be severed moments before they were shoved into those casings and cast into the workings at the sea bottom. Would the new dull heads grow faster that way? I didn't know enough about the process to have any idea.

Possibly the Queen didn't either. Possibly it was simply easier to have the bodies she'd collected walk to their doom. She wouldn't want to parade *those* heads, the heads of citizens who'd done nothing wrong but happen to be in the guards' path at an unfortunate time, through the streets, putting her clearest villainy on display for all to shudder at.

What was she pearling all those people for? I couldn't think of any purpose that sat remotely well with me.

My stomach still churning, I forced myself to turn and head back toward the city. Lyssa and Theo—and all the rest of the Spades—needed to know about this development.

As I reached the edge of the city, I pulled my mask up over my face against the stink of doctored roses. I was meant to wait for the Spades who were attempting to usher a few of the city folk down to the caves by the exit we'd decided on, in case they needed assistance. Freeing them from the Queen's influence in dribs and drabs might not make much of a difference to the larger battle, but I couldn't blame Lyssa for wanting to try. Especially after I'd seen what was happening to their neighbors.

Music warbled around me, punctuated by giggles and sighs. I stuck to the smaller streets and alleys where the Clubber crowd wasn't generally drifting as much as I could. Even invisible, dodging those swaying, dazed bodies wasn't much fun. When I had the chance, I ducked into a shop the owner had abandoned and grabbed what food I could to bring back for our stores along the River Down.

I reached the crimson-and-blue rear end of the candy

shop that had a hidden trap door in its basement just as a similarly masked figure came into view down the back alley. Doria was urging along a couple of young women who didn't look much older than she was—friends from the days when we could enjoy Caterpillar's Club at least a little, I suspected.

"I want to go back to the music!" one of them said in a slurred voice. "I wasn't done dancing, Doria."

"Mmm. I just want to lie down a moment," the other mumbled.

"There's lots of room to lie down where we're going," Doria said. She had her chin high, but even through her face mask, I could hear the waver that had crept into her voice. It was one thing to see the Clubbers in their constantly high state from the sidelines and another to try to reason with people you'd really known face-to-face. "And there's more room to dance over here. Don't you hate constantly bumping into people? Let's mix things up."

The first woman made a disgruntled sound, but she didn't appear to have the motivation to put up more of an argument. I eased back beside the building and drew myself into being fully present, the sounds sharpening and shapes steadying around me. Then I stepped out to greet them.

"This way, this way," I said with a grin, motioning them to the shop's back door with an entertainer's air. Might as well make the trip seem as appealing as possible while I could. "An exclusive lounge only for the most select patrons. Let's keep it hush hush so it stays limited to our special guests."

"Oooh," the second woman said, her eyes going overly round. "This does sound cool. How did you get in, Doria?"

Hatter's daughter shot me a grateful look. "You just have to know the right people," she said. "So aren't you lucky you know me?"

They were, more than they knew. Doria led them through the door and down to the basement. One of the other Spades would be waiting below in the caves to help take the Clubbers the rest of the way. Doria must have decided her part of that job was done, because she poked her head out a minute later.

"Should I stick around up here?" she asked. "Do you need me for anything else?"

Did *I* need her? The question sounded so bizarre that I didn't immediately know how to answer it. What did any of this work have to do with my needs?

She meant whether I thought there was any other way she could pitch in with the mission Lyssa had sent us on, of course. As I considered, Kip ducked into the alley, nudging along a middle-aged man who appeared already half-asleep. Kip's face looked pinched.

"I had two," he said under his breath as he reached us. "But a bunch of guards barged into the street while I was convincing the other—I think they're taking more people now, just over there." He jerked his head back the way he'd come, and a dazed sound of protest filtered to us at the same time.

Doria stiffened. "Should we do something?" she asked. She glanced not at Kip but at me. He did too.

I blinked at them, and it struck me like a bucketful of

water in the face. Oh. She *had* been looking for actual orders—from me. It made an odd sort of sense, now that I'd cottoned on. They'd seen me at our true queen's side regularly from the moment they'd learned of Lyssa's heritage. I'd stepped up as well as I could when we'd been gathering everyone in the caves. Now the other Spades took me for one of the leaders of this rebellion.

The thought provoked much the same emotions as a dosing of water might: a discomfort at being out of my element twined with a weird sort of thrill in the new sensation.

Was I a leader? I'd never meant to be, never thought to be. I'd served as one of the White Knight's tools, and that had been plenty involvement for me.

I supposed I'd better contemplate this unexpected turn later. Right now, two of my comrades were looking to me for an answer, and I had to come up with one quick.

What would the White Knight have said? What would Lyssa want us to do? Those two guiding impulses merged into a course of action that sent a nervous quiver through me even as I felt the rightness of it.

"Send him down quickly," I said to Kip. "Then we'll scout out the street. If we see an opportunity to put the guards off, we will, but no jumping in if we're too outnumbered."

The two of them nodded as if they'd been following commands from me all along. Kip hurried his Clubber into the basement, and then the three of us set off in the direction the shout had carried from.

We stopped in the shadows at the end of the alley. The

urge prickled over me to slip back into the in-between, out of view, but the awareness that my companions were looking to me for guidance kept me in place. I wasn't sure how much I liked the weight that responsibility came with, but I'd taken it at least for now, so I'd better own it.

Eight—no, nine—guards were weaving through the scattered crowd of revelers on the wide street ahead of us. A few Clubbers already paced in the back of the cart parked near the corner. My hands balled as I watched the guards grab a couple more, not too old or too young and in reasonably good health, like we'd observed before.

I couldn't see any way we could intervene that would help anyone, though. They had three times our numbers, and given the compliant way the Clubbers were going along with them, I suspected the city folk would push back against us before they'd turn on the guards. The drug hadn't made them any braver.

Hatter would never forgive me if I led Doria into a skirmish with the odds so far against us.

"I don't think we're in a position to stop them," I murmured. "But watch everything they do. It may be useful in defending against them later."

The other two nodded as if I'd offered words of great wisdom. I followed my own instructions, noting the construction of the vehicle, the way the guards moved among the Clubbers. In a matter of minutes, they'd herded several more onto the cart and jumped up themselves to move on.

"Let's go!" one shouted to the last of the helmed figures, who was still in the crowd.

"I've got one more," he called back, tugging a woman

with him. At the sight of her oval face with its billow of red hair, my heart stopped. Doria flinched beside me. She grasped my arm.

"We can't just let them take *her*," she said.

"Wait," I said, holding her back. Was there a way to dislodge her without this scene turning into a bloodbath? I hesitated, trying to see it, willing my mind to narrow to tactics and logistics the way Theo's might have. My head started to ache, and the guard had already reached the cart. My lips parted as he hauled the woman up, but I had no useful words to speak.

And then they were rattling away, the remaining Clubbers swaying with the pulse of the music on as if they'd never been disturbed.

"I'm sorry," I found myself saying. "There wasn't any — I couldn't tell—"

"We'll get them back," Kip said. "When we're ready."

Whenever that would be. I swallowed hard. "Let's return to the camp," I said. "We've got a lot to report."

We trudged back to the candy shop and through the trap door into the caves. The sentry standing guard there nodded to us as we passed by. With each step toward camp, my feet grew heavier. Doria rubbed her mouth, unusually quiet.

I hadn't been quite the leader they'd wanted just now, had I?

The twins were the first people I saw when we reached the alcove. My legs stalled as they looked up from the devices Theo must have set them assembling. The former White Knight himself emerged from one of the cabins a moment later. Lyssa came just behind him, holding her ruby-marked sword. Despite the bad news I was bringing, my heart still leapt at the sight of her, so sure of herself now in the role that was meant for her.

She would lead us right. I trusted in her if not myself.

"I know why they're rounding up the Clubbers," I made myself say. The words tried to stick in my throat. I turned my gaze toward the twins. "And we've got even more reason to stop them as soon as we can. We just saw —They've taken your mother."

Dum's face grayed. Dee stared at me for a second. Then he swore and dashed the instrument he'd been working on to the ground as he leapt to his feet. He stalked off toward the cabins, but stayed within hearing.

Lyssa's lips slanted into a frown. "Tell us everything."

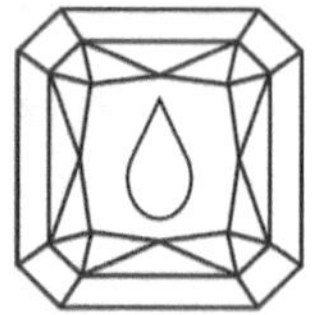

CHAPTER TWELVE

Lyssa

We walked nearly as far as the oddly shaped hills I'd passed when Hatter had taken me out to the Topsy Turvy Woods what felt like years ago. Theo stopped at the edge of a small clearing surrounded by the vibrant trees and nodded, finally declaring the spot safe enough for the training I was meant to do. Like when I'd run from Hatter's home, I had the ruby-marked scepter in a bag slung over my shoulder and the sword in my hand.

The weapon's weight didn't drag on my arm the way I remembered it doing before. My fingers seemed to fit around it perfectly. But before we started this training, I needed to address a different weight that had filled my stomach since Chess had arrived back from his patrol. I hadn't wanted to ask these questions in front of Dee and Dum.

"Why wasn't she with us—with the Spades?" I asked.

"The twins' mother, I mean. She asked you to look after them from when they were kids… She obviously trusted you and believed in the cause."

Theo grimaced. Before he could answer, Chess piped up where he'd leaned against a nearby tree. "She sent Dee and Dum to the White Knight because she was afraid of the Queen. Saving them was the most important thing. Saving herself, of lesser importance. I heard her say once that if she ran with the Spades and was identified as a rebel, the Queen's wrath might come down on all of them. Better for her to play along and not draw any additional possible ire."

And now she'd been drawn right into the palace—to be made into one of those dim "pearl-heads"? I hugged myself with one arm across my gut, my sword hand dipping. The blade brushed the grass.

"You don't have any idea how quickly the Queen is sending people out to the cove or what she's using them for after?"

Chess shook his head. "It takes at least a few days, normally, for the pearling to finish. She can't have been gathering people from the city for very long, or we'd have noticed sooner."

"No doubt we'll find out her aims soon enough," Theo said grimly. He tipped his head to me. "Which is all the more reason to help you find the full extent of your powers."

"The artifacts' powers, you mean," I couldn't help saying.

One corner of his mouth twitched upward. "They don't work for me. That sword burned my hand trying to get away from the wrong wielder. It's your power feeding them."

"So far that power hasn't done much more than light up the rubies," I muttered. I'd spent an afternoon practicing sword strokes and trying to figure out what to do with the scepter after we'd first retrieved them, with the Red Knight who'd served my however-many-greats grandmother guiding me, and hadn't gotten anywhere. The Red Knight who'd since fallen under a guard's sword, protecting me when I couldn't protect him—or even myself.

But as those doubts started to rise up inside me, a sense of iron conviction pushed back against them. I was Lyssa, the heir to the Red Queen. I *was* the Red Queen, now that anyone else who might have claimed that title was gone. This sword felt right in my hand because it was, by all rights, mine. So was the scepter, and the armored vest I wore, and the ring hanging from its chain around my neck that glowed with my blood in proof of my heritage.

This was my land, and I had thousands of people to save. I was ready to claim the role that had made me hesitate when the Red Knight had told his story.

It hadn't been safe to try out the artifacts properly in the caves around the stream—I might have hurt someone or brought the ceiling down on us. Here, far enough from the Queen's reach that my worries about discovery had faded too, anticipation hummed through my veins. I set down the scepter and hefted the sword. Warmth streamed from the grip into my palm. The ruby gleamed, and a smile crossed my lips.

"You're holding it well already," Theo said. "Maybe you won't need much of my help after all."

"The Red Knight taught me a few things," I said, with a twinge as I thought of the eccentric old man. He'd been clinging in his devotion, but he'd believed in me before I'd believed in myself. He'd given his life to save me. I wasn't sure what I believed about spirits and an afterlife, especially in a place like this, but I hoped there was some way that he was watching now. That I'd give him a victory to show his sacrifice had been worth it.

"I'll just stay here and admire the view," Chess said with a playful smirk. He'd volunteered to join us so he could stand guard while we were focused on testing the artifacts. I'd gotten the feeling he felt uncomfortable hanging around in the caves while the twins murmured together about the horrible news he'd had to bring them.

I swung my arm, the sword guiding my hand as much as my hand guided the sword. Its tingling energy spread up my arm and through my chest. Suddenly I was picturing the Queen and her tiger-headed Knave who led the Hearts' Guard, the Duchess and the other haughty Diamonds, standing across from us at the other end of the clearing.

I wanted to be rid of them. I wanted them and their influence lifted from *my* people. I wanted the joyful Wonderland I'd thought I'd landed in way back when returned to me.

My arm whipped out. The blade sang through the air. The warmth against my palm turned into a blazing heat—and a sharp ripple of magic shot from the gleaming edge.

A shimmering light raced across the clearing. It

walloped the trees so hard their branches shook and the bark dented around a slash across their trunks, leaving a cut deep enough to leak sap.

The hum of power reverberated in my chest for a few seconds before it faded. I sucked in a ragged breath, staring at the damage I'd done. Excitement and horror jarred together inside me, making my lungs tighten.

"Wow," Theo said. "That was spectacular. Can you summon that magic again?"

A good question. He'd probably also like to know whether I could summon even more. I gripped the hilt harder and tried to gather the anger I'd felt in that moment, but the sight of the scored trees dampened it.

I hadn't really hurt our enemies with that slash. And even our enemies, I didn't really want to defeat by spilling their blood all over the palace, the way they'd slaughtered my ancestors centuries ago.

I sliced the sword through the air again, but this time the ruby only glowed faintly—like before. I frowned at it, but I didn't need to ask what the problem was.

"I have to be fully committed," I said. "I *am* now—to being queen. I'm just not sure I want to be the kind of queen who wins that way."

To my relief, Theo didn't push. "You know more of what you're capable of," he said. "If the moment comes when you need to use that power, you'll be ready. Do you want to go through a few basic exercises to get more comfortable with the sword in general?" He grabbed a fallen stick about the same length as my blade. "I can make do with this for training purposes. I'd like to know you can defend yourself the old-fashioned way too."

I couldn't argue with that. We circled the clearing one way and then the other, practicing parries and feints and jabs, until sweat was dampening my blouse under the metal vest. Chess was still watching us, his head cocked to listen for any sounds of approach.

"What about that ruby rod of yours?" he asked, pointing his foot toward the scepter in its bag. "Got any idea yet what magic that can stir up?"

"No, but I'd certainly like to figure it out." I set the sword down in the grass and took out the scepter. Like the sword, it felt more secure in my grasp than it had the last time I'd tested its powers. And the warm wood topped by its crown of gold and ruby spoke of a power less violent than what I'd get with a blade.

"The Red Knight said he saw his Red Queen use it once to tame... some kind of creature. I didn't recognize the word he used for it." I tipped the scepter one way and then another. Even before I'd found it, I'd worked a sort of power like that on a jabberwock on the Checkerboard Plains. An echo of that sensation quivered through me—the sense that I could connect and calm, compel the fear and anger from another being's mind, convince it to see me as a friend rather than a foe.

With that memory thrumming through me, I stepped toward the trees, looking for any animal I could test the magic out on. I held out the scepter as if the intensifying glow of the ruby might light my way—and the shadows fell back from the base of the tree trunks.

I stopped, blinking. At another wave of my hand, the patches of darkness retreated farther into the forest. It wasn't that the ruby's light fell that far. Its glow was condensed around the stone, and no red shine colored the trees or grass. No… I'd simply urged the darkness to give way. Cleared it the way I'd cleared the rage from the jabberwock's mind those weeks ago.

Chess let out a low whistle. "That's something and a half."

I didn't know how useful it would be, but I had to smile anyway. "It isn't what I meant to try. Now, where…"

A sparrow fluttered from one branch to another. It peered at me warily with beady black eyes. I raised the scepter between us, holding its gaze over the top of the ruby and its gold enclosure. A tremor of encouragement traveled over my tongue.

"Hey, there," I said. "There's nothing dangerous here. Come to me?"

The bird hopped to one side and then back again. I extended my hand slowly, willing my good intentions to flow with it the way I had with the jabberwock. Theo and Chess didn't make a sound.

The ruby glowed softly, its light drifting over the sparrow. The bird ruffled its feathers. Then it sprang off the branch and swooped down to land on my outstretched hand. Its tiny clawed feet gripped my finger.

I beamed at it with a rush of giddiness. "Thank you," I said. "Go safely."

It darted away into the forest. I let out the breath I'd been holding, and a laugh came with it.

"They work," I said. "The artifacts respond to me. I really—I really am the Red Queen."

Somehow, despite all my conviction and

determination, that fact hadn't felt totally real until this moment.

Chess stepped away from his tree. He rested a hand on my waist as he lowered his head next to mine.

"Of course you are, lovely," he said. "This land will be yours, and you're going to make it the wonder it should be. I can already see how it will be every time I look at you."

His touch, his words, and the admiration in his eyes sent a flush of heat over my skin. "Is that why you're here?" I said teasingly.

"No," he said, his voice dipping. "I'm here because you're you, wondrous as that is, queen or no. Whatever you want. Whatever you need. How can I brighten your day, Your Majesty?"

I made a sound of protest at the title, and then the desire swirling through me took over. I set down the scepter, brought my hand to his jaw, and drew his mouth to mine.

Chess grinned into the kiss. Then he tucked his arm around me and pulled me right up against him, angling his head with a slide of his lips that set off sparks through my nerves. His kisses were always sweet, but there was something a little more urgent to this one.

It had been only days since we'd fallen into each other like this in my memory. For him it'd been weeks, and for most of that time he'd thought I was dead. Knowing that loosened any hesitations I might have had about seeing this moment through to the end I was already yearning for.

I curled my fingers into the rumpled waves of Chess's

soft hair, kissing him harder. Aiming to make up for the time apart, to show him how much I did want him. With a pleased rumble in his throat that was almost a purr, he flicked his tongue across the seam of my lips. They parted for him. A needy whimper worked its way up my throat as his tongue twined with mine.

Chess's hand slid to my side and tugged at the base of the armored vest. As I stepped back to pull off that much too solid barrier between us, my gaze caught on the other one of my lovers here with us.

Theo was watching from a few paces away, his expression unreadable. I thought I saw hunger flash through his eyes, but he schooled them back to their usual steady warmth so quickly it was hard to be sure. He wet his lips and flipped the stick he'd been using as a makeshift sword in his hand.

"I can give you some space," he said, his attention never leaving my face. Waiting to judge my reaction so he knew what course I needed him to take. "If you'd feel more at ease without me here."

Something twisted at the base of my heart. The doubts I'd felt about getting close to him again snapped and shattered. All they left behind was a pang of longing.

What more did he have to do? He'd gone through weeks of torture rather than give in to his mother, he'd declared his loyalty to me in front of the people who'd mattered most to him, and now this man who could be so commanding was tossing away any intimate claim he might have put forward, not even asking, just assuming when I was ready, I'd let him know.

Chess's hand lingered on my side, his thumb tracing a

teasing line over the silky fabric of my blouse. *He* wouldn't mind the company. He'd told me he preferred having another man there, taking some of the pressure to perform off of him. He hadn't been intimate with anyone one-on-one since the Duchess had nearly murdered him for her own gratification.

So there really wasn't any reason to deny myself.

I dropped the vest beside the other artifacts and motioned Theo over. "I'd feel best with you right *here*."

The elation that lit up his handsome face only reinforced my decision. He crossed the space between us with two swift strides. Chess eased to one side of me, trailing kisses from my cheek to my jaw, and Theo captured my mouth.

I'd never been with two men at the same time before I'd come to Wonderland. It should have been overwhelming. But having two pairs of lips branding my skin, two sets of fingers tracing over my body, only made me feel more solidly in place.

Yes, this was where I belonged. Right here, between these two very different but oh so enticing men.

Chess's hand traveled up over my blouse to cup one breast and then the other. His thumbs circled my nipples and drew them to stiff peaks. Theo grasped my hip. He released my lips to kiss a path down my neck to my collarbone, and then Chess was devouring me again with a light pinch of his fangs. The tiny prick of pain amid the pleasure left me moaning.

Theo continued his journey downward. He yanked my blouse and bra aside and sucked the tip of my breast in his mouth. I gasped, clutching Chess's shirt, Theo's shoulder. The heat of their bodies on either side of me was like a furnace, but if I burned up, I couldn't help thinking it'd be an amazing way to go.

Theo's tongue worked some kind of magic against my skin, and Chess lifted my hair to nibble his way around to the back of my neck, and oh God, I didn't know how I'd spent so many years satisfied without this rush.

My White Knight, my prince, lifted his head just long enough to brush his lips against mine once more. "I promised you I'd worship you," he murmured in a voice rich with promise. Then he sank to his knees, charting a path farther down over my belly to my waistband. Chess nipped my shoulder and eased up my skirt, clearing the way. My hips swayed toward Theo instinctively with a desire I couldn't suppress. He smiled, tugged down my panties, and pressed his mouth to my core.

"Oh, fuck," I muttered, and then all I could get out was a sigh. Chess ground against me from behind, his cock temptingly hard against my ass. He kept one hand splayed against my thigh, holding up my skirt. The other brushed over Theo's dark curls, half caress, half urging him on. Theo didn't seem to mind, and the sight turned me on even more.

Theo grazed his teeth over my clit and swiveled his tongue around it until I was panting. Pleasure pulsed from my core, making my legs wobble. He reached past my hip to yank the fly of Chess's slacks open, and I just about caught fire right there.

Chess chuckled and slid his fingers over my slick folds. I edged my feet apart to give him more access, leaning into Theo's mouth, braced between the two men. With the utmost care, Chess aligned our bodies and eased his straining cock into me one delicious inch at a time. Theo suckled my clit harder.

The dual sensations of being filled within and worked over without tipped me over the edge. I came with a hitch of breath and stars behind my eyelids. Theo steadied me, Chess pulled back and drove into me even deeper, and I shuddered around him with a sharper cry.

Theo drew back with a gleam in his dark eyes. Chess's thumb replaced my other lover's tongue in an instant. The Prince of Hearts looked ready to rise up again, but as the aftershock of my orgasm trembled through me, another desire took hold. That wasn't where I wanted him.

I nudged him down and bent over him. Chess followed me, lowering himself to his knees as I did, adjusting his angle and driving into me far enough to hit the most sensitive spot inside. I gasped at the wave of bliss, but I wasn't going to be deterred from my current mission.

"Lyssa," Theo said as I snapped open his slacks over the bulge of his own erection. His voice was ragged. "I— You don't—"

He sounded like he was considering trying to talk me out of it. I caught his gaze. "I want to have you. Let me see how much you're mine."

Putting it that way appeared to release any concerns he'd had. He sank back on his elbows as I freed his cock. I ran my tongue up the hard, faintly salty length of it from base to tip, and a groan escaped him.

The leader of the city folk, the Spades, and the Queen

of Hearts' chosen heir. I had him sprawled back and lost in pleasure, completely at my mercy.

I took him all the way into my mouth, and then I felt filled from head to toe, Theo's musky rose flavor tickled over my tongue while Chess set off fresh bursts of pleasure with each thrust behind me.

Chess's breath stuttered as he leaned closer to my back, one arm looped around my waist, the other stroking over Theo's thigh. A thought hit me, sending my desire spiking higher even as it brought a lump of emotion into my throat: We were in this together. Not just them with me, but all of us, finding bliss in each other.

"So fucking lovely," Chess said around a hitch in his voice, and then his hips were jerking, heat flooding my core. Those last few thrusts of his cock sent me crashing into my second release. Ecstasy crackled through my body, and I closed my lips tighter around Theo's length as I rode out the wave. He groaned again, bucking to meet me. Then, with a whirl of my tongue, he was flooding my mouth with his cum.

We sprawled on the grass together, me between my two lovers, but not separating them. Theo kissed me hard and then glanced over at Chess as if checking in, giving the other man's arm a brief caress before offering me the same. Chess kept his arm around my waist and nuzzled the side of my neck. He alternated between trailing his fingertips over my belly and grazing his knuckles against Theo's chest in a languid gesture of affection.

"Our queen," he said, brightly but so firmly you'd have thought I was sitting on the throne right now. I started to squirm toward him, wanting another kiss from those sweet lips, but his head snapped up. He knit his brow.

"Someone's coming this way," he said.

I scrambled up, straightening my clothes and grabbing my sword as quickly as I could. Chess had barely zipped his pants when his shoulders relaxed. "One of ours," he said.

A few moments later, one of the Spades from the secondary camps emerged through the trees. If he noticed anything odd about the three of us with our flushed cheeks and mussed hair, he was too caught up in his own concerns to react.

"We thought you'd want to know," he said, looking to Theo first, and then to me, as if he wasn't sure who he should be addressing. "It looks like Dee has gone missing."

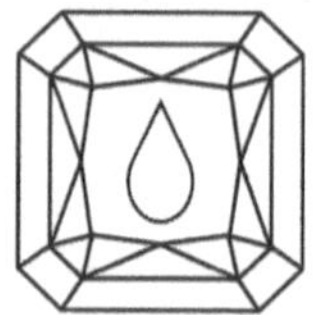

CHAPTER THIRTEEN

Lyssa

When we reached the main camp in the caves, a few of the Spades, including Mallo, were standing around Dum, all of their faces tense. Dum was shaking his head as if in response to something one of them had said. He looked up as the three of us came into the alcove, but his expression stayed dour.

"What exactly happened with your brother?" Theo said without preamble, his stance rigid and his voice taking on that princely commanding tone. I didn't mind him jumping in to take the lead here. He'd seen the twins as his responsibility, and he knew both of them way better than I did.

"We gave him some space, seeing as he was so upset," Mallo said. "He went into one of the cabins. But he was supposed to go up to the city with me an hour ago, and when I went to see if he was up to it, he wasn't there."

"He must have slipped off without talking to anyone," said the man beside her, a young guy who went by Kip. "No one's seen him since the morning. We looked through all the passages nearby before we thought we should let you know."

My stomach knotted. The usually cheerful twin had been distraught about his mother's capture—of course he had, especially after Chess had revealed where he'd seen the guards taking their earlier captives. Whatever he'd decided to do, he probably hadn't been thinking very clearly.

"Where do you think he'd have gone?" I asked his brother.

Dum rubbed his mouth. He glanced at his companions. "Give us a moment?" he said.

The others eased back. Chess waved them over to the other side of the alcove, asking a question about the latest Clubbers who'd been brought to our recovery area and snorting at something Kip said. Theo and I turned to Dum. He looked at the stone floor and then fixed his gaze not on Theo but on me. Somehow that choice made me proud and nervous at the same time.

He was putting his faith in me, even above the man who'd guided him since he was a kid. I had to be worthy of that trust.

"He talked to me before he left," he said in a low voice. "Tried to convince me that we should go on a mission to get Mom out of the palace. He wasn't properly in his head—he could hardly stand still, he was so agitated. I told him there'd be a mission, that we were working on it, but he didn't want to wait. He thought just the two of us should make a run at it."

The two of them against the entire Hearts' Guard? Nausea pooled in my gut. "That'd be a suicide mission."

"I know," Dum said. "I told Dee that, in softer words. I told him Mom was safer if we stuck to the plan, stuck together with the rest of the Spades, so we could see the rebellion through. If the guards caught us, which they almost definitely would, they might torture us for information before taking our heads. It'd put the whole cause at risk. I love my mother, but I don't see how that would help her. I couldn't calm Dee down, though. He was still all worked up when he walked away."

"Did you see what direction he went in?" Theo asked.

Dum shook his head. "He went back into the cabin then. It must have been later he snuck off. I never thought—I'd have stayed with him if I'd realized he was frantic enough to make a go of it on his own. But that has to be what he's done. He must have gone off to the palace."

At the rustle of fabric, I realized we had company again. Doria had come over, Hatter right behind her, and Kip and Mallo had drifted back toward us too. From the looks on their faces, they'd heard at least the end of Dum's account.

"If they get it out of him where we've been hiding…" Mallo said, so pale her beady eyes stood out even more starkly than usual. She didn't need to finish that sentence.

"Dee wouldn't tell them anything, no matter what they did," Doria insisted. Her cheeks had flushed. She'd kind of admitted to me that she'd had a crush on the guy for a while, so I couldn't blame her for wanting to stick up for him. But it wasn't as if anyone could easily predict what they'd find themselves doing if pushed to the brink through torture.

Theo must have been thinking along similar lines. His mouth set in a grim line. "I hope that he won't, but if the guards get their hands on him and realize he's one of us, there's no telling how they'll force the issue."

"Maybe he'll think better of rushing in there once he's out at the palace alone," Kip said. "It's one thing to think about taking on the whole lot of them on his own and another to be faced with the reality."

I hoped he was right, but my stomach stayed tight. Mallo spat on the ground.

"We're all going to end up stir-crazy stuck down here like rats in a warren while the guards pick off the city folk a batch at a time."

She gave me an accusing look that might have made me wince with guilt not that long ago. But I had a queen's sword in my hand, a queen's armor over my chest, and a queen's scepter at my back. Less than an hour ago, I'd commanded more magic than most of these people had witnessed in their lifetime. I'd commanded the desires of two of the most powerful men I'd ever met.

If the Spades needed to know that we'd do more than cower in tunnels under my rule, I could show them that now. Still careful, still weighing the risks, but taking the chances we could afford to keep everyone's spirits steady.

"He might be out there working up his nerve," I said. "Let's go for him. Hatter, Chess, you come with me the shortest route through the city with the masks. Theo, you take the fastest Spades around along the fringes to meet up with us in case we end up with a fight on our hands. We'll circle the palace grounds and bring him back if we can."

Theo's eyebrows arched as if he was a little startled by my taking charge, but he didn't argue. After that split-second hesitation, he spun on his heel and swept his hand through the air.

"Mallo, Kip, you know who to round up. Grab a few small weapons too. I'll bring some of those devices we've been working on. We move out in five minutes."

He bent over the supply pile and offered me a couple of the dark metal eggs I knew would explode with a billow of smoke. "You should have some extra tools on hand too."

"I'll carry them," Chess offered. "I believe our queen has her hands full." He winked at me as he tucked a smoke bomb into each of his pant pockets.

"All right." My breath snagged in my throat now that we were putting this plan into action. It still felt like the right thing to do, for both Dee and all the people looking up to me now. "Let's go."

As we hustled to the cave entrance closest to the palace, Hatter adjusted his suit jacket sleeves where he kept his stealthy hatpins. "Isn't it about time you got yourself a real weapon, oh mad one?" Chess teased.

Hatter rolled his eyes with a tweak of his top hat. "I've got one of those too." He patted his hip, where I noticed the end of a hilt protruding, the line of a dagger visible through the fabric of his slacks. "What weapons are *you* bringing, madder one?"

Chess grinned. "My fists do well enough when the bastards can't see them coming."

The spot where the caves slanted upward into a narrower passage led us into the cellar of what Chess had told me was a pillow-stuffing factory. Stray feathers drifted through the air as we clambered up the ladder into the back room where a few heaps of fabric and bags of down lay.

We were still several blocks from the road leading from the city toward the palace. Beyond the door, music thumped and wavering voices carried back and forth. I tugged my mask tighter over my face against the chemical scent of the roses.

We eased out right by the corner of the street and darted down the alley in the opposite direction. When we had to cross the main roads, we ducked our heads and bobbed with the music as we wove between the bodies as if joining their dance.

The sun was sinking by the time we left the irregular buildings of the city behind. In the sparse forest between the city and the palace, I tugged my mask down and drank in the fresh warm air, the smell of the dry earth clearing the last lingering hints of rose from my lungs. Until we got closer to the palace, anyway.

"We need to find Theo the material to make more of these," I murmured.

"Dum's been trying to track down the supplier he used to go to," Chess said. "The woman hasn't turned up. Either the guards have taken her or she's wandered off in her reveling. He'll keep looking."

My mind started spinning through other possibilities

for protecting ourselves from the rose's drug so we could move around the city more freely, but every plan that came to mind seemed more ridiculous than the last. The Queen of Hearts had the upper hand here.

We couldn't let her gain even more of one.

The tall stone walls around the palace grounds came into view up ahead. We slowed, scanning the forest and the area along the wall for both Dee and any patrolling guards.

"He might have gone to the looking spot by the laughing trees," Hatter said. "Let's head that way first."

As soon as we came near the trees with their long thin leaves that vibrated together to create an eerie chittering sound, the hairs on the back of my arms rose. It wasn't hard to figure why no one liked coming through this part of the forest, which was why it made such a good hiding spot for a rebel lookout. Hatter darted up the holds on the one tree's trunk and descended a few moments later with a frown.

"No sign of him there, and I couldn't spot him anywhere I could see from the platform. Theo's group is getting close—we could intercept them if we continue that way." He pointed in the direction we'd already been heading.

"All right," I said, my throat constricting. The platform didn't give a perfect view around the whole palace—Dee could have been around the other side, or in a particularly sheltered spot amid the trees. But every step we took without finding him, the more likely it was that he'd already gone into the palace grounds.

Hatter touched my arm as we walked on, waiting

until I met his green eyes. "If he's out here, we'll find him," he said. "He was upset, but the twins aren't stupid. He'd *have* to realize rushing in there on his own would only lose him his head."

"They might have caught him even if he changed his mind," I said, and then raised my chin. "But we can't think that way. We'll cover all the grounds around the palace just in case, like we decided."

"That's our queen," Chess said, with a pleased glint in his eyes and his grin.

Hatter had directed us well. He paused and rapped on the truck of a tree three times, and an answering knock came from deeper in the forest a second later. With only the slightest rustling, Theo and the six Spades he'd assembled strode forward to join us.

He hadn't brought Dum along, I noticed. He must have been worried about the guy's emotional state, potentially losing both his mother and his brother in the same day. Dear God, please let us save at least one of them.

I pointed with my sword for us to keep along our circuit of the walls, and Theo nodded without a word. We walked on quietly, the Spades fanning out a bit between the trees to scan more ground.

The trees thinned up ahead where a road passed through the forest. As we slowed, a distant creaking sound reached my ears. I froze, my head jerking toward it. Toward the palace gate that opened onto this road.

With a shout and a thunder of booted feet, a horde of guards spilled onto the road and charged toward us. If I'd had an instant's hope that they were stampeding off to tackle some other foe, it was destroyed the second several of them veered into the forest on our side, their gazes sweeping the shadows. Someone on watch must have spotted us.

"Shit," Kip muttered, taking a step back.

The words rose in my throat to yell at the others to run. But even as my lips parted, doubt gripped me. There were dozens of guards rushing toward us. I couldn't say for sure we'd make it to one of the cave entrances without them catching any of us—and even if we did, we'd have led them straight to our shelter.

And all the Spades would have seen of their queen was a woman who turned tail and fled rather than defending them.

My legs balked for just a second, and then I leapt into the road, raising my sword high. "Go!" I said to the others. "As fast as you can. I'll slow this bunch down."

"Lyssa," Hatter said, his eyes wide, but I'd already swung around to face the onslaught of guards. Several more shouts were ringing out at the sight of me. Blades flashed in the fading sunlight, but they were nothing compared to mine.

My fingers tightened around the grip with all the conviction I had in me. The ruby flared. I didn't want to spill blood, but if it was my people or the Queen's, I had to protect mine.

When I'd sent out the sword's magic before, it'd both walloped and sliced. Maybe I could control those effects more consciously. I focused all my intent on driving the guards back, and slashed the blade through the air in a sweeping arc.

Power surged through my body and across the road, radiating into the trees. It slammed into the wave of guards, a more concentrated punch than the deflecting magic my vest had protected me with in an earlier battle. They stumbled backward, doubling over, blood springing along cuts on their arms and their pleated uniforms waving tattered where some of the cutting magic had slipped through.

"I am the true queen of Wonderland," I hollered at them, pitching my voice as forcefully as I'd heard Theo use his. "I will take back what's mine from the people who stole it from me. I will protect the people you've abused. You know I don't want to hurt you. If you'll give up your loyalty to the tyrant on the throne and join the Spades, we'll welcome you. But if you attack us, I have no choice but to push back."

The guards at the front of the rush had taken the brunt of my magical smackdown. Many more pushed past their wounded companions. Their expressions were warier now, but they raced at me with swords and daggers drawn anyway. A few of the faces I glimpsed looked more terrified than furious, so much that my heart ached.

Then the Knave appeared by the top of the wall by the gate, jabbing his sword toward me and letting out a roar from his tiger maw. "Strike them all down. Kill the usurper!"

The guards' faces hardened. They were making their choice. I'd already told them what mine would be.

I whipped my sword in front of me again, letting it sharpen this time. The magic crackled from its shining blade and sliced across the front line of the charge. The forerunners stumbled and toppled with a gush of blood down their bellies. The punch of power drove the figures behind them backward onto their asses.

My stomach turned at the sight of the men I'd likely killed, and my breath burned in my throat from just those two swings of the sword. I had to buy us a little more time to safely make our escape. Setting my jaw, I glanced around and made two swift jabs through the air toward the sides of the road.

Two massive trees toppled across the cobblestones to block the road, their emerald-green leaves shivering. As the Knave screamed at his men, I swiveled around. Chess tossed his smoke bombs over the fallen trees to cover our escape even more. Theo was waiting farther up the road. He waved us on, and Chess and I dashed to him, to flee the way he'd sent the other Spades running.

We hadn't found Dee. I guessed we'd have to hope he found his way back to us on his own. But I'd staked my claim on Wonderland, and I'd shown the Queen's defenders that I was a true force to be reckoned with.

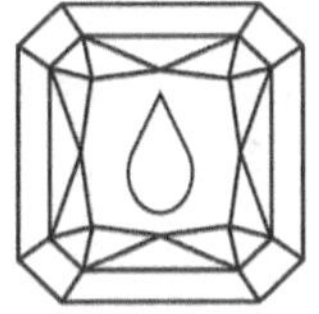

Theo

Lyssa's brainstorm had grown from a small bit of company to a crowd in the course of a day. Sixteen of the city's citizens sprawled or wandered around the shallow branch of cave where we'd laid out blankets and food for them. With only hours having passed since their last dose of that mind-muddling drug, the dazed look hadn't completely left their eyes, but a few of them were starting to register that this wasn't just some exclusive club they'd been invited to experience.

"I don't understand," said the woman I was crouched down in front of. She pulled her blanket closer around her trembling shoulders. "My head aches. I don't remember what I've been doing for… I don't know how long. How did I *get* here?"

"You know the smoke and 'shrooms you'd sometimes take in Caterpillar's Club?" I said, keeping my voice calm. "The Queen of Hearts has filled the whole city with intoxicants like that. Everyone up there has been partying like they're constantly at the club for weeks." I pointed to the stone ceiling.

The woman's chin wobbled. "Why would the Queen do *that*? I don't—I have my shop to check on. I—"

She shifted forward, and I grasped her shoulder. "You'll need to stay here a little longer," I said. "We brought you down here to get you away from the chemicals so you can clear your head. Your shop won't be safe yet. But we're working on it."

I tipped my head toward Lyssa, who was at the other side of the cave talking with an older man with a hound's head whose hands twitched in jerky movements. "The Queen of Hearts is afraid because Wonderland is finding out that she isn't a real queen after all. Her family stole the throne from the true rulers, the Red royal line. And our true queen has come back to us. The Red Queen is going to lead our way back to the world we're meant to have."

The woman peered a Lyssa with a puzzled but awed expression that brought a smile to my face. "Our true queen," she murmured.

"It's never really seemed right, having one we're afraid of, has it?" I said gently. "That's because it wasn't right at all. All along, a cruel imposter has been on the throne. We can have so much better than that."

The puzzlement melted into pure relief. I gave the woman's shoulder a light squeeze and stood up to see who else might appreciate exchanging a few words.

Looking at the people gathered there—*my* people, part of me still insisted—the impulse bubbled up to step into the middle of the room and command their attention, to guide them more like the White Knight than one of many Spades. More like a prince. The thought made me cringe inwardly.

Whatever influence my mother and the line of Hearts before her had inflicted on me, through exposure or genetics, I wanted to shed all of it. I could use those princely airs to reassure and to direct these people toward the ruler they ought to be focused on.

Lyssa caught my gaze on her and shot a small smile my way before stepping to welcome the next of the city folk. That woman's head was lolling on her shoulders, but her eyes held on Lyssa for a few seconds as the Otherlander spoke. You'd hardly know she grew up in the Otherland, seeing her now. She'd found her true self here with us. Pride filled my chest, seeing the results of that transformation, even though I couldn't really claim much credit for it.

I helped a goat-like man whose hands were shaking around his cup drink some water and reassured a teenaged boy who was still pretty out of it but had started mumbling about where his sister might be. "We'll keep an eye out for her," I told him. "If we see her, she'll be invited here too, I promise."

Lyssa finished her rounds at about the same time I did. I stepped into the passage beyond the cave with her, blinking my eyes against the brighter glow of the water there. Then I reached for her hand, as naturally as if I had no reason to think the gesture would be anything but welcome, but ready inside to pull back if she stiffened.

She'd wanted me earlier today—she'd given herself over, and then taken me over in a way I remembered with a fresh bolt of desire through my groin. But that didn't mean every sore point between us was fully healed.

To my joy, Lyssa's hand welcomed mine, her fingers curling to grasp my palm.

"You're doing well," I told her. "Every bit a queen—all the queen they could ask for."

She smiled, but this time it looked tight. "I hope so. This afternoon… I wanted the Spades, at least, to see how committed I am. And now the Queen of Hearts knows for sure what I'm after. And I—I killed at least some of those guards…"

Her voice dropped with the last words. I stopped and turned her to face me. She hesitated, but only for a second before leaning into my embrace.

"You were brilliant out there," I said, my heart wrenching at the thought of her feeling guilty over that moment of glory. "They meant to kill as many of us as they could."

"I know." She nestled her head against my chest. I knew it was only for a moment, but I wished I could hold her like this, protect her with my arms around her, through everything that lay ahead. "I did what I had to do. It was the right choice—I'm not doubting that. I just… I hate having to make that choice."

"And that's why you're the queen we need," I said. "Just remember, we're fighting a woman who's mad as they come. Sometimes you have to get a little mad to fight back against madness. The more you can hold on to sanity in the fray, the more impressive it is."

"I'll try to keep that in mind," Lyssa said. When she exhaled, she sounded more settled. She pulled away from me and swiped her hand over the pale waves of her hair, rumpled from all the rushing around she'd been doing today. Her blue eyes still held a glow of their own even though weariness was starting to color her expression.

"How are you doing?" she asked me. "Are you sure you shouldn't be getting more rest, after the way they treated you in the palace?"

"I think all this running around has been good for me, actually," I said honestly. The spasms of my muscles, the startling flashes of images, and the pains in my head had all retreated behind adrenaline and motion as the day had gone on. "She only had me for a couple of weeks, after decades of going my own way. It shouldn't take too long for me to shake whatever she did completely."

Lyssa squeezed my hand. "All right. I don't want my White Knight running himself ragged."

"I won't," I said, with a twinge at the name I wasn't sure I could really own now. "And *you* need to rest," I said. "The guards haven't shown any sign of discovering our hide-out. We can decide how to tackle them next in the morning."

Lyssa's lips pursed, but she nodded.

Not entirely trusting her to actually get that rest once we reached the camp, I walked her all the way to the cabin she'd been sharing. She narrowed her eyes at me, but she tugged me in for a quick kiss before she opened the door. The press of her mouth against mine even for that brief moment left me hungry for more. I wasn't sure I could ever get enough of her.

When she'd ducked in, I turned away and noticed Dum's slouched posture where he was spooning up soup from a bowl outside his own cabin. The cabin he'd been sharing with Dee, as well as Chess and Hatter. Dum had always been the more down-to-earth and solemn of the twins, but he'd rarely acted outright glum. The gloom of his current situation hovered over him like a storm cloud. Even his red hair appeared to have dulled.

I'd failed him. I'd sworn to their mother I'd keep both of them from harm, and I'd lost his brother. Why hadn't I seen that Dee was shaken enough to take drastic action?

All of Mother's damned "treatments" had been addling my thoughts and my senses. Perhaps I was mostly healed now, but I'd been distracted too often since I'd returned. I needed to make sure I kept control of my mind and my body from here on.

I grabbed an apple from our food supply and hunkered down on the cool rock next to Dum. He looked up from his bowl and made an effort to straighten his stance, as if he thought I'd be offended by his downcast demeanor.

"I'm sorry," I said. Best to get that out there first, especially if he was acting as though he owed *me* something. "I really hoped we'd find him. He may return to us yet. He's never let the Hearts' Guard catch him before."

"That's true," Dum said. His lips slanted at a crooked angle. "But I think something has shifted in him. I don't know how it'll have shifted his reactions in turn."

I tipped my head to the side. "What do you mean?"

Dum shrugged. "I wouldn't have said anything to you before. It didn't matter. Maybe you already noticed anyway. But since we were kids, when we first started helping with the Spades on the sidelines, it always seemed to me like Dee saw the whole rebellion as some kind of game. An adventure where we just had to play well enough and we'd win, like the games in your apartment in the Tower. I could never get him to take things totally seriously. He didn't have to. No one we were close with ever got caught. We never got really hurt. He could always keep that delusion going to stop himself from getting too scared."

I hadn't gotten quite the same impressions Dum had, but he'd know his brother better than I did. His suggestion explained how Dee had managed to stay in such high spirits throughout the missions, even when we'd faced setbacks. In some ways, the approach had served him well.

"But you think that's changed," I prompted. "Because of your mother being taken?"

"That," Dum said. "And you being gone before that. He was having trouble keeping up that carefree face he always wanted to show the world. He wouldn't talk to me about it, but I could see it. The fears were creeping in, and he couldn't push them back the same old ways. I'm just worried that finding out about Mom pushed him over some sort of edge. I don't know *what* he'd do if he really panicked."

"We'll do our best to find him and bring him back," I said, which was the best I could really say. "All of us. If we can save him, we will."

"I should have talked him down when he was here," Dum said. "He's *my* brother. Even I couldn't figure out the right thing to say." He raised his head. "It won't be your fault if he's gone too far for us to bring him back, is all I'm saying."

His whole family's lives were at stake, and he was trying to reassure *me*. My throat constricted. I clapped him on the back. "It won't be yours either. Don't you ever doubt that."

I left him to his meal, the talk of siblings and fear leading me across the camp to the new cabin the Spades had set up for my own sibling's use. I wasn't sure Mirabel could have tolerated sharing such close quarters with anyone else. As it was, she'd barely left the small structure since I'd arrived here.

As I'd used to when I'd arrive at her apartment in the Tower, I knocked on the door. "Come in," Mirabel said immediately, as she would have then too. I eased open the door and ducked inside to check in on my older sister.

She was sitting against the back wall, her legs drawn up under the soft white folds of her woolen skirt, a book propped against her knees. After a second, I realized the volume was upside down. I decided not to mention that fact. For all I knew, she'd managed to read it just fine like that.

"I didn't think I'd see you so soon," she said, with that dreamy air that made me wonder whether she was viewing time backwards or forwards right now. Or maybe a little of both, as seemed to becoming increasingly common these days.

"I wanted to make sure you're settling in all right," I said. "I know this is pretty different from the Tower."

Mirabel let out a light laugh. "Anywhere is fine if it's

not where Mother is." She paused, her gaze searching mine. "She comes close. I don't like her that close."

Before or after now? I swallowed hard. "I'll do whatever I can to make sure she never touches you again. You know you have my word on that."

"Yes. Yes." The urgency left her expression. She relaxed back against the wall. Then her forehead furrowed, a more melancholy shadow crossing her face. "We survived it, didn't we? As much as it hurt. As many as we lost."

A chill ran over my skin. I couldn't help asking, even though I knew my chances of getting a straight answer were slim, "What do you mean, Mirabel? What did we survive? Who did we lose?"

She rocked slightly from side to side. "Queen against Queen, Spade against Spade, family against family, friend against friend. We all turn on each other in the end. And only one can come out the other side."

CHAPTER FIFTEEN

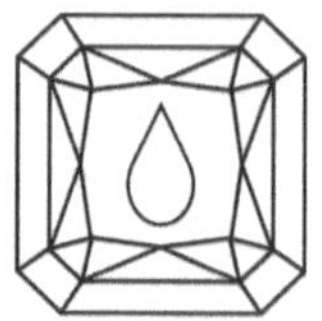

Lyssa

My mind felt more alert, if no less cluttered, after the exhausted sleep I'd toppled into. I rolled my shoulders as I considered the city people the Spades had gathered in the cave room. They seemed to be waking up in their own way too.

A few newcomers, brought in early this morning, lounged in the hazy blue light that reached the back of the cave room like they might have in one of the club's shallow pits, a faint rosy smell drifting off their clothes. The ones who'd spent the night with us were starting to ask a lot more pointed questions.

"The Inventor was here last night, wasn't he?" said one of the women Theo had talked to yesterday, peering around me as if I might be hiding him. Her gaze focused back on me, and she knit her brow. "He said you're a queen."

"I'm the Red Queen," I said. The words came more

easily every time I said them. "A long time ago, my family ruled Wonderland—without anyone losing their heads. The Reds believed in spreading happiness, not fear. The Hearts slaughtered all of them except one princess who escaped to the Otherland. That was hundreds of years ago, and the Queens of Hearts wiped out every trace of us they could. But they couldn't wipe *us* out. And now I'm here, to set things right."

A woman I'd talked to yesterday stepped closer with eyes much sharper than they'd been before. "Do you really think you can do that? It's the Spades down here, isn't it? They've only made trouble the whole time I've been alive."

The man with the hound's head shuddered where he was hunched by the wall. "The Spades? If the Queen finds out we've been taken in by them, she'll have all our heads."

Several others in the cave stirred nervously. My chest tightened. Before anyone else could start fretting, I held up my hand.

"Don't you remember all those years you were stuck repeating the same day over and over? The Spades freed you from that magic. We're helping you now, bringing you down here so you can clear your head from the drug the Queen of Hearts was forcing on you."

"As if we had any choice about it," the skeptical woman said.

"*Now* you have a choice," I pointed out. "You can think properly. Do you want to go back up to the city and be taken over by that drugged daze again? You can if you want to, and the guards will never know you were gone. But you won't be able to look after yourself either. They've been stealing people from the city, you know. Grabbing cartfuls of you and shipping you out to the Oyster Cove to be pearled. Down here, you're safe from that too."

"Pearled?" the first woman repeated. She hugged herself. "Why would the Queen want *that?*"

"I don't know," I said. "We're trying to figure that out. But it can't be good for anyone. I've seen the guards with my own eyes—they were taking dancers off the street, people who hadn't done anything wrong. The guards weren't even pretending they had a good reason. Everyone up there is so out of it, they didn't even think to protest. That's what you'd be going back to."

The houndish man glanced toward the ceiling with a pensive expression. "I don't like that. But I'm not ready to join some kind of fight. That'd get us killed even faster."

I inhaled slowly, willing my nerves to settle. The most important thing was convincing the Clubbers to stay down here where they couldn't betray our location. Where we'd still have a chance of convincing them to join the cause. As long as they were with us, the rest could wait— forever, even, if that was what they wanted.

This had been my idea. I couldn't let it become the Spades' downfall.

"You don't have to join in any missions," I said. "You don't even need to help out with our camp down here if you don't want to. We'll keep you as comfortable as possible and make sure you're fed. All we want is to know you're safe. As your queen, I serve *you.* I'm not going to demand your help when you hardly know me. There'll be no pressure on you. Just stay here, stay protected, at least until we can make the city up there safe again."

The jitters that had passed through the bunch of them faded. The houndish man sucked in a breath.

"All right," he said. "I don't like how I felt up there—I don't like anything the Queen's done to us. If you're not asking anything from us, I'm in no hurry to throw myself back on *her* mercy."

The skeptical woman frowned. "I'm not either. But if you're some kind of queen, you're going to do more than this, aren't you? What about our friends? Our families? My father must be wandering around up there still. Are you going to stuff all of us down in these caves before she has the chance to pearl any more of us?"

I swallowed hard, my thoughts slipping to Dee, who I *hoped* was only wandering around up there and not already locked in the palace dungeon or being shipped to the Cove. "We're doing everything we can to stop the Queen of Hearts completely," I said. "I don't want any more people taken. If I can stop her *today*, I will."

I had no idea whether that was even remotely possible, but the answer seemed to satisfy the woman for the moment. She bobbed her head to me and sat back down on her blanket. I hurried back through the tunnels to see what kind of plans I could actually make.

As I came up on the main camp, the blue glow of the stream caught on the shiny fabric of Hatter's top hat farther down the passage. He'd been off on sentry duty, if I remembered right. It reassured me a little, seeing the bit of jaunt in his stride as if he wasn't all that fazed by the fact that we were now fighting our rebellion literally from underground. The smile he gave me warmed me even more.

"How are our refugees doing?" he asked when he reached me.

"About as well as I could have hoped, I think," I said. "I've managed to convince them they're better off staying down here for the time being."

"I happen to know you can be very persuasive," he said, an amused glint in his eyes.

"I wouldn't have needed to persuade you so much if you'd been more helpful to begin with," I reminded him.

"Fair point." He leaned in to kiss me as if he couldn't quite help himself, and I was more than happy to return it. But as much as I might have liked to lose myself in that heady sensation for longer, I had come back here with a purpose.

"Do you know where Theo is?" I asked. He normally got up early, but I didn't see him around the camp.

To my relief, Hatter nodded. "I passed him on my way here. He was heading out to take his turn guarding the entrance near the palace. I think he wanted to check up on the protections he set up last night."

After our close call with the guards, the Prince of Hearts had made whatever use he could of the materials and devices the other Spades had scavenged to hopefully buy us some time if the guards traced our path. Since they hadn't turned up yet, we seemed to have gotten off scot-free, but it couldn't hurt to have the defenses in place.

"All right," I said with a rush of purpose. "Then that's where I'm going too."

Hatter raised an eyebrow at me. "What are you up to, looking-glass girl? You almost look a little mad."

I made a face at him. "Maybe I need to be a little mad

to go up against a Queen who couldn't be madder," I said, remembering Theo's words last night. "You're not exactly one to talk, Mad Hatter."

He let out a laugh, but concern had softened his gaze. "Which is exactly why I know the risks involved in letting loose that way."

"You should also know by now I'm not the type to go right off the rails. I actually have a very good track record with trains." I gave him a teasing shove. "Go do whatever else you're supposed to be doing now. Maybe I'll come back with a crown on my head."

His eyebrows rose even higher. "I'll look forward to that, then," he said, and stole one last kiss before heading into the camp.

The Spades had marked the passages around the stream with chalk symbols long before I'd made it back to Wonderland. I was becoming familiar enough with the usual routes now that I barely needed to look at them as I treaded over the rough stone beside the rippling water. Getting to the palace exit required a scramble across a makeshift bridge and a few turns.

The mineral scent in the air thickened as the stream narrowed until I could have hopped across it without any bridge at all. It veered to the right. At my left, a narrow passage slanted upward into a room about the size of my apartment kitchen back home.

Theo was standing by the far wall where carved footholds led up to the trap door, fixing slim silver rod just beneath the door with a faint squeak. He gave the base one last twist and turned to face me as I slipped into the small space.

"Everything's still as you wanted it?" I asked.

"I made a few adjustments I thought of overnight," he said. "I may not be the Inventor anymore, but my mind still leaps into those ways of thinking automatically."

"Good for us that it does," I said with a smile.

Theo studied me. "You didn't come out here just to find out about that," he said. "What is it, Lyssa?"

He'd always been able to take a quick read of my mood. I guessed there wasn't any point in beating around the bush.

"I want us to move on the palace as soon as we can," I said. "Too many people are being hurt. I want the hold the Queen of Hearts has over Wonderland severed as quickly as possible, not with a drawn out war. When we found you, in the palace, you said something about clearing the way to the throne for me. What exactly did you do? What do we need if we're going to see that plan through?"

I'd thought Theo had recovered his balance yesterday. Now, with the abrupt clenching of his jaw, I knew he hadn't completely shaken the effects of his mother's torment yet. He closed his eyes for a second, his throat working as he composed himself. The obvious strain made my heart ache for him.

"My apologies," he said, his voice only slightly rough. "Yes. I—The Queen of Hearts has more than one throne. There's one most people never get to see her sitting on, farther into her inner chambers than the looking-glass I sent you through. Seeing it while I was there these past weeks, I realized it's another artifact of the Red royal rule. I believe my family has harnessed the magic in it somehow to their own ends—it's the source of her magic. If you can reclaim it, I don't think defeating her will be difficult after that."

My heart leapt, but only for an instant before I thought of all the obstacles still in the way. "How do I reclaim it?"

"Once you get to it, I managed to fix a small device to one of the panels, that when triggered should crack through the cage of sorts she's built around it to control it. Then all you should need to do is sit on it and let it welcome you." Theo gave me a crooked smile. "Of course, the greater trouble is getting you that far into the palace to begin with. And not just you, but enough of us to protect you while we subdue my mother. Even without any magical power, some of the guards will still listen to her. You couldn't take her and them on alone."

"Okay," I said, mulling her words over. "So we really just have one problem—how to get me and at least a few Spades into the Queen's inner quarters. That's a *tricky* problem, but at least it only needs one solution, and then we're ready to go."

Theo chuckled. "You do know how to look on the bright side. We'll get you there. *I'll* get you there. Those city folk you've been collecting may sway the balance too."

"I don't know. They didn't seem too enthusiastic about the cause this morning." But that could change. I opened my mouth to ask another question, and a raised voice filtered through the trap door above us, far too close for comfort.

"This is it. I'm telling you."

My mouth snapped shut. Even muffled by the layer of

wood, it sounded like… Dee. Another, deeper voice was already answering him.

"You'd better not be yanking us around. If this is a trick, your head will be on a pike within the hour."

That growl was the Knave—I was almost sure of it. My eyes caught Theo's and found his expression was as distraught as I felt. Then Dee spoke up again.

"Why would I come to you and make this offer if I was lying? I just want the deal we made—I want my mother freed—you promised that, didn't you?"

A dismissive guffaw from one of the other men above didn't dislodge the horror that swelled inside me in an instant.

The Hearts' Guard hadn't forced Dee into giving us up. He'd gone to them intending to betray us.

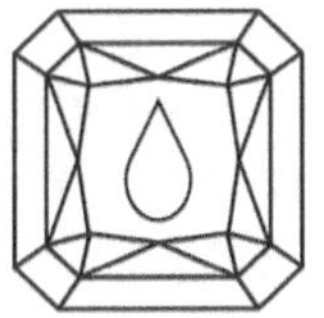

CHAPTER SIXTEEN

Lyssa

Theo grabbed my arm. "Let's get out of here," he said under his breath. "*Fast.* We have to warn the others."

As I scrambled after him into the longer passage with the glowing stream, the trap door's latch was already grating to the side. Shit. My heart thumped with a lurching beat. How could Dee have given us all up like that—even his own brother?

We broke into a run along the side of the stream. "What are we going to do?" I said to Theo.

His mouth had gone tight. "The measures I put in place will slow them down exactly as I intended. I just didn't expect one of our own to be helping set them off. Damn it."

Nausea coiled around my stomach. "What else do you think he might have told them? What if there are guards at all the exits?"

Theo shook his head. "I have to believe he still had some concern for us and the cause. The way he was talking up there—he'd have known that by pitching his voice that loud, anyone standing guard down below would hear it. And he knew there'd be a sentry at that entrance. He sold us out, but he purposely gave us a little warning. I don't think he wants us dead. He just wanted a big enough bargaining chip to save his mother."

It was hard to picture the happy-go-lucky guy I'd been getting to know scheming like that, but I hoped Theo was right. "Do you think the Queen will keep up her end of the deal she made with him?"

Theo's lips curled into a grimace. "I wouldn't count on it. Even if he'd served us all up on a platter, she'd probably enjoy laughing in his face and sending him off to be pearled with the rest of them. He'll have admitted he was a Spade. That's a death sentence right there. She'll never trust him to stay in 'her' kingdom."

Then we'd better make it my kingdom before it came to that. My breath ragged in my throat, I pushed my legs even harder.

A crashing sound echoed through the passage behind me. I startled, nearly tripping over my feet. Theo steadied me.

"That's the main trap," he said with grim satisfaction. "It'll take them at least a few minutes to work their way through that."

A sentry from one of the smaller secondary camps came into view up ahead. "Get everyone to move out!" I hollered to her. "Right away, take only what you have to. The guards have found the way into the River Down." I paused for a second, searching my whirling thoughts for the right strategy. "Leave through the forest exit. We'll regroup on the other side of the mushroom fields." Please, let that be far enough.

Between our fight and flight yesterday and the stress my body had been through in the weeks before that, I couldn't keep up the same pace as Theo for much longer. A burn nibbled at my legs and chest. He slowed as I did, but I nudged him onward. "I'll catch up. You get to the main camp and sound the alarm there. As soon as I've got my sword, I can push back anyone who comes at us down here."

We still had to leave, though. Now that the guards knew that the Spades were using these underground passages, we'd never be safe down here again.

Theo squeezed my hand and forced himself to let go. I kept up a steady lope as he pulled ahead. The prickling burn spread on through the muscles in my calves.

When I made it to the main camp, everyone was already grabbing their things and heading farther along the stream. Theo had retrieved my sword and my scepter from my cabin where I'd left them. I didn't have anything else here that mattered all that much to me. Theo handed the artifacts to me and gripped Mirabel's arm where she was standing wide-eyed next to him to urge her along. Chess fell in with us at my other side. Hatter glanced back from up ahead where he was hurrying Doria along, and the mass of us hustled on through the caves.

The stream's blue glow wavered over our bodies. The Spades stayed quiet, but the noise of so many hurrying footsteps echoed through the cave. I kept glancing back over my shoulder, waiting to see a flash of red-and-pink tunic. How long would it take the Knave and the other guards to break through Theo's defenses?

He was fiddling now with a round device about the size of a coaster, with a shell of dark gray metal and a clump of tiny wires protruding from its upper edge.

"What's that?" I asked him in a hushed voice.

"Something to cover our escape," he said. "I didn't think I was going to be using it down here, but if I adjust the intensity of the shock…"

That sounded a little ominous. We passed the third camp and stirred everyone there into action. My pulse stuttered at the thought of the city people we'd brought down here, the ones I'd been talking to no more than an hour ago. I'd promised them they'd be safe, and now the guards were coming right down here.

"The Clubbers," I said. "We can't leave them."

"Of course not," Theo said. "Chess and I will get them. That'll be the perfect place to cut off the charge anyway."

The fork in the passage opened up ahead of us, one side leading to the Clubbers' room, the other to the forest exit. Theo motioned to my sword. "Hold off anyone who comes this way. We'll be back as soon as we can, and then I'll blockade the guards completely."

There wasn't time to ask him how he was going to do that. He motioned to Chess, and the two of them dashed down the left passage toward the cave where the Clubbers had been recovering. In front of me, the other Spades kept running. I stopped at the fork and spun around, sword at the ready.

The hasty footsteps on either side of me faded away. I stood braced, my fingers clutching the sword's hilt, my ears pricked for the slightest sound of our pursuers.

It didn't take long. Theo's traps might have slowed the guards down, but they hadn't needed to stop to warn anyone or grab anything. The distant rasp of dozens of boots scraping the rocky ground carried to me, getting louder by the second. My gut knotted. I raised my sword a little higher.

They emerged into the hazy light like a mass of crimson, the mix of red and pink reminding me of butcher's meat. At first it was hard to pick apart individual forms. They barrelled toward me along both sides of the street, their blades flashing with the blue light, and I made out the Knave's tiger head at the front of the pack. He wasn't hanging back shouting orders today. No doubt after yesterday's embarrassment, he wanted to sever my head from my body himself.

Too bad, buddy. I intended to keep it right where it belonged.

My muscles ached with tension, but I held myself still, poised. The thunder of their feet and the warble of harsh breaths and muttered curses filled the passage. There was no point in playing my hand too soon. I didn't want to wear myself out. Only when I had to, I'd press them back.

Chess and Theo had better get those city people over here fast.

There was no sign of Dee in the midst of the guards. They must have left him behind, either suspecting he might try to sabotage their efforts at the last second or not wanting him to get in the way. It wasn't as if the guy was a fighter.

Something else struck me about the faces scattered around the Knave as the horde came more clearly into view. Not just a few but at least a dozen of those I could see had the glazed look of the pearl-heads I'd noticed before. Their expressions were slack, their eyes fogged, as dazed as the Clubbers were when under the influence of the rosy drug. Their bodies moved in a relentless forward charge as if nothing existed inside them except the impulse to carry out the orders they'd been given.

No doubt those orders included slicing through any Spades they encountered.

I shivered with a sudden, chilly certainty. *This* was why the Queen of Hearts had commanded her guards to round up people from the city—people healthy and strong. She was expanding her army by the day with unwilling soldiers. With innocents she'd murdered.

If I'd lacked conviction before to strike back with all the power I had in me, that realization would have summoned it. I adjusted my grip on the sword and tensed my muscles. They were only thirty feet away now. Twenty. Fifteen—

I lashed out, snapping the blade in a swift arc, the need to defend all the people fleeing behind me rolling off me and surging out through the air.

The sword's power smacked into the advancing force as if a sheet of metal had slammed into their middles. The guards buckled over and heaved backward at the same time, knocking into each other in a domino effect down several rows. Some stumbled and fell into the stream.

Blood spilled across the floor where the sharpest edge of the magical blow had hit them.

I sucked the still air into my lungs and readied myself for another strike. The sound of pounding feet reached my ears again—from the passage beside me this time. Theo and Chess were urging our twenty or so recovered Clubbers toward me.

"Go!" I called to them. "Hurry! I can hold them off for now."

The woman who'd expressed so many doubts when I'd talked to her earlier glanced past me down the caves toward the horde of guards. Panic washed across her face, followed by a startled expression as she realized the men were struggling just to get up. Her gaze fell to my sword and then rose to my face. In that instant, for the first time, she looked at me like I really was a queen. Similar surprised relief lit up the expressions of her companions.

I waved them on down the tunnel, and they dashed the same way the Spades had gone. Chess loped with them, calling directions. Theo came to a halt beside me. He reached into his pocket and yanked out the coaster-shaped device he'd been tweaking earlier.

"It's time for you to go too," he said. "Let's see how well this works underground. Get ready to run."

He flipped a switch on the device and jammed it into a nook in the rocky wall. Hooking his hand around my elbow, he tugged me down the passage. I raced with him, but I couldn't stop myself from looking back over my shoulder at the eerie crackling that reverberated through the cave.

Sparks were shooting from the device. A bolt of

searing white electricity leapt from its top and arced across the cave ceiling. Everywhere it touched, the stone cracked and split open.

The Knave roared on the other side of the device's path. He rushed toward us, one arm pressed against his abdomen where my sword's magic must have cut him, the other gesturing for his men to follow. He wasn't fast enough.

The ceiling shattered. Rocks rained down with a boom that rattled my ear drums. In an instant, that entire section of cave had collapsed in on itself, cutting us off from the rest of the underground.

Pebbles plummeted down even where we stood. At Theo's noise of warning, I started running again.

We darted through increasingly narrow passages until a familiar top hat came into sight in a streak of sunlight spilling down from an opening above. Hatter let out a relieved sound at the sight of us. "Everyone else is up," he said. "Come on, slow-pokes." He paused as he gripped the rungs of the ladder. "What in the lands was that noise back there?"

"I carried out a minor renovation to the caves' layout," Theo said, breathlessly wry. "There's now a wall where there once was a passage heading this way. If the guards want to catch us, they'll have to find their way back aboveground first."

Hatter's lips curled into a smirk. He scrambled nimbly up the ladder. Unwilling to let go of the sword that had saved us twice now, I heaved myself after him one-handed, the blade clinking against the rungs.

In the thick forest above, the fresh green smells of the

vivid leaves filled my nose. Most of the Spades were already hustling off between the trees, aiming for the land beyond the mushroom field like I'd told them.

When I turned in the other direction, all I could see of the city amid the foliage was a sliver here and there of bright paint. My legs locked for a second. That city was part of *my* Wonderland. We were fleeing it, leaving it behind—abandoning all the people there who still needed my protection.

"We should get moving," Theo said, firmly but with sympathy in his eyes. "The Knave knows which direction we fled in; he'll suspect we came to ground somewhere. He'll send troops this way as soon as he can."

"I know." I did, but turning my back on the city still wrenched at me. I set my jaw and strode toward the mushrooms. We'd regroup and sort ourselves out, and then we'd come up with a plan for how to reclaim the ground we'd lost—and more.

No workers chattered and giggled in the mushroom field today. The giant orange-and-pink spotted forms loomed beside the path completely untended. I guessed Caterpillar didn't have any need to harvest his crop when the Queen was getting the entire city high with her doctored roses and the ingredients Rabbit was bringing from the Otherland.

More forest sprawled beyond the mushrooms. A cloud drifted over the sun as we tramped along, and a cool breeze tickled over my skin. How far did we need to go to make sure the Hearts' Guard didn't find us? *Could* we go far enough? They might track us all the way to the Topsy Turvy Woods with its massive upside down trees. The Queen wanted us all dead, one way or another.

I needed to make sure I could protect the people already with me before I could even think about the rest of the city.

Our companions had gathered in a clearing just out of view of the mushrooms. It might have been the same one where I'd trained with my sword and scepter the other day. The city people paced or swayed in the middle of the meadow while the Spades stalked along the perimeter as if on patrol, but they were here. A few of them had even picked up spare weapons the Spades had brought with them, watching the forest just as warily. A little awe touched me, looking at them.

The Clubbers might not be all the way ready to fight yet, but they were coming around to the cause. They'd chosen to stay with us rather than take their chances heading back to the city. We had more than twice the number of allies we could have counted on a few days ago. It was the start of a real army.

The thought sent a quiver of nausea down to my gut, but it steadied me at the same time. We *needed* an army. That much was clear. Even what we had now wasn't going to be enough.

"Where to now?" Dum asked, his gaze on me expectantly. "What should we do?"

Oh, fuck. It was up to me to figure that out too, of course. I had the urge to glance at Theo for guidance, but that might destroy the confidence I'd spent the last two days building in all these people watching. They'd want to know their queen could make her own call.

The guards might be coming behind us. Ahead of us lay that stretch of bizarrely shaped hills and then the Topsy Turvy Woods. Would it be easier to hide out there? Of course, I also had to consider that the last time I'd ventured that far, Hatter and I had nearly been lunch for a jabberwock…

Oh.

A smile leapt to my face with the spark of inspiration that had just lit in my head. I wanted to laugh, but I hadn't pulled my new plan off yet.

I reached behind me and tugged my scepter from its carry bag. Theo watched me with obvious curiosity.

"What are you going to do with that?" he asked.

"We don't want the guards catching up with us here," I said. "I'm going to put something between us and them that they won't want to tangle with. I'm going to call a jabberwock."

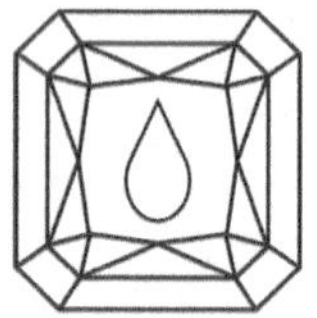

Hatter

"This is fucking *amazing*," Doria said, her face glowing with excitement as we moved through the forest. She bent to grab another stick to add to the pile of firewood in her arms. "Isn't it? Can you imagine the looks on their faces when they realized they'd have to go through a jabberwock to get to us?"

"It's pretty incredible," I said, maybe a little more dryly than she'd have hoped to get from my response. The truth was that an anxious twitch had been tugging at my ribs from the moment Lyssa had declared her intentions. Not even the evergreen tang in the warm summer air or the brightness of the sun—more sun than I'd gotten to experience in weeks—had managed to soothe it.

I was the one who'd once earned the name "Mad." If anyone around here could say a plan was completely bonkers, it should be me. Ordering jabberwocks to serve as our guard dogs was one hundred percent, beyond a doubt, utterly insane.

And yet our queen's first attempt had worked out so well, she was summoning a few more of the monsters right now.

I scooped another two thick branches into my arms and judged I wasn't going to be able to carry much more back to the camp without my arms falling off. Also, it was a good thing I'd become accustomed to my suits getting ruined on a regular basis, because this one's sleek blue fabric was now polka-dotted with bits of bark.

My daughter's arms looked heavily laden too. "I think this is enough for now," I said to her. "Let's head back before they start thinking a stray jabberwock has eaten us."

Doria gave me an amused look as we tramped through the brush toward the clearing where we'd set up a new sort of camp. "Once Lyssa brings more of them, she's going to start pushing the guards right out of the city, you know. That's what she said. But she'll need people on the ground helping the Clubbers stay out of the way and watching her back. I'm planning on going with her."

She kept eyeing me warily as she said the last bit. I didn't need any psychic powers to know she suspected I was going to argue about her plans.

A month ago, I probably *would* have argued. Even now, after everything all of us had been through together, after everything we'd survived, something deep in my chest screamed *No!* at the thought of Doria going up against the Hearts' Guard directly, even with a bunch of us and a herd of jabberwocks at her side.

I swallowed that scream down. If I'd learned anything from all those close calls, it was that these days hearing a "No" only made Doria more determined to follow through. She was coming up on fifteen, coming up on adulthood soon after. I'd taken plenty of mad risks with the Spades at her age.

March and May had wanted me to look after her, not lock her in a cage.

"Of course you do, Mouse," I said fondly. I'd have ruffled her hair for good measure if my arms hadn't been occupied with the heap of firewood. Doria made a face at me for the childhood nickname, but I wasn't done yet. There were things I should say that maybe I should have said even earlier.

"You don't need permission from me to run missions or pitch in however you think you best can," I went on. "I've seen how well you can handle yourself, especially in the last few weeks since we've come underground. I'm still going to worry, because as far as I know that's what parents are for, but I'll try not to inflict those worries on you too often. All I ask is that you make sure you're working *with* us, not running off to try something on your own like you did with that fiery sign outside the club."

Doria blinked at me. A slow smile spread across her face. "Yeah. Okay, I can handle that. I'm not in any hurry to revisit the palace dungeon anyway." She paused, and her voice softened. "Thanks, Dad."

Damn, she had grown into a capable young woman right in front of me, hadn't she? I found I had to add, "I'm proud of you, you know."

She brightened even more, and then a teasing glint lit in her dark eyes. "I'm proud of you too, Pops," she said, bumping her elbow against my arm. "You proved you're not just a stick in the mud after all."

I laughed. "I suppose I deserve that."

She grinned, but a moment later a shadow crossed her expression. Her gaze slipped away toward the forest ahead. I knew her well enough to guess what she might be thinking about.

"You and Dee were good friends," I said. "I know it must be hard—if you want to talk about anything to do with that, you can."

Her mouth tensed. "I'm not even totally sure what happened. Did he really sell us out? He *offered* to bring the guards to the River Down?"

The twins had been not just good friends but her best friends in the Spades. I wished I could save her from the pain of that kind of betrayal, but I had to be honest.

"I wasn't there, but from what Lyssa and Theo have said, there isn't much doubt. He didn't have anything else to bargain with, and he was frantic to save his mother." And he'd been shaken, no doubt, by all the revelations about the man he'd looked to as a leader. None of that excused him turning traitor, but the circumstances explained his betrayal at least a little. "Theo did say it sounded as if he tried to give warning, to make sure we'd get out in time. And that worked."

"Still." Doria kicked at a fallen twig. "I would never have thought... We could all have been *killed*. How could he trust the Queen's people enough to even try to make a deal?"

"I don't know." I'd run missions with the twins and joked around with them afterward for a few years before my life had become focused on parenthood, but I couldn't say we'd really been close. "People can always surprise you. Sometimes in good ways, but sometimes in bad ways too."

She let out a sharp chuckle. "I still hope he makes it back to us in one piece. If only so I can shout his head off myself."

"Well, I don't think anyone would blame you for that —either part of it."

To my relief, the conversation appeared to have taken a small weight off her shoulders. She strode over to the pile of firewood in the camp with her usual energy.

Most of the city folk we'd taken in were sitting near the fire, gnawing on pieces of roast pigeon. Dum and a couple of the others had gone off on a hunting trip not long after we'd set down here. A prickle of annoyance passed over me looking at the bunch of Clubbers as I set down my wood in the pile too.

They were sitting on their asses enjoying our efforts, happy enough that we'd gotten them away from the Queen's influence but too scared of the consequences to really join in.

It was going to take time, I reminded myself. A lifetime of playing along and following the rules couldn't be switched off in an instant. It'd taken me long enough to recover my sense of righteous courage after holding back in caution for twelve years, and I'd had plenty of years of running wild before that.

Chess strolled over to meet us, the bright sun sparking

in his auburn hair. He rubbed his hands together with one of his familiar grins.

"Are you ready?" he asked Doria. "We're heading out now."

Despite the way I'd talked myself down when she'd mentioned the impending mission, a flicker of panic shot through me. "Are you going to the city already?"

Chess tipped his head in that direction. "Our queen headed over with her first jabberwock not that long ago. She said she expected she could summon a few more before too long. They do move rather quickly when they're motivated. She wanted us to be ready to press on toward the city right away."

I supposed that was better than having a horde of jabberwocks prowling around *here*. I worked my jaw for a second and then said, "I'm coming along too."

"The more the merrier," Chess said. "We'll show the guards how the Spades throw a party." He beckoned, and a few more of the Spades joined us: Dum and Kip and a newer woman whose name I couldn't recall. There wasn't any sign of Theo around, but probably our former Inventor was conjuring up new tools for us wherever he could find the means.

With at least one monster making sure no guards came this way, we could take the faster path of the road rather than weaving out of sight through the forest and the mushroom stands. I spotted the jabberwock before I made out Lyssa. Or rather, jabberwock*s*. One sat right at the side of the road, its searing violet gaze aimed at the city as if daring anyone to try to travel this way. Another stood closer to the nearest buildings, ruffling its gold and scarlet feathers impatiently.

A third of the immense creatures was leaning right over Lyssa where she stood in the middle of the cobblestone lane. Streams of smoke trailed up from the jabberwock's wide nostrils as it nudged its snout against the scepter she was holding up. Its lips drew back, revealing the jagged teeth I'd seen another clamp around a guard's body just a few weeks ago.

Lyssa's lips were moving too, forming words too soft for me to make out across the distance. As we approached, her attention didn't waver from the beast in front of her. My pulse kicked up a notch as the sour stench of the creatures' breath reached my nose.

I'd watched Lyssa tame jabberwocks before, but I'd also seen one snap from her hold in an instant. That one was so close, it could have snatched her in its maw before she could so much as blink.

Just as that thought crossed my mind, the beast's head jerked up and then down again. My heart outright stopped. Before I had a chance to think anything else, my feet were already flinging me forward to grab Lyssa, to fling myself between the monster and the woman I loved if I had to.

The moment I leapt, a shudder passed through the jabberwock's bulky body. Its eyes flashed, and its head jerked again—toward me.

"Hey!" Lyssa said, a little louder now but still gentle. "Hey. Here. With me."

I stopped in my tracks. My heart thumped so hard it echoed through my head, every nerve insisting I had to get my queen, my lover, to safety, but I clenched my hands against the urge.

Lyssa knew what she was doing, I reminded myself. I had to trust her. My attempt to intervene had only incited the creature.

Chess came up beside me, touching my shoulder. I forced myself to take a slow step backward, and then another. The jabberwock shifted its focus to Lyssa again, and Doria let out a shaky breath, as much excited as relieved.

Lyssa rubbed the creature's muzzle with the gold-and-ruby end of the scepter, and the muscles coiled beneath its feathered skin appeared to relax. The jabberwock exhaled with a putrid huff. A satisfied sound reverberated in its throat. It blinked slowly and gazed down at the new Red Queen with a look I'd almost call adoring.

Now that we were closer, I could see there was a fourth jabberwock, already tamed, waiting amid the trees on the other side of the road. Its gaze was trained on Lyssa with a similar expression. She had won them over well, hadn't she? I never would have thought I'd see a jabberwock look at anything like that.

If she could keep them that loyal, we might really get somewhere.

Lyssa slid her scepter into the bag at her back and pulled her sword from the belted leather sheath Theo had hastily constructed for her. She pointed the blade toward the city. "We destroy the roses and clear off the men in the uniforms of the Hearts. Everyone else is our friend. Watch me and listen."

She glanced back at us and gave a quick nod. I

couldn't blame her for not being able to spare us more than that brief gesture. By all means, let her stay focused on the massive beasts that could slaughter us all in a matter of seconds.

Three of the jabberwocks lumbered toward the city with our queen. The one farthest back stayed in place to watch over the path to our camp. It narrowed its eyes at us as we passed, but apparently we passed muster. I wasn't keen to find out what it was going to do to anyone who didn't. How well could they identify the guards' uniforms, exactly?

As we passed the first few buildings, the revelers up ahead caught sight of the jabberwocks. Even in their dazed state, a few of the Clubbers shrieked.

"Go inside," Lyssa called out. "They won't hurt you, but it'll be easier for us to protect you if you're off the street. As soon as we've passed by, you can come back out. The Red Queen is here to take your city back for you and free you from the spell of the Queen of Hearts' roses."

With her last words, she pointed her sword toward a nearby heap of roses. One of the jabberwocks snorted and spewed out a spurt of flame. In an instant, only cinders and a faint burnt smell remained.

If we could burn up all the drugged roses and stop the guards from bringing more, the whole city *would* be freed.

I walked on with lightening spirits, pausing to reassure a trembling woman who'd frozen by the door of a shop, carefully slipping past the monsters to usher a few gaping kids into the shelter of a nearby house. In the Clubbers' current state, no one was likely to care which building belonged to whom.

Lyssa strode on between the jabberwocks without a hint of nerves. My gaze kept sliding back to her, wanting to revel myself—in the power she commanded, in the confidence she was finding in herself. She'd always been pretty, but now, with her eyes bright and her mouth set in a determined smile, she was more beautiful than I'd ever seen her.

It made me want to offer her more than meandering along here dealing with the stragglers.

When we reached the street with my hat shop, a tiny inspiration hit me. It wasn't much, but hopefully it'd give her a little comfort when she took a break from her work.

A few of the guards who'd been stationed there charged out and then fled with jabberwock fire scorching their heels. Lyssa directed one of the beasts to bring its head to an open second floor window, and I heard more scampering out the back of the building with shouts of alarm. I exchanged a glance with Chess.

"Let's make sure they're all cleared out?" I said. "We don't want any enemies lurking at our backs."

Chess nodded, and I pushed past the shop door. "Everyone out," I hollered, "or the jabberwocks will have you. This building belongs to the Spades now."

It turned out only one guard had stood his ground. He rushed at us on the stairs, and Chess heaved him on past us, leaving him crumpled in a heap at the bottom.

"Off with you," he said. "And run fast, or the beasts with have you for dinner."

I brandished my dagger in one hand and a hatpin in the other. The guard looked from one of us to the other, and then out the shop window at the feathered beasts beyond, and must have recalculated how much he valued his life. He darted out the back door.

A couple of now-stale scones sat on a plate in the kitchen. The bakery would be closed, the baker as muddled by drugs as the rest of the city, or I'd have grabbed more of those to bring back to the camp. Too bad.

On the top floor, I opened up the wardrobe Lyssa had been using and picked out a couple of the dresses I thought she'd favored. Since she'd arrived here, she'd been relying on her Otherlander clothes and a blouse and skirt one of the Spades had been able to lend her. Something clean and familiar should give her a least a bit of joy.

"For Lyssa?" Chess said from where he was leaning against the doorframe.

"It's the least I can think to do." I stared at the fabric in my hands, and suddenly this effort seemed ridiculous. "She's out there with jabberwocks looming over her on all sides, taking on all the guards in the city practically on her own. Doesn't it bother you that she's having to put herself through so much, and there's hardly a thing we can do to protect her?"

"I don't think Lyssa takes more onto her shoulders than her shoulders can hold," Chess said in his typical offhand way. "When she needs us, we're here."

"It doesn't seem right to simply wait on the sidelines." Not for the woman I loved. Not when there was so much danger still ahead of us.

"It's hardly right to jump into the line of fire either, I expect." Chess cocked his head, and his tone turned more serious. "You know, when our queen heard of threats still hanging over me, the best thing she did for me was to simply ask what I needed and give me that. She didn't go charging off trying to take on the spirits of my past as if she didn't believe I could attend to them myself. She has my back, and I have hers, but we don't step in front of each other in our eagerness to prove our devotion. Treat her like she's whole, not like she's broken."

I couldn't help thinking of the state Chess had been in when he'd first come to me, years and years ago, after his torture at the Duchess's hands. The resetting of the day had ensured his body had returned to its previous state, but he'd flinched at almost every touch, at random noises. He'd spent five days holed up in my guest bedroom before he'd come back to himself enough to join myself and March and May even for dinner outside those four walls.

The buoyant, carefree man I'd always seen him as hadn't taken long to re-emerge, but perhaps that wasn't the whole story. The pain of the past could haunt a person a long time—I should know. Had he still felt broken?

However much he was speaking from his side of the experience as well, his words rang true. I'd only diminish the confidence I'd been admiring in our queen if I hovered around Lyssa braced for any possible catastrophe. Trying to guard Doria that avidly certainly hadn't helped anyone.

"That sounds… very reasonable," I said. "Even if I wish I could take more of the blows to come."

"Ah," Chess said, his smile coming back, "but she wouldn't wish that, don't you see?"

Perhaps not well enough, but I'd have plenty of time to practice shifting my inclinations during the battles to come. I bundled up the dresses and headed back down the stairs, stopping only to duck into my bedroom and grab a fresh suit for myself as well.

My gaze roved over the shelves beside my bed automatically and halted. I frowned, stepping closer to check the floor.

The sketch of Alicia's house—the house Lyssa had since inherited—wasn't sitting where I'd left it. It didn't appear to have fallen, either. Where had that slip of paper gotten to?

A roar echoed through the walls, and the hairs on the backs of my arms jumped up. That minor mystery could wait for another day. I dashed toward the street to see how I might have my queen's back now.

CHAPTER EIGHTEEN

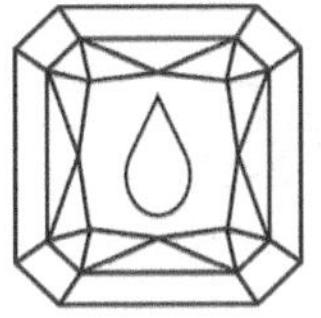

Lyssa

In the morning, we'd fled the city. Now, between streaks of amber lamplight, I was bringing the Clubbers home. While I watched their faces as we walked past the first buildings, as they breathed in the clearing air and took in the burnt piles the jabberwocks had reduced the Queen's roses to, a glow lit up inside me —a sense of accomplishment more potent than anything I'd felt before.

In some ways, the Queen of Hearts had stolen these people's home from them. She'd turned it into a place where they had no choice but to live in a drug-addled daze. I'd freed them from her and given back everything she'd taken from them.

Almost everything she'd taken from them. I couldn't say they really had their freedom until I'd managed to strip her guards of their weapons and her of all her power. But for now, this felt like a pretty epic victory.

The jabberwock lumbering along beside me let out a faint snort. I patted its feathered leg. When I'd first called out to the creatures I'd thought of as monsters, I'd been terrified underneath. But the connection I'd been able to form with the ones we'd encountered on the Checkerboard Plains, to calm them and tame them, had come even more easily now that I held the scepter and believed in my right to use it.

As the cleansing glow of the scepter's ruby had dispelled the storming emotions behind the blazing eyes and the teeth like shards of glass, I'd gotten a taste of their turmoil. The jabberwocks were more anxious than raging. I had to wonder whether they'd always been monstrous or if the tyranny of the Hearts' rule had driven them to viciousness like it had warped so much else in Wonderland.

I sensed a faint impression of the other three I'd summoned, which I'd asked to patrol the fringes of the city on the palace side and to frighten off any guards who tried to journey along those roads. If the guards didn't frighten, they might find themselves barbequed or skewered. I was leaving the choice up to them.

A thin wail caught my ears. The jabberwock shivered but stayed at my side. I peered down a side-street and spotted a little girl, no more than six or seven, hugging her knees where she sat at the side of the road.

The jabberwock would probably only scare her more. I looked into the violet eye closest to me and made a motion for it to stay put. Then I hurried over to the girl.

"What's wrong?" I asked, crouching down in front of her. "Do you need help?"

She swiped at her damp cheeks. Her hair was tangled and her face smudged with dirt, presumably from weeks of roaming around amid the revelers. The drug had left the city people barely able to look after themselves.

"I don't know where my mom and dad are," she said, and jabbed her thumb at the building behind her, a spindly yellow structure that zigzagged back and forth across its five storeys. "This is my house. I came back a couple hours ago, but they aren't here. Maybe they went off somewhere without me. Everything's gone so confusing." She rubbed her forehead.

An ache closed around my heart. "We'll try to find your parents," I said. It was possible they were among the Clubbers the guards had taken to be pearled. I couldn't bring myself to mention that to her, though.

One of the city people, the woman who'd been so hesitant to trust the Spades before, came up beside me. "I can help her look," she said, with a tight but warm smile at me. "And if we can't find them tonight, I'll make sure she has somewhere comfortable to sleep."

"Thank you," I said, with a swell of resolve. I hadn't been totally sure what to say to the city people we'd rescued now that we were here. Why not give them a purpose?

I let my gaze sweep over the crowd when I came back into the main street we'd been walking along. "You can all go back to your homes, of course," I said. "If you want to help the city recover, though, I'd be grateful if you could check in on your friends and neighbors and help anyone in need as much as you're able too. We've destroyed all the roses, but the effects of the drug aren't likely to wear off completely until sometime tomorrow, and even once people's heads have cleared, they're going to be confused. Let's really take back the city."

A murmur of agreement spread through the Clubbers. A few of them headed off down other streets right then, I guessed toward their own neighborhoods.

The man with the hound's head sidled closer to me. "Are you sure the guards won't come back to take some sort of revenge?"

"They won't know any of you were ever with us once you're back at home," I reassured him. "And I've got more of my new friends protecting the city for us so that the guards can't get this far anyway."

He gave the jabberwock a glance that was both awed and horrified. I'd take that combination.

Most of the Spades had come back to the city with us too, some of them scouting along the edges to make sure we hadn't missed any guards and others here with me. Theo ambled over as more of the Clubbers dispersed.

"Where are you planning on spending the night?" he asked. "We'll want to make sure *you're* fully protected."

"I haven't decided yet," I admitted. He'd probably like it if I joined him in his Tower, assuming that was where he was going, but like often before, it felt too claustrophobic to me. Too difficult to escape from if the guards managed to break through. And now, on top of that, I couldn't help thinking of how distant it would put me from the people I wanted to have faith in me.

It'd be better if they could see me as much as possible, better if they knew I was standing right here with them, ready to defend them the moment any threat raised its head.

"I have a few ideas for adding to our protections along the city borders," the former Inventor went on. He rubbed his jaw, his eyes going distant with thought. "I think some of the Clubbers who came with us are ready to take on some minor responsibilities now. We can get more people on rotation around the most vulnerable points of entry. I'll equip them as well as I can."

"I don't plan on us having to hold the city like this for very long," I said, lowering my voice. "Once everyone in the city has had time to recover, we're going to gather as many willing volunteers as we can, and then we're marching on the palace. I'm sure a lot of them will be ready to step up after how the Queen of Hearts has treated them and after we've saved them. Between them and the jabberwocks, we've got to be able to make it to the throne."

Theo nodded, the corners of his lips curling upward. "I believe we will," he said. "If not tomorrow, maybe the next day. We just want to be sure of holding the city that long."

His vote of confidence gave me another burst of assurance. It lasted about half a minute. Then Chess came dashing down the street toward us, his face flushed, running so fast he'd lost most of the grace his brawny body usually held. My heart skipped a beat.

"We scouted closer to the palace, keeping a safe distance," he said between pants for breath after he'd reached us. "We saw—they're preparing fresh carts of the roses. The first ones were already heading out when I left.

They've assembled some new weaponry, too—arrows and a few catapults—I think they mean to try to fight the jabberwocks directly."

A memory flashed through my head of the previous Knave, the one with the sharkish face, charging at one of the jabberwocks on the Checkerboard Plain after I'd distracted it in my attempt at calming it. I was pretty sure he'd killed the poor creature. I couldn't let the ones I'd summoned, the ones who'd offered me their help at the sight of my scepter and the sound of my voice, meet the same fate now.

At the thought of projectiles flying through the air, heat crept over my chest. The rubies on my armored vest had started to glow. I gazed down at them, a tingle of power racing over my skin. Before I'd been sure of myself as queen, before I'd been able to get the Red royal artifacts to work for me consistently, this vest had propelled back a bunch of guards who'd been racing to attack me. It'd protected me from the worst of a speeding truck's impact.

I didn't let myself second-guess the idea that had popped into my head. I rubbed the jabberwock's leg, and it lowered its head to peer at me.

"So, they're not scared of the jabberwocks anymore," I said. "I'll give them something even more terrifying to deal with."

Chess raised his eyebrows, and Theo cocked his head. "What's that?" the Prince of Hearts asked.

I shot him a nervous grin. "An avenging queen *on* a jabberwock."

It was probably a good thing that Hatter was off on patrol elsewhere in the city, because I suspected he'd have had a few critical remarks to make about this decision. I slid my hand up to the jabberwock's shoulder above my head and tugged lightly on the gold feathers there, holding its gaze at the same time.

"I'd like to ride you," I said. "We're going to take on more of the people who'd want to hurt you. But I'll make sure they can't touch us at all. We'll send them all running or burn them up. What do you say?"

I wasn't sure how much the creature comprehended my words or just could read my meaning in my expression or tone. One way or another, it understood me enough. It sank down until its broad belly rested on the cobblestones. The Clubbers still with us stared as I climbed onto the massive feathered form using the bends in its front leg for leverage.

A rumble trembled through the jabberwock's body when I'd settled into what felt like the most secure position I could find, between its stunted wings just above its shoulder blades. My legs dangled on either side of its long sinewy neck, and the scabbard with my sword rested on the feathers beside me. I rubbed the beast's tensed muscles. "I'm ready. Let's go teach them a lesson."

The jabberwock heaved itself to its feet at those words. I swayed a little but kept my balance with a squeeze of my legs and my hands gripping the coarse feathers in front of me. My pulse thumped faster as the beast rose to its full height. I was level with the third floor windows on the building beside me.

Oh, yes, those guards had better be afraid.

At my nudge, the jabberwock lurched forward. It fell into a shuffling jog, a little faster than its earlier walk. But

Chess had said the guards were already on their way, and we had a lot of ground to cover. As soon as I felt stable enough at that speed, I patted the creature's back behind me to urge it faster.

It broke into a full-out run. The buildings in all their vivid colors whipped by on either side of us. The wind tossed my hair.

When we came to the next major cross-street, I directed the jabberwock in the direction of the palace with another light nudge. The thrum of its pulse and the anticipation shivering through its body echoed into me. I wasn't sure it needed my touch at all to pick up on where I wanted it to go.

We rushed on, taking another turn, and another, the quickest route to the palace road I knew where my unusual steed would fit. Ahead of us, the buildings gave way to the sparse forest where I'd spent more time than I'd have liked in the last couple months. I urged the jabberwock even faster.

We charged past the last of the buildings in time to see a swarm of guards who'd just come up over the crest of the hill. Several clusters of them pulled carts of roses and others were hauling the catapults Chess had mentioned.

The jabberwocks I'd sent on patrol prowled closer at the sight of me. One of them looked toward the guards and hissed through its jagged teeth. Blood seeped over the golden feathers on its neck where it must have taken a hit. They were hanging back now, waiting for my instructions.

I didn't think I could shield all of them, and I didn't want to send them forward to be battered. We'd have to see if my steed and I could manage this on our own.

I stroked the jabberwock's shoulder encouragingly. "Go for it," I said. "Burn up the flowers, the carts, the weapons. Burn the guards up too if they won't fall back. I'll keep you safe."

The rubies on my vest flared hotter and brighter. A ripple of energy ruffled the jabberwock's feathers. It hummed through the air around us.

Please let it be enough to ward off their attacks.

The jabberwock barrelled up the road toward the guards. The ones at the forefront gave a shout. Panic blanched some of their faces—and others just trudged on with the same dull expression. How many pearl-heads did the Queen of Hearts have fighting for her now? Had Carpenter sent back even more since this morning?

My gut twisted, but I couldn't focus on that now. The people they'd once been had already been murdered. I had to protect the city's people, the ones still living, first.

I pointed toward the nearest cart. "Light them up!"

My body swayed with the hitch of the jabberwock's stride. A burst of flame shot from its mouth to swallow up an entire cart and all its contents. The guards hollered to each other, the ones at the catapults fumbling with the controls. A line of pearl-heads strung bows with arrows and raised them toward us with robotic precision.

The jabberwock managed to cough out another spurt of flame that turned one of the catapults into charred wood. Three more of the massive weapons launched spiky metal balls at us while the arrows whined through the air. I dug my fingers into the jabberwock's feathers and willed all the power I had in me through the rubies on my vest.

The weapons hurtled toward us—and the energy of

my vest slammed them backward a few inches from the jabberwock's snout. One of the spiked balls smacked a guard in the chest, knocking him over with its force. The arrows rattled against the ground. The jabberwock released a furious belch that lit up another of the catapults —and a couple of the guards scrambling around it.

Their screams made me cringe, but I held on with my jaw clenched. "This city is under the Red Queen's protection," I shouted. "You cannot touch us. I don't want to hurt you, but if it's that or see my people hurt, I will. Go, before I have to."

The other jabberwocks sprang to my side without any orders, emboldened by our success. The guards might have taken them out, but they didn't know that, and the sight of their enemy suddenly quadrupled must have been too great a test for their resolve. The hollers turned more frantic. A couple of pearl-heads tried to launch one of the remaining catapults, and my jabberwock scorched them in an instant.

"Retreat and regroup!" a call went up. The remaining guards dashed for the palace grounds, leaving their carts rather than be slowed down hauling them. I gestured to the jabberwocks, and they turned the rest of the drugged roses into a massive flaming pyre.

My whole body was quivering with exhilaration when I had my jabberwock turn back toward the city. I hadn't expected to see anyone there except maybe a Spade or two who'd been patrolling with Chess.

A small crowd of Clubbers, a few Spades mixed in with them, had gathered at the edge of the city. They all stood stock-still in shock. As the reality of our victory must have sunk in, one and then another raised their hands with a breathless cheer.

A smile stretched across my face that had nothing but joy in it. We hadn't won the war yet, but damn, winning this battle had felt fucking good.

I could beat the guards on our ground. Now I just had to figure out how to beat them on theirs.

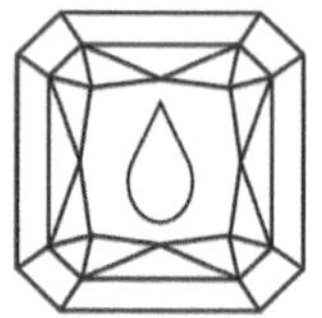

CHAPTER NINETEEN

Lyssa

Chess was waiting for me on the road when I slid down off the jabberwock—a little less gracefully than I'd have preferred. He caught my elbow when I landed off balance. I shot him a grateful smile and patted the creature's side. It studied me with its fiery violet eyes. They were actually kind of pretty amid the gold and scarlet feathers, once you got used to their intensity.

"Keep watch on the palace," I told it. "Come looking for me if more like that bunch head this way."

I could feel in the quiver of energy that had summoned the jabberwocks to me that they would be able to seek me out the same way. No further guards had emerged from the palace grounds as evening had darkened into night, but I doubted that attack would be their last.

The jabberwock bobbed its head in apparent

understanding. Chess gave me an amused grin when I turned back to him.

"When we first met, you told me you didn't have many interesting stories to share, lovely. I can't imagine anyone will ever top the one you just gave me."

"We'll see about that by the time this rebellion is over," I said, but under my bravado I was way too worn out to even imagine attempting any more epic activities today. I let out my breath, my shoulders sinking from their tensed stance, and Chess slipped his arm around me.

"I heard some of the Spades were going to meet up in the city park. It would be my pleasure to escort you there."

"Sounds good," I said. My hands instinctively moved to check my sword at my hip and my scepter at my back. My vest's rubies had cooled again against my chest. Everything was where it should be.

The crowd of city people who'd gathered to watch me scare off the guards from the jabberwock's back parted to let us through. Their faces still shone with the elation I'd seen when they'd cheered, but they looked awfully weary underneath that too. For nearly three weeks, they'd been partying and only sleeping in brief spells when they'd gotten exhausted enough to overshadow the high of the Queen's drug.

But they seemed unwilling to head off to bed even now. As Chess and I headed toward the park, most of the Clubbers drifted after us.

I'd just saved them twice over in one day. Maybe they were taking comfort from keeping me in sight. Hopefully that meant Theo was right about more of the city people taking up arms with us, even if right now I found their devotion a little uncomfortable.

I didn't want them to swap their blind fear of the Queen of Hearts for blind loyalty to me. I wanted them to believe I'd have their best interests at heart even if they were off doing whatever made them happy.

Lights glowed on posts here and there throughout the sprawling park, which was where I'd first met Chess ages ago. It didn't look as if any of the revelers had bothered with the chessboard other than to fling around the pieces, most of which were now missing. Someone's dress fluttered where it hung from a branch it'd been tossed over. The ashes of burnt roses floated off in the breeze like dark snow. A lingering hint of smoke mingled with the crisp scent of the grass.

I recognized a few of the figures already in the park from the Spades—Kip was there, and a couple others from one of the side camps, as well as a few of the city people who'd fully recovered in our care. It wasn't much of a meeting, though. Really, we all needed to get some sleep at this point. I could figure out where Hatter and Theo had gotten to in the morning.

Kip and the others were moving among the Clubbers who were slumped or meandering here and there across the park's lawns, most of them hazy but waking up enough to look confused. The bunch who'd followed Chess and me ambled into the park and glanced around uncertainly, their posture wary.

The excitement I'd been able to generate in the battle with the guards had waned, and now there wasn't much left but fatigue and anxiety around me. That was about all I had left in me, too.

I groped for something to say, some gesture to make, that might put them at ease enough that they'd find somewhere to rest. Nothing emerged from my tired brain.

Chess peered around us and at me, and a wider grin stretched his lips. He bounded away from me and leapt onto a nearby hedge, catching the attention of everyone around the park as he teetered on the landing. He caught his balance and dipped into a bow as if that had been part of the performance—which knowing him, maybe it had.

"What a day!" he called out in his playful tenor. He sauntered along the top of the hedge with a bit of a sway as he found his footing. "Did you see all the exploits of our Red Queen? It's enough to make you wonder why we've been dodging the Hearts' Guard all this time, isn't it? The look on their faces when the jabberwocks came trotting into the city…"

He let his jaw drop and clutched his chest in mock panic before scrambling backward so frantically leaves flitted off the hedge from under his feet. A tittering spread through his audience. A smile slipped across my face.

"And then," Chess said, righting himself, "they think, 'Ah, well, we can handle a few jabberwocks if we come out with every bit of weaponry we own." He lumbered forward with shoulders up to his ears in a joking imitation of the guards' march. "No match for our queen, though. She just hops right up on one of those jabberwocks and sends them running back home like they've got fire at their heels. Because they do." He made a panicked dash across the hedge and spun around with a wink.

The crowd watched him avidly, clapping in encouragement. Chess gave another little bow. "I think we deserve to enjoy ourselves while they're shivering in their pretty palace," he said. "Take a load off and make the most of what true freedom can be."

He tipped over, falling onto his back with a delighted smile as if he meant to fall asleep right there. The second he hit the hedge, he blinked out of sight. Then his grin appeared, gleaming as it floated against the night.

More laughter carried through the gathered Clubbers. Someone found a guitar leaning against a nearby tree and started playing it—not the frenetic music that had filled the city before, but soft strums of a city at peace. People sank down on the grass, talking in quiet voices, their faces light again.

Chess turned visible again as he hopped down from the hedge. He strolled back to me with his light blue eyes twinkling. I beamed back at him, a surge of affection washing away every other emotion inside me.

I might have protected these people from the guards, but Chess was already bringing them back to the joy they deserved. The joy I wanted Wonderland to be made of.

"It's amazing what you can accomplish by playing a fool," he said. "Make much of how little our enemies really are, and we feel like a whole lot more."

"I don't think there's anything foolish about that," I said, and then I couldn't help myself. I gripped the front of his shirt and bobbed up on my toes to kiss him.

This intimacy didn't feel as urgent as yesterday's, that first real coming together after a painful separation. This time, his kiss and his touch was all another sort of joy. I leaned into his well-muscled body, wanting to soak in his warmth and his tenderness with every particle in me. Chess teased his fingers into my hair and tipped my head to claim my lips at an even more enticing angle.

There were people all around us who might be watching, but I found I didn't care one bit. Wonderlanders didn't appear to have any qualms about enjoying each other where their neighbors could see. I wasn't about to do the full horizontal tango in front of dozens of them, but I had no problem with letting them see how much I wanted this man.

They should know their queen had as much love in her as she did defiance.

Desire unfurled through me with the heat of Chess's mouth against mine. I gripped his shirt harder, the ache of need in my core bringing my hips against his. He hummed low in his throat, his tongue darting out to part my lips, and I knew I wasn't going to want to stop.

But he might. I couldn't make assumptions, not when the last woman he'd dedicated much of himself to had torn him apart so badly. He'd told me, the first night we'd come together—when he'd surreptitiously arranged for Hatter to join our interlude—that he didn't trust himself to be able to offer enough on his own.

I kissed him back hard, my tongue tangling with his, and then I eased back a few inches. It took me a moment to recover my words.

"Is there somewhere nearby we can talk without any spectators?" I asked quietly.

Chess's eyebrows rose, but after a pause, he nodded.

"Why don't you come see the closest thing I've had to a home, for many years past?"

He had a home—near here? I'd gotten the impression he just roamed around, resting wherever he felt like it with whatever company he felt like keeping.

He tucked his hand around mine and led me beyond the hedge and past a stand of saplings. Not far from the park's fountain, we reached a dense thicket, nearly as tall as Chess and maybe fifteen feet across, the spiny leaves such a dark green they were almost black.

Chess prodded his fingers into the brambles and opened up a gap with some careful shifting. I followed him through the narrow gap into a hollow in the center of the thicket. The brambles pulled back over a stretch of grass only slightly larger than Chess would have been lying down.

He sat on the thin grass at one end of the hollow and motioned for me to join him. I sank down tentatively. A faint glow from the nearest lamp seeped over us.

"This is where I'd taken a mind to sleep the night the Queen froze time," Chess said, his gaze drifting over the brambles around him. "I suppose it was for decades I woke up here every morning. Not a bad bit of shelter, as shelter went in times like that."

Oh. That was what he'd meant about it being his "home."

My throat tightened in sympathy. Hatter might have ended up in his armchair every morning rather than a bed, but at least he'd been inside his apartment, on a cushioned surface. Theo had managed to arrange a bed of his choosing inside the Tower. Chess had cycled back to a bit of ground in the middle of the park every morning.

Maybe it wasn't so surprising he'd had trouble believing he deserved better than the Duchess. Or that he'd been tempted by the extravagances of the palace in the first place.

I took off my sword and set down my scepter at the far end of the hollow, and then scooted closer to him. Chess wrapped me in his embrace from behind. With his intoxicating licorice-and-wine smell making my mouth water, it felt perfectly natural to tilt my head back against his shoulder so he could recapture my lips. He kissed me so easily I started to think we might not need to talk at all.

Chess claimed my mouth slow and sweet, deeper with each kiss, his fingers trailing along my jaw. Fresh desire quivered through my body. I turned in his arms to face him, just slightly taller than him when I knelt between his thighs. He ran his hands down my side as I kissed him again, but only a hint of that contact carried through the woven metal of my armor. *That* definitely needed to come off.

As I leaned back and pulled the vest up over my head, hunger darkened Chess's eyes, but his shoulders stiffened at the same time. I tossed the vest over to join the rest of my royal equipment and hesitated. When he leaned in for another kiss, I stopped him with a gentle hand on his cheek.

"I want you," I said. "I want— It's been good, before, with Hatter and Theo joining in. I'll be happy to do that again. But I want us to have our moments that we don't share with anyone else. I love you, Chess. Every bit as much as I love them. You don't have to give some perfect performance. I want *you*, nothing more or less. If you're not ready to be with just me, that's okay. It's up to you how far we go. I just thought you should know."

Chess stared at me. His throat worked. For a second, like in the moment weeks ago when I'd first asked to kiss him, I thought he was going to turn me away. Then in one swift motion, he slid his hand over my hair and tugged me to him, rising to meet me at the same time.

We kissed with a hot tangle of tongues, his other hand roaming under my shirt, searing my skin with need. When he tipped me over on my back, looming over me, I settled into the grass eagerly. He gazed down at me, the light in his eyes giddy if a bit frantic.

"My queen should have everything she desires," he said, his voice gone smoky with his own desire.

Something in me balked at those words. "I don't want you to have sex with me because I'm your *queen*."

His gaze softened. "No," he said. "You're right. I'm here because you're my lovely. My Lyssa."

Then he was kissing me again, urging my hips to arch toward him. The hard length of his erection fit against my core through our clothes, and an eager noise burst from my throat. Chess smiled against my mouth. He pressed against me with soft, rhythmic hitches that sent pleasure and longing sparking through every inch of me. I scrabbled at his shirt, needing more of him.

Chess peeled his shirt off and eased up my dress. As he reclaimed my lips, one of his hands traveled over my chest with a teasing flick over my breasts, across my belly, to settle between my legs. He stroked over my clit with a more precise pressure than the bulge in his pants had offered and then dipped his fingers beneath the fabric of my panties, lower, until they could slick right up inside the place where I was most wanting.

I whimpered into his mouth. He groaned in response at the feel of me, already soaked with desire. His fingers worked deeper, the heel of his hand rubbing my clit. I squirmed as I ran my fingers over the planes of bare muscle down his back, solid and smooth and coiled with effort focused completely on me in this moment.

"Mmm," he murmured, and ducked his head down to kiss my neck with a scrape of his fangs. A gasp escaped me, and his fingers plunged right to the sweet spot inside me. I came with a burst of bliss and a cry I couldn't contain.

Chess beamed down at me, looking the very picture of satisfied, as if it didn't matter to him at all that his cock was still straining for attention.

"Happy with that, are you?" I asked, breathless and teasing.

He chuckled. "I think it'll do for a start."

"In that case…"

I yanked at the button on his pants, and he kicked them off. Somewhere in the middle of another scorching kiss, I lost my panties. Good riddance. I slid my hand between us and gripped his erection through his boxer-briefs. Chess growled, and a moment later his undergarments were no longer in the picture either. I raised my legs to his hips instinctively, and he drove into me so hard and fast I saw stars.

"Chess," I gasped, and he chuckled again, rawer this

time. We rocked together in a blissful muddle of stuttered kisses and shifting limbs, his cock thrusting deeper with each brilliant pulse, his heat and his scent engulfing me. If it wasn't perfect, then it was perfectly Chess, unpredictable and jubilant. Another wave of ecstasy built up inside me sharp and swift, as much as I wanted to linger in this pleasure.

My peak shuddered through me, and my core clamped around him. As I rode out the wave of bliss, my head tipping back against the grass, Chess let out another groan. He came with me, his face buried against the crook of my neck, his hand clamped on my thigh to lock us even more tightly together.

He stayed braced over me as I came trembling down from that high. A grin I suspected looked rather goofy curled my lips. Chess grinned back at me.

"*Now* I'm happy," he said, in a voice that held nothing but joy.

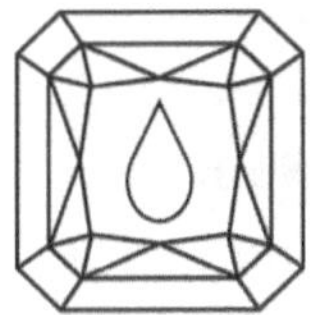

Chess

Somehow the Tower apartment looked more familiar with its owner in it. Although perhaps Theo wasn't truly its owner anymore. I supposed the city would have to sort out the matter of whether a Prince of Hearts could also be the Inventor once we could say the city was fully ours.

Theo rifled through the drawers of his worktables and the bins on the shelves with the efficiency you'd expect from a man who could construct a bomb—a small one, anyway—in fifteen minutes flat. The contacts rattled and clicked. We'd already filled one sack, now slung over my shoulder, with materials he thought he could make good use of. All the rifling had sent a sharp metallic sent into the air. Familiar as they were, the blank white walls around us left me uneasy.

All right, it might not have been *just* them causing my

uneasiness. I shifted my weight from one foot to the other. The pleasure I'd shared with Lyssa yesterday night had started my thoughts off on other tracks, some more welcome than others. But even as I'd dodged the memories of less pleasant intimacies, it had occurred to me that tools used once could serve fresh purposes.

"Theo?" I said. His claimed name tasted odd on my tongue after all those years referring to him by the title White Knight, but I'd noticed he got a bit twitchy when anyone directed that label at him since his return.

He swiped his dark curls back from his face and fixed his gaze on me, puzzled but with his full attention. That was why he'd made a good White Knight—and a good Inventor, I supposed. No matter what else was occupying him, he could pick up on how important a matter was to someone else, and then it became important to him too.

He could have been the Prince of Razorweed Town for all I cared, as long as he was still that same man.

"Is something wrong, Chess?" he asked.

"Not exactly," I said. "Possibly the opposite. I only—I got thinking last night… Do you remember, quite a lot of years ago, Hatter asked you to make a device that could siphon a memory from a person's mind?"

Theo straightened up. "He told you about that? It was an experiment. It seemed to work somewhat on the Spades who volunteered for testing, minor memories I constructed and then removed, and I assumed it ended up working well enough, since Hatter was never arrested for the crime he said he had to wipe, but I wouldn't have tried if he hadn't said the situation was dire. I don't like meddling with minds."

Ah. I supposed it was too late to retreat from this line of inquiry now.

"The dire situation was actually mine," I admitted. "One of the Diamonds, one who had shown an interest in hurting me, knew something about me that would have made me a very wanted man if she'd chosen to share it with the Queen. Hatter said you might be able to help." I had the cat-like urge to swipe my hand across my face in embarrassment. "I would have come to you myself, but we hadn't exactly moved in the same circles back then."

And then, as our lives had shifted, I'd ended up one of the White Knight's most regular companions, and Hatter had withdrawn from the Spades into domesticity. Funny how these things turned around.

Theo considered me for a long moment. "I have to wonder what you had to hide before you were involved with the Spades, but I'd imagine if you wanted to tell me, you would have. It doesn't really matter who used the device. I'm glad it helped you. Why do you bring it up now?"

My innards unclenched. Part of me had been expecting him to ask the question he'd just dodged for me. That wasn't how Theo usually operated, though. He wasn't his mother's son, not really.

"I just thought—there was a lot of power in that device. And what Lyssa wants to do is change people's minds, not bludgeon them into submission or slaughter dissenters. I'm not sure what other ways you could use the general concept, but perhaps there's something useful there."

Theo's expression turned thoughtful. "That's a good

point. Let me make sure I have the supplies I used for that. I think there were a few things Dum had to pick up specially…"

He rummaged through the drawers and then wandered off to his other rooms. When he returned, the sack he'd been carrying was bulging even larger than mine. His mouth was curved in a subdued but pleased smile.

"I think we've got everything I'm likely to use in the next few days."

"You don't expect to move back in here any time soon?" I asked as we headed for the elevator.

Theo grimaced. "We'll see what the future holds when we get there. For the time being, the people I want to be helping are down on the ground. I spent too long watching over the city from afar up here, I think. I'll be back to visit Mirabel, since I think she'll be happiest here for now, but otherwise I'd like to stay close to the streets."

When we came out into the warm mid-morning sun at the base of the Tower, Mallo was waiting for us. She darted over with furtive twitches of her eyes along the road, even though there'd been no sign of a renewed attack from the palace since the one Lyssa had pushed back last night. The only sounds I could hear were relaxed voices of recovering city folk chatting with each other down the street, but I braced myself for bad news all the same.

"The Otherlan—The Red Queen already knows," she said, looking at Theo. "But I thought you should be part of the discussion too. A representative has snuck out of the palace to try to strike a deal with us—between us and the Diamonds."

At the word "Diamonds," my blood ran cold. "What representative?" I said, even though she hadn't been directing her comments at me. "Who came?"

Mallo's gaze jerked to me, startled. "It's—you know. Unicorn." She gestured over her head as if indicating the gentleman's shiny horn. "I know he helped us before, but I still don't entirely like it."

"It's good that you told us, although I'm sure the Red Queen would have asked to consult with us before making any decisions anyway," Theo said.

My mind was still whirling. "Unicorn came alone?" I said.

Mallo nodded. "He said it was a lot of trouble getting out without the Queen catching on. I'd imagine it'd have been harder with more."

"Did he say which other Diamonds were involved in the offer?"

"I didn't hear much," Mallo said. "It sounded like all of them."

I could think of a large number of the Queen's pampered courtiers who would have sooner chopped their own heads off than ally themselves with the common city dwellers. Unicorn *had* helped us—I trusted him well enough. But so many of the others... My gut couldn't quite sit right with the idea.

"Do you think this is some kind of ploy?" Theo asked. "They have plenty of reasons to want to see the Queen of Hearts overthrown. Who knows how she's been terrorizing them during this latest furor."

"All true, all true," I said, taking a step away. "But having spent as much time among them as I have... I think I'd like to look into a few things before I report back to our queen."

I slipped into the in-between without another word. If I was going to make it to the palace and back in time to share any news I could bring, I'd have to hustle.

The Duchess had rambled on sometimes in a bragging tone when I'd gone to her rooms with her. Back then, she'd known a little stone cottage near the edge of the palace grounds that was overgrown with vines as if no one ever went there. Which made it, she'd told me, the perfect place for her to meet with other Diamonds if they wanted to have discussions without any fear of the Queen overhearing.

They'd just sent Unicorn off to us. Where else would they be waiting for him to return with the answer we gave him but there?

I jogged through the streets, speeding up as I left the city behind. One of the first things we would need to do once we had our land back was replenish our stock of horses and carts. Maybe we could even claim some air trolleys for city use. I didn't think Lyssa would object to speedier transportation options.

I skirted the wall around the palace grounds until I was in the area of the cottage, between the west and the north gates. Getting over the wall would have been easier with Dee along. But he was somewhere on the other side of that wall already, making his own deals. My hackles rose at the thought.

In the end, I took a running start and simply flung myself toward the top. My fingers managed to hook around the edge of the highest stones. I hauled myself up, hoping no guards inside had been close enough to hear my scramble even if they couldn't see me.

To my relief, no one was in earshot. I stalked along the top of the wall until I spotted the viney mass, only the door, a window, a chimney, and patches of worn marble stones visible amid the leafy tendrils.

I leapt down from the wall and hurried over to the wooden door. In my invisible state, I leaned my ear close.

Someone was in there. Muffled voices reached my ears, but the door was thick enough to muddle their words. I couldn't make out a thing they were saying.

I frowned and stalked to the window, but it had been covered with some kind of fabric on the other side to prevent any outside eyes from peering in. The stuff dampened their voices too. I circled the whole building, but there was no way I was finding out what was going on in there short of opening the door and strolling in. Somehow I didn't think I'd get a particularly warm welcome. The Duchess had gone to some effort in recent months to see my head ended up on one of the Queen's pikes.

My gaze drifted up to the roof and settled on the chimney. My chest tightened.

There was another way I could get into the building— a way that, if I was careful, would ensure they'd never know their center of conspiring had been breached. The trouble was that even the idea of doing it made my skin prickle with discomfort.

I sucked in a breath. I'd shifted before, to save Lyssa,

even though the sensation had brought too many awful memories back to the surface. It had been easier to make the leap in that moment of panic, though. I might not hear anything useful in there. Lyssa hadn't asked this of me.

She shouldn't have to. Whether I'd planned it or not, I was more than just a rambler helping the rebellion on the side. I was at the fore of the struggle now, and I had to act like it. It wasn't just Lyssa but all the people in that city back there whose lives could rest on the information I discovered.

A hero wasn't someone who only pitched in when it was easy. I hadn't seen myself as a hero before, hadn't wanted the title particularly, but when I remembered the way my queen had looked at me last night, I wanted to earn it. For her sake and mine.

Holding myself in the in-between, I hunched down on the ground and gritted my teeth. With a mental shove, the change rippled through my body. I seemed to contract and expand at once, shrinking but changing shape, fur sprouting all over my suddenly rotund body. My whiskers twitched. My tail lashed behind me instinctively.

The ghosts of long ago fingers, pins, knives traced over my skin. I shuddered and sprang at the vines.

If I just thought about Lyssa—if I could let those better, fresher memories drown out the old ones, even if they came from my human form...

As my claws dug into the tendrils and I clambered up the side of the cottage, I urged my mind back to last night. To the gentle caress of her hands, the eager slide of her mouth. The fondness so clear in her voice and in her eyes…

Fondness? No, I should be honest. It'd been love. Love that she'd spoken of, love that she'd shown.

Even my cat heart in my cat chest thumped eagerly in response to those recollections. The words to return her sentiment had been there at the back of my throat. But I hadn't said them. Even now, a shiver passed through my nerves imagining doing so.

The shiver rippled deeper in this form. It connected with the older memories and sparked a flare of understanding that burned all the way to my bones with the phantom echoes of ropes tied tight and slicing knives.

I did love her. Oh, how I loved her. More than I'd ever cared for anyone in my entire existence. It was fucking terrifying.

Saying those words, admitting the depth of that emotion out loud… somehow that felt like tying myself to her in a way I might not be able to break.

Why in the lands would I *want* to break it? Hearts take me, I should be honored if she wanted me by her side for as long as we both did live. I didn't enjoy the roaming. I got nothing but joy at her side. The Duchess would have the ultimate triumph if I let her perversions sour everything good in my future.

I needed to be brave for Lyssa, and not just here, in this private mission.

My resolve coursed through me. I climbed up the side of the chimney with a steady grip. Then I eased my way down inside, thanking the powers that be that it was far too warm a season for a fire.

It was slow going, because while no one would see me if they looked up the chimney, they'd catch the scrape of my claws if I wasn't careful. Also, it wasn't the widest chimney in the world, and I had plenty of bulk for a cat. After several tight and tense minutes, I'd edged down far enough to make out the voices in the room.

"Do you really think that's wise?" a man was saying.

The laugh that answered made my fur stand up all across my back. "Make what you will of it," the Duchess said. "We can always leave you behind."

Were they talking about going to the city, as if they truly meant to go through with that plan? It was impossible to tell from a comment that vague. I wasn't inclined to trust a word that came out of her mouth, besides.

There sounded to be at least a dozen people in the room. A few murmurs went around about the chocolates someone had brought for snacking on. "How long will they take to hash it out, do you think?" someone asked.

Apparently the Duchess was leading this endeavor, because she answered immediately again. "The poor things, no doubt the offer has sent them into quite a tizzy, picturing an alliance with us. We must give them time."

Her patronizing tone set my teeth even more on edge.

"It is a gamble," another voice pointed out. "Either way you slice it."

"You wouldn't be here if you didn't agree that appeasing her is our only hope of survival," the Duchess replied. "*Any* way you slice it, we all know what the greater threat is here. "

The greater threat. A prickle ran over my skin as the

words sunk in. Was that the place they were making this offer from? Their sense of a great threat?

Knowing the Duchess, knowing the Diamonds, I couldn't imagine them fearing anyone more than the Queen of Hearts.

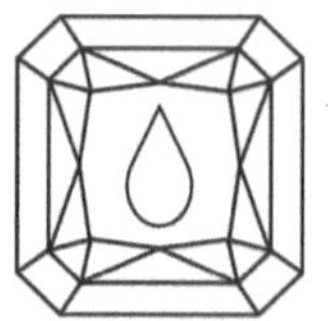

CHAPTER TWENTY-ONE

Lyssa

It should have been totally bizarre seeing a horse-like figure sitting at a table like a man, but somehow Unicorn perched on his chair, resting his hooved arms on the tabletop, as if it was a perfectly natural pose. Here in Wonderland, I guessed it was.

He shook back his glinting mane with a quiver of the muscles in his graceful white neck. He didn't look totally at ease with the proposal he was making, but then, I wasn't sure I'd ever seen Unicorn really relaxed. Every time I'd talked to him, we'd been making illicit plans behind the Queen's back, after all.

The woman who owned the ice cream café that'd been a convenient spot for our sit-down lingered by the back counter, watching us with wide eyes. Several of the Spades, including Theo and Hatter, stood along the walls around us. Hatter periodically whirled the hatpin he was holding with a faint hiss of motion. Having them at my back put me a little more at ease, but my heart was thudding harder than usual anyway.

The decision I made here could win or lose us the war.

"All of the Diamonds would help us push back the guards?" I said, turning over what Unicorn had already told me about the theoretical alliance in my head. The flavor of the shop's sweet cream laced my tongue. "How many of you are there?"

"Around a hundred," Unicorn said. "Not as many as there are guards, but combined with your numbers here, and the jabberwocks, and the fact that we can move on the inside to stem the charge before it truly begins... I think we could make a useful contribution."

I did too, though I wasn't sure how much of that impression I wanted to share with him. Even though Unicorn had helped us before, he'd spent most of his life at the Queen's beck and call. How far could we really trust him?

And if I couldn't completely trust him, how could I trust the Diamonds who'd never shown any interest in supporting our cause at all?

"What exactly would I need to promise in return for that contribution?" I asked, watching him carefully and paying careful attention to my ring. So far it hadn't woken up as if there was danger to combat, but it had been pretty selective in what it decided to respond to in the past, so that wasn't a total comfort.

"We'd ask for forgiveness for our association with and prior support of the Hearts' rule," Unicorn said. "No charges laid, no punishments dealt out. Those who wish to will keep their homes in and around the palace until equivalent accommodations are found or built."

That didn't sound unreasonable, even though the idea of living in the palace with the glammed up Diamonds all around made my skin crawl. We'd have to come up with those "equivalent" accommodations quickly. Let the Spades have the run of the palace for a change.

"And they'll trust my word?" I said.

Unicorn shrugged. "I trust it. I vouched for your credibility. They were all there when you broke the prisoners free—they know you're not the bloodthirsty type by nature."

I ran my thumb over my chin. "Why would they take this risk at all, though? They've had an extravagant life living the way they do under the Queen of Hearts."

"I don't see that any amount of extravagance is worth the constant tension having her right at our backs," Unicorn said. "If I could put you on that throne right now in her place, I'd happily do it. Her latest strategies… We can't be sure how long she'll even let us keep our free minds as her paranoia grows."

His shudder as he said that convinced me that he meant every word. But he was speaking for an awful lot of others.

"Do you trust all of the Diamonds you're here on behalf of?" I asked. "You believe that they'll follow through? They haven't always been all that considerate of you, from what I've seen."

Unicorn grimaced, but he nodded at the same time. "All the talk that happened when I was part of their discussions sounded genuine enough. I wouldn't have come to you if I doubted them."

"Fair enough." I exhaled slowly, trying to hide my tangled emotions, and eased back my chair. "I'd like to discuss the offer with my companions, and we might have more questions after that. Do you mind waiting here?"

"That's fine," Unicorn said. "But I'd like to bring your answer back as quickly as possible. The Diamonds may have meant the offer, but they do tend toward impatience… If they start to feel you're not committed to working with them, I don't know what directions their minds will go in next."

Well, that wasn't exactly reassuring. I got up, and most of the Spades followed me out, Kip and Dum staying behind to keep an eye on Unicorn.

We walked across the sunny street into the shadows of the buildings on the other side. Hatter passed his hatpin from one hand to the other, his expression tight. I could guess how he felt about the possibility of allying with the Diamonds. Theo looked more thoughtful.

"What do you think?" I said. "Is it worth trusting them?"

The Prince of Hearts rested his dark gaze on me. "I think we should hear what you make of this first, my queen," he said. "Better that you have a chance to sway my judgment before I give it than the other way around."

I wasn't so sure about that, considering he'd spent way more time around the Diamonds and the palace than I had, even if that'd been decades ago. But I *was* supposed to be queen here. I still had to get used to acting like it.

"I'm thinking that *if* we can trust them, allying would

give us a huge advantage. We'd have people helping open the way for us on the inside. And with more numbers, with people who can step in early on, we might be able to avoid a lot of the violence that'd be inevitable otherwise if we're going to get to the throne. I like all of that."

"If we can trust them," Hatter muttered.

"Exactly." I wet my lips. "They haven't found the courage to stand up to the Queen in an awfully long time, even though they were in the best position to do it. They might resent her, but they've always enjoyed the benefits they get from sucking up to her a lot more. But they *could* have been shaken up enough by the way I challenged her during the trial and the way she retaliated afterward to rethink their position. I'm not sure how we could tell."

"I'm inclined to think we should take the chance," Theo said. "The Diamonds, from what I knew of them— my mother didn't have me mingle very much—are selfish but often smart. If they see more benefit in supporting you than her now, they'll switch sides in an instant. If they're lying, then we're in exactly the same position we were before. We'll just have to be prepared to make the full push ourselves, and any way they assist will be a welcome gift."

My gaze slid to Hatter. "Do you feel okay about that?"

His mouth twisted. "I don't like making any promises to those boot-lickers. Why should they get to keep everything as they've had it at the expense of everyone else, just for finally doing what they should have done ages ago? If they really cared about setting things right, they wouldn't put conditions on their help."

Theo spread his hands. "Like I said, they're selfish."

"I don't like that part either," I said to Hatter. "But at least we can put specific conditions on how they need to help, and if they don't do enough, then we don't have to keep our end of the deal either."

"It may be worth it, then," he admitted. "I know how much you'd like to reclaim the throne without bloodshed."

My stomach knotted. "I realize there'll end up being some no matter what I do." I just had to keep reminding myself of all the blood the Queen of Hearts would continue shedding if I didn't take this stand. "All right. Let's work out exactly what we want the Diamonds to do for us, and see what Unicorn—"

"Wait." Chess's voice leapt from the air a second before his form blinked into sight. Sweat dampened his rumpled auburn hair, and his broad chest was heaving as if he'd run all the way from the palace. A chill raced through me. Theo had said Chess had gone to do some scouting. Obviously he hadn't liked whatever he'd seen.

"What's wrong?" I said.

Half a dozen pairs of eyes fixed on Chess. He tensed a bit under that scrutiny, and a flicker of uncertainty crossed his face.

"I—I'm not entirely sure," he said in a careful tone. "I was able to listen in on some of the Diamonds' conversation, but they'd already discussed the particulars of their plan, of course. They didn't say anything that clearly revealed their intentions." He studied my face. "You want to accept the alliance."

"I think it would make the battle ahead much easier if it's real," I said. "But if you heard or saw anything that made you uneasy, Chess, I want you to tell me. You know those people better than anyone, even Theo. I trust your judgment."

His mouth twitched, as if caught between smiling and frowning. He wasn't used to people relying on his judgment, was he? All this time, it'd always been him following Theo's directions—or not caring what anyone thought at all. It seemed like a simple request I was making of him, but maybe it wasn't after all.

"It doesn't sit right with me," he said after that momentary hesitation. "The Duchess sounded as if she's in charge, and she's never cared about anyone other than herself in all the time I've known her. And... they were talking about appeasing someone, about avoiding the greater threat. They didn't say enough for me to be sure what they meant, but... I think they're more likely to assume the Queen of Hearts will win against you and to be coming up with a scheme to prove their loyalty to her, than to be afraid of you beating her. They don't know you like we do. They've always been terrified of her."

"They saw how Lyssa took her on during the trial," Theo pointed out. "And how could they hope to turn this in the Hearts' favor?"

"I don't know," Chess admitted, his head ducking. "If they know when we mean to march or what signal to look for, they could betray us. But that was only my impression. I'll admit I may have biases at play."

I didn't think his feelings about the Duchess were biases. They were instincts created through experience— horrible experience. An ache crept through my chest at the thought of giving up this chance, but I believed in *him*. He wouldn't have tried to sway my hopes if he hadn't been awfully worried.

"All right," I said. "We do this without the Diamonds. That way we don't owe them anything. A little more bloodshed on the Hearts' is worth it if it means we don't have to worry about getting stabbed in the back. Come on. We'd better let Unicorn know." I paused, my mind spinning. The ache dug deeper, but I felt the rightness of my next thought all the way down to my bones.

I glanced at Theo. "Do you have enough of your devices ready for us to have a real shot at making it to the throne?"

His eyebrows rose, but he nodded. "I haven't put together everything I was thinking of, but I started with the most important pieces."

I dragged in a breath. "Then *I'll* tell Unicorn. Chess, you stay with me—you've done enough running. Everyone else, round up all the city people who are willing to march on the palace, and set them up with whatever weapons and armor you can. Right now the Diamonds expect us to be considering their offer, not already marching. So we march now and take them all by surprise."

Unicorn looked briefly startled when I told him my decision, but his expression quickly steadied with determination. "I can't blame you for hesitating," he said. "If we're not fighting alongside them, then I'm staying here to fight on this side with you. If you'll have me."

It was my turn to be startled. "Of course," I said. "We'll need all the help we can get. Thank you."

A hint of a smile curled his equine lips. "Thank *you*, Red Queen, for coming back to us before the Hearts completely destroyed Wonderland."

Outside the ice cream café, a crowd was already gathering. Spades ran this way and that, bringing equipment to the city folk. Most of the Clubbers had shaken off their drugged daze, but those who'd agreed to join us for the march shifted nervously as they shrugged on makeshift armor and tested the weapons the Spades had found for them.

We were really doing this. We were going to take back the palace, take back the throne the Hearts family had viciously stolen all those years ago. Despite my nerves, a rush of exhilaration filled me. *Now* my ruby necklace glowed against my chest, but its heat was encouraging, not alarming.

Chess had followed me out. He touched my arm to draw me to the side. "Can I talk to you for a moment before we rush into the fray?" he said.

Did he have some other concern he hadn't wanted to mention in front of the others? I followed him to the edge of an alley away from the noisy activity on the main street. Chess stopped in front of me. He touched the side of my face, bowing his head so his nose brushed mine. My pulse hiccupped giddily as his breath grazed my lips.

"I should have said this last night," he said. "But precision has never been my specialty. Let's just pretend I did."

"Chess," I said, meaning to reassure him, but he shook his head gently to stop me.

"This is what's true," he said. "For most of my life, I've never known where I was going, so the path didn't matter much. You changed that. From here on, the only way I want to go is where I'll find you, for as long as you want me with you. I love you too."

I hadn't needed to hear the words, but the sincerity in his voice washed everything away except the love I felt in return. I tipped my head up to kiss him hard. He kissed me back just as passionately. Then his arms slid around me to hug me close.

"Now let's see you all the way to that throne," he murmured.

"I wouldn't have a chance of getting there without you," I said.

He made a dismissive sound, but he was beaming when we rejoined our growing army.

The crowd was ready within an hour. I hopped up on a crate to look out over the swarm of figures who'd joined our cause. Yes, we could do this. And we would do it now.

"We'll march together up the road to the palace as quickly as we can. I'll take the lead with the jabberwocks to blast open the gate and push back the nearest guards. The Spades will handle as many of the others as they can. All the rest of you need to do is defend yourselves and keep going until we reach the palace. This will be the last day the Queen of Hearts reigns through fear!"

A nervous cheer rose up. I caught Theo's eye at the other end of the crowd, and he nodded.

We set off through the streets, the thump of footsteps

behind me gaining confidence with each block. When I held up my hand and the jabberwocks moved to join us at the edge of the city, another cheer rose up, more forceful this time. We barreled on toward the palace.

Guards massed around the main gate as we approached. Some of them were no doubt pearl-headed Clubbers. My stomach twisted at the thought of them charred or sliced by my sword's magic, but I squared my shoulders. There was no way to help them now, and I'd given the guards who still had their real heads plenty of opportunities to come over to our side.

Our charge sped up. I slid my sword free from its hilt. Just as I was about to order the jabberwocks forward, the striped head of the Knave appeared on the parapet next to the gate.

"Halt, Red Queen," he hollered, "or lose what you love most."

What I loved most? I had no idea what he was talking about, but he sounded so sure my pace faltered.

A guard hauled a man into view beside him—a bearded guy in a logo-etched polo shirt who looked only vaguely familiar at that distance. Then the Knave's comrades shoved two more figures into view, and my heart stopped.

Standing side by side, their faces bruised and arms bound behind their backs, my best friend and my mother stared back at me.

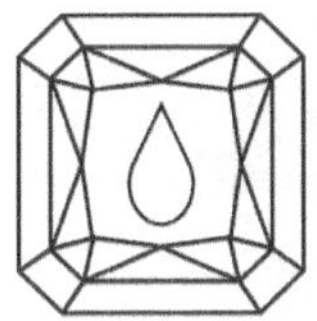

Lyssa

My sword arm sagged, dropping my weapon to my side. At the same time, the Knave gestured, and the guards brought the blades of their daggers to the throats of the three hostages along the wall. They weren't careful about it. A bead of blood streaked down Melody's pale throat. She winced.

Around me, the jabberwocks shuddered with uneasiness. "Hold," I murmured, my voice coming out hoarse. I could hardly pay attention to them, hardly think of anything except the faces of my mother and my best friend in the last place I'd ever have expected to see them. The last place I'd ever have *wanted* to see them.

The guy next to them… It was one of the movers who'd been helping haul the furniture out of Aunt Alicia's house. The Knave must have gone back there and grabbed whoever he could find.

How had he— *Where* had he— When—

The questions jostled in my head, but none of them really mattered. All that mattered was getting those deadly edges away from Mom and Melody's throats. And the mover guy's. He didn't deserve to be here anymore than they did.

I had no idea how to save them, though. The guards could slit their throats in an instant. No one, not even Hatter, could move that fast. Fuck. The smell of the roses in the palace garden drifted over the wall, clogging my nose and making me want to vomit.

The army behind me was stirring restlessly, the metal pieces of their makeshift armor clinking. They had no idea what was going on. I didn't know what to say. The Knave must already be able to tell he'd landed his blow well. Did I want him to know just how much?

He'd managed to get his hands on the two people on the other side of the looking-glass I cared about most.

"Not so hasty now, are you?" the Knave called down. His tiger mouth pulled back into a sneer, his fangs glinting in the midday sun. "Will you sacrifice these three in your bid for the throne?"

He didn't know that only two of them were particularly important to me, then. I didn't see how I could use that fact either. My thoughts were too scattered; my chest clenched tight.

Theo eased closer behind me. "Lyssa?" he said under his breath.

"My mother and my best friend, from back home," I said, just as quietly. "The guy, I don't really know." My gaze didn't leave them for a second. The words "back home" felt strange coming out of my mouth. I'd claimed

Wonderland as my home. My bond with the ground beneath my feet rang through me even now when I reached for it.

But the Otherworld had been my home for much longer. I'd already been torn up with guilt over running off on Mom and Melody, leaving them wondering where I'd vanished to. Now they knew where I was, and that was so much worse.

I was a queen here. I had to remember that. I was *the* queen. I tried to summon the resolve and certainty that had carried me to the palace.

"If you have any honor at all, you'll release those three," I said, raising my chin. "You know they have nothing to do with our conflict. Or is your supposed queen so afraid of me that threatening random civilians is the only way she can think to protect herself?"

Some of the Clubbers snickered at the jab. The Knave's sneer tensed, but he didn't care about the Queen of Hearts' pride half as much as she did.

"It looks as though you're the one afraid now," he shot back. "You call yourself a queen, do you? Interloper. Otherlander. What do you think the ones you left behind feel about the danger you've brought down on them?"

He motioned to the guard holding my mom. My stomach dropped as the guy eased his sword a little lower and shoved her right up to the edge of the wall. Mom blinked hard, her face sickly pale. Her shoulders trembled.

"Lyssa?" she said. "What on Earth... What is this place? Who are these people? What have you gotten yourself caught up in?"

A lump filled my throat. "There's too much to explain right now. I'm so sorry. I had no idea… I'm sorry."

"Can you make them stop? Tell them we're not part of… whatever this is. Give them whatever it is they want. Whatever you're doing here, it can't be worth it."

Her voice wavered with the last sentence. I swallowed hard. She had no idea how much rested on my shoulders. What the men holding her and the woman who commanded them wanted was to crush every person behind me, every person in the city. They wanted another two hundred years of battering Wonderland's spirit, if this place survived that long.

It was worth almost anything. But how could I say it was worth these three lives? Mom had raised me, even if she'd needed some help along the way. Melody had been there for me every time I'd turned to her, even if she'd turned to me more often. I'd shared so much of my life with them. I loved them.

The guard behind Melody shoved her forward next. "This is crazy, Lyss," Melody said. "These fucking people —whatever they think they're doing, they've gone way over the top. I really think they'll kill us. This is some scary shit. I don't know what to do."

I didn't know what to tell her either.

Was I a queen or wasn't I? The answer felt suddenly out of reach. How could I say I was the Red Queen, the ruler of all Wonderland, if I'd give up the whole battle for three people who weren't even of this place?

How could I say I was a human being worth living if I let them die?

The moving guy sputtered when the guard nudged

him. "She's right, this is fucking crazy," he said. "I don't even know who *you* are. Why the hell am I even here?" He twisted his head toward the Knave. "You've got to let me go. I was just there on a job."

The Knave raised his hand with a jerk, and the guard silenced the guy with the touch of his dagger to the guy's throat.

Another restless rustling spread through the crowd behind me. A prickle ran over my skin. The Knave hadn't made any demands. He hadn't even told me to stop fighting in so many words. His threat was obvious, but he wasn't pushing the issue—why?

My heart started pounding even faster. What else could he want from this stand-off?

"Well?" he shouted. "What will you do, little queen? Would you like to chat with them some more about how they've been treated here? Get a better idea of their fate?"

Of the men I trusted most, Hatter was the only one I could see nearby now. He might know where Theo had moved to in the crowd—Theo could get a better read on the Knave. "Hatter," I said in a low voice. "I have a bad feeling. Can you—"

I was cut off by a torrent of motion. A squad of guards burst from the trees along the side of the road, swinging swords and spears at my army of Clubbers.

I whirled around, my fingers clutching the grip of my sword. The force must have left through a farther gate and slunk through the woods while the Knave distracted us. *No.*

A woman near me shrieked. A teen in a metal helm that looked like it'd once been a pot toppled as a guard stabbed him. More cries rang out from the other side of the road where a matching force was charging at us. We were boxed in by enemies on both sides.

I slashed out with my sword instinctively, but my heart was heavy, my emotions in disarray. The ruby didn't flare to life. No magic leapt from the blade. I only managed to cut a tear through the red-and-pink tunic of a guard right in front of me.

The royal artifacts didn't respond unless I was completely committed.

My shaken confidence rippled through the other connections I'd forged. The jabberwocks spun around, their violet eyes flashing with a testy light, their maws snapping. One lashed out at the incoming wave of guards, but another sent a frantic spurt of flame into the crowd of Clubbers. Someone screamed.

No. I had to get control of the beasts I'd summoned. Planting my feet on the cobblestones, bracing myself in the midst of the chaos, I grasped my scepter and held it up over my head.

Maybe I was afraid of the consequences of this battle, but I knew this land belonged to me. I knew every creature living on it should respond to my command.

"Jabberwocks! Only the ones in pink and red. Only the guards with their helms. The rest of us fight with you, not against you. Please."

The last word dropped from my throat as the jabberwocks wheeled and groaned in clear confusion. The road had turned into a mass of struggling bodies. Billows of smoke puffed up where someone had tossed several of Theo's smoke bombs. The creature closest to me gouged its claws through the road, wrenching up cobblestones in its wake. Another whipped this way and that, more flame dancing over its lips.

They were trying to listen, but the commotion was too much for me to get a proper hold. One snapped its jaws around a woman from the city, and my heart wrenched.

The best I could do was get them out of here before they did our side any more damage.

I waved the scepter in the air. "Jabberwocks—away! Into the trees! Leave us until I call on you again."

Smoke coated my throat. I coughed and stumbled as a body collided with mine. I could barely make out who was friend and foe with the haze swirling around us and sunlight glancing off blades in every direction.

We'd lost our advantage. The thought of abandoning Mom and Melody to the Queen of Hearts made me queasy all over again, but I'd really have abandoned them if I died here and there was no one left to fight for them at all. All I could think to do was pull away, retreat from the crush of guards on either side, back to the shelter of the city where we could regroup and decide how to deal with this new threat.

If we even could make it back.

"Retreat!" I cried out raggedly. "Spades and Clubbers, back to the city, now, as quickly as you can move!"

The crowd shifted one way and another. I smacked aside a lunging guard with the flat of my sword. The mass of bodies heaved a few steps in the direction of the city, but it was hard to tell if that was even on purpose or just part of the turmoil of the fray. More smoke surged up from somewhere to my left.

My straining eyes couldn't make out anyone I recognized. Theo, Hatter, Chess—they were all lost to me in the chaos. If my heart had been heavy before, now it weighed on my gut like a boulder.

I'd led all these people here, and if I didn't pull them together fast, this march would turn out to have been an invitation to a slaughter.

CHAPTER TWENTY-THREE

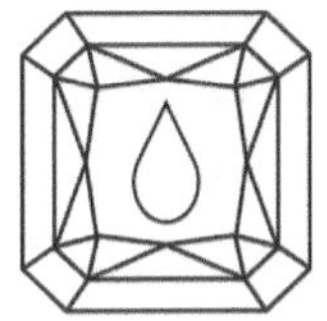

Theo

The Knave on the wall today might not have been the Knave I'd grown up with—my mother had gone through at least a couple in the time I'd lived in the palace, and more since then—but I could sense from his stance as he had the guards prod their captives to call out to Lyssa that there was more at stake here than rubbing his ruthlessness in my queen's face. He was making some kind of play.

I took a step back from Lyssa, scanning the road. We were surrounded by sparsely forested hills on both sides with the main palace gate looming straight ahead. I couldn't see far enough along the wall to make out the next gates farther away. While we'd been charging forward, our force had seemed unstoppable. Now, as the gathered city folk waited on restless feet for further orders, the sensation of being boxed in crawled over my skin.

We'd lost our element of surprise. Our enemies could

watch our every move while our line of sight was cut off in every direction except behind us. No, this didn't feel secure at all. I didn't like it one bit.

We'd stopped closer to the wall than I'd usually come on my furtive missions in days past. The smell of the roses grew more pungent, trickling down my throat with every moment we stood here. Flashes of images and the doctors' muttering voices jostled my mind, with an undercurrent of more distant impressions from the pomp and callousness of my childhood. Rich fabrics. Raised voices. The crimson splash of fine wine and the scarlet of fresh-spilled blood.

I stiffened my shoulders, holding myself in the present. I had to focus. I had to *think*.

Breathing shallowly, I eased through the crowd toward a head of red hair that stood out amid the Clubbers. Dum caught my eye and drew himself straighter the second he saw my expression. The Knave was taunting Lyssa again, but I tuned his voice out. He was trying to keep our attention on him—to distract us from other things.

"Go along the east side of the road, watching the woods," I said, and handed Dum a few of my smoke bombs. He closed his fingers carefully around the egg-shaped devices. "If you see any movement, shout a warning and slow them down with the smoke and those sprightly legs."

A tight smile curled Dum's lips. "I can do that."

"And the west side?" a light voice said at my shoulder. Chess's grin flashed for a second before he shimmered into view.

Just the man I'd wanted to talk to next. I gave him a

few smoke bombs too. "You can put those stealthy fighting skills to good use, if you need to."

"Here's to the very slim chances I don't," Chess said with a salute, and vanished.

I was just turning on my heel, watching Dum reach the edge of the road and feeling decently satisfied with my preparations, when the forest on either side of us exploded with a flurry of movement.

Guards careened down the slopes on either side, red and pink flooding toward us between the trees. There wasn't time for Dum or Chess to really slow them down. Smoke burst on either side of the road, but too close to our haphazard army. It flowed over us as well as through the trees, and the guards were already on us.

I caught glimpses of my Spades dashing to the defense, wielding the electrically charged batons I'd given out. Sparks flitted through the smoke. The city folk, who'd never really had to or been inclined to fight before, jostled against each other with panicked faces. A few steps away from me, one of the guards speared a young man straight through. My gut lurched.

"Hold tight!" I shouted, even though I wasn't sure they'd even know what to make of that suggestion. I squeezed through churning crowd to zap and smack aside a few of the closest guards with my own baton. My other hand wrenched my short sword from my belt, but I hardly had room to use it without risking slicing through my own people too.

With a warbling roar, one of the jabberwocks reared up over the clouds of smoke. Its head shot into our midst and snatched up a guard. Before I could feel grateful for that, another of the feathered monsters let loose a stream of fire over a clot of Clubbers. Shrieks and the odor of burnt flesh mingled with the rose stink in the air.

Lyssa's bright voice, fraught with tension now, broke through the chaos. I couldn't make out anything more than the word "jabberwocks," but whatever she'd said and done, it at least made them back off from the fray.

I snapped my baton left and right, sending one guard to the ground and another wheeling backward, but more were battering us from all around the road. Farther down, Mallo's hair clung to her sweaty forehead as she exchanged blows with a guard holding a spiked club. Unicorn pummeled another pleated figure with his hooves. Hatter's hands whipped out, one with his narrow dagger and the other with a hatpin. He caught one guard in mid stab, but he wasn't quite fast enough to stop another from slashing through a woman's stomach.

My pulse rattled through my veins. What if they got to Lyssa? Hearts take me, what if they took down all of us? The rebellion we'd built over so many years might fall apart in the space of an hour. And then what would Wonderland be left with?

Lyssa's voice rang out again, this time clear enough to split through the clatter of the battle.

"Retreat! Back to the city, now, as quickly as you can move!"

The idea made me balk down to my core, but in the same moment, I understood it was our only real option. We were hemmed in here—we had no real chance of making it through the gate, let alone across the grounds to the palace. Our best hope was to pull back and regroup.

The Clubbers around me bumped against each other as they tried to orient themselves. Fear still whitened their faces. "This way!" I hollered with a sweep of my arm. Several of those anxious gazes locked onto me.

"Inventor!" one woman said, with a sob. "What do we do?"

Even more of the city folk turned toward me, a hint of relief touching their expressions.

"The Inventor will know what to do."

"Should we go?"

"You've got to help us!"

My stomach twisted at the barrage of hopeful but frantic voices. Their queen—their *true* queen—had just told them what to do, but that wasn't enough.

They'd known me, turned to me for help, for ages. She'd only revealed who she was a few days ago. How could I blame them?

I dragged in a breath, and the scent of roses saturated my lungs. A cool thread of thought bloomed in the back of my head and curled tight around every other intention.

I could spin this in my favor—have all the power I'd once assumed was mine in the space of a few heartbeats. Win their loyalty now even more than I'd ever had it before, and they'd turn to me every time afterward too. Lyssa might sit on the throne, but I'd be the one truly in command.

Even as the idea crossed through my mind, the rest of me rebelled. Nausea coiled in my stomach. A chill raced over my skin.

Lyssa and the others hadn't really rescued me when they'd hustled me out of the palace a few days ago, had they? Its hooks had been in me still. If I was going to be free of the horrors of my family's reign, I was going to have to rescue myself, once and for all.

My gaze sought out Lyssa's form through the haze and the turmoil. Her pale hair streamed around her, tinted with the reddish glow from the rubies on her vest. My mother's treachery had battered and overwhelmed her just like my family's had all of Wonderland, but she was still standing, unbroken.

Like Wonderland itself.

The understanding clicked into place like a wire into its slot. I'd wanted to champion Wonderland, to build it back into the realm it had once been. I could still do that with everything I had in me. Our queen *was* Wonderland. The realm's fate lay within her. Being her champion was all I could ever have wanted.

With that realization, the treacherous urge inside me crumbled away. The poison laced through my bloodline disintegrated. I raised my voice with all the conviction I had in me.

"Friends!" I called out. "We must follow the Red Queen. Retreat toward the city, quickly, as she said! Listen for her commands. She'll guide us true. We can overcome our enemies yet if we stand with her and do not falter."

I moved down the road, jabbing at the guards who tried to stop us as I went. One knocked my sword from my hand as I swiped at him, but I sent him stumbling backward with a thrust of my baton. The crowd surged around me, really moving now, displacing the guards from the road just with the force of so many bodies. We'd lost some, but most were still standing.

I dug into my pouch and produced a handful of skitter cubes. "Toss them at the ground by the guards," I shouted, passing some along to the figures around me. "It'll slow them down." I hurled one of my own, and several of the new guards running at us skidded and fell on the silvery shards of metal that slipped beneath their feet.

Our army swarmed along the road back toward the city, pulling away from the main force of the guards as they stumbled and tripped and our batons forced them back. The Hearts' force gathered together between us and the palace, but we had no intention of making another attempt at it now.

They pressed forward as we kept hustling on. They'd follow us all the way to the city if we let them.

That realization sent a fresh chill through me. Lyssa's jabberwocks had dispersed. There was nothing to stop the Hearts' Guard from pushing any advantage they gained today even farther. We'd needed this retreat, but we couldn't outright flee, not if we wanted to keep our freedom after.

I wove through the crowd, gripping shoulders here and there to offer words of encouragement, toward where the sunlight glanced off Lyssa's white-blond hair near the edge of the fray. The rubies on her armored vest still cast her with their ruddy glow, and relief rushed through me to see her unharmed other than a shallow cut near her elbow. Several of the Spades had gathered around her to help fend off the guards following our retreat.

I motioned to Chess, and he leapt in front of her to shield her completely. Lyssa glanced back at me, her face so stark with tension it made my heart ache for her. I grasped her arm and leaned close to speak over the clang of blades.

"We've survived the worst of it. We can hold our ground here. We have to show the guards they can't push us back completely. *You* can show your people that this retreat isn't a full-out loss."

"I don't want any more of the Clubbers getting hurt because of me," Lyssa said, doubt coloring her voice. My heart squeezed tighter.

"Not because of you," I said fiercely. "Because of the villains we're fighting. No matter what else happens, you've been amazing, Lyssa. You're our queen. You're *my* queen, as long as I live. It's an honor to stand here with you. Don't let the bastards take what belongs to you."

Her grip on her sword tightened. I felt the power moving through her body as her spirit stirred to action. She shot me a quick glance, grateful and determined, and raised her sword to catch the sunlight, high enough that our whole force should have seen it.

"We stand here!" she cried. "Fall in behind me, protect each other's backs, and don't give up your ground. They can't move us if we won't be moved."

Then she sprang forward, sweeping the sword down and across. A crackling wave of magic surged from the blade. It slammed the guards several feet back, blood welling through the rents in their uniforms, bodies crashing into those behind. When the ones farther back tried to surge past their injured companions, Lyssa lashed out again, toppling them too.

The crowd pulled tight around me. The Clubbers still

looked nervous, but their chins were high, their eyes bright. We'd survived this long, and they weren't so scared any more that we wouldn't survive longer.

They believed in our queen.

The guards spread out, attempting to circle our army again, but the Spades along the edges battered them with stones and tossed skitter cubes into their midst. Those still on the road between us and the palace milled around uncertainly.

Our Clubber allies probably should have still been scared. The guards wouldn't hesitate much before they came at us again, and we would run out of tricks like the skitter cubes soon. But for now, we'd shown we weren't that easily cowed. That might just be enough.

I wove through the crowd once, handing out my last few skitter cubes, nodding to my Spade companions. My pulse thumped with a ragged rhythm driven by adrenaline and hope. Then a choked hush fell over the fray.

A grand figure had appeared on the wall by the gate, her tall crown gleaming and her eyes glimmering even across that distance. I stopped in my tracks. My innards tangled into knots at the sight of my mother, but my feet held steady against the ground.

She knew what I was now. I'd only lied to her before to get where I needed to go. That time was past. All that mattered now was how to stop her from dealing out even more terror.

She grazed her elegant hand over the heads of the Otherlander hostages the Knave had gathered. Her lips pursed into a tense smile. When she let them part, her cudgel of a voice carried all the way up the road.

"False queen and false queen's disciples, you have twelve hours to make your surrender. If the one of the line of Alice does not present herself to me for my justice within that time, the three on the wall will meet their deaths instead. And then the rest of you will follow them. Guards, to me!"

She spun with a whirl of her massive skirts, and the guards drew back to congregate by the gate, leaving us with her ultimatum and her threat ringing in our ears.

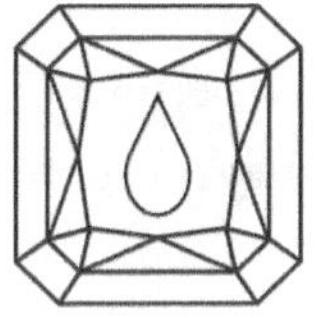

CHAPTER TWENTY-FOUR

Lyssa

A couple of days ago, Wonderland's city streets had been filled with partiers. Maybe those people had been caught up in drug-fueled whims they couldn't control, but they'd given some appearance of being happy.

Now we were laying out the wounded along the road beneath the gleaming silver tower. Dozens of Clubbers and Spades sprawled on blankets and mats or simply pieces of clothing laid out for a bit of comfort. Mallo, it turned out, had some medical skill, so she was moving from person to person checking on their needs, bandaging or sewing up wounds as need be, with Doria acting as her assistant. A few of the city people had volunteered their services too. Dum passed around tubes of the healing cream Theo had used on my bad cut weeks ago.

The scent of the roses, even the smoke of their burning, had dispersed completely. A fresh bready smell wafted from the bakery on the corner, where the owner was hard at work making loaves to feed this crowd.

I walked along the street with my sword at my hip and my scepter at my back, my nerves jumping despite the comforting warmth of the afternoon sun. But even though no music was playing and I heard more groans than laughter, this was better. These people had made their own choice, and they'd fought for what they believed in.

They'd believed in me.

The patients sat up a little straighter when I approached. Their faces lit up in spite of whatever pain they were feeling. Any friends or relatives keeping them company gazed at me with no hint of blame for the injuries dealt under my watch, only awe and an eager sort of hope.

"Red Queen," one woman said. "Thank you. We're going to take Wonderland back for ourselves."

"Yes, we will," I said, with all the confidence I had in me. "And thank *you*. I couldn't do it on my own. We're only succeeding because we're willing to face the danger together."

"We were always in danger before," the man beside her muttered. "It doesn't matter how hard we tried not to notice. *She* was always looming over us—one wrong step, one wrong word…"

"It won't be like that when I take back the throne," I promised him. "I don't want anyone hurt. This isn't about power or vengeance. When we free Wonderland, you'll truly be *free*. A ruler is supposed to serve their country and their people, not the other way around."

"No one could watch you and not know you're doing all you can for us," another woman said, cradling the sling around her broken arm. "I'll fight again if I can."

I went on down one side of the street and then up the other like that, giving everyone a chance to talk to me, letting them see how much I cared. My heart still weighed heavy in my chest, but I tried not to let that tension show on my face. I smiled and kept my voice mild. I thanked everyone for the risks they'd faced in the battle. It was all I could think to do, right now.

It was hardest when the questions came. "Red Queen, when will we march again?"

"What will we bring to the Hearts' doorstep next?"

"How will we finally bring her down?"

"I'll talk with my advisors in the Spades, and we'll have a new plan soon," I told everyone. "Before the end of the day, we'll hold the palace."

Or the palace would hold me, probably without my head. I didn't think it'd help spirits any to comment on that possibility, though.

Dum came over to me as I finished my circuit. His mouth was twisted as if he wasn't sure he should be saying what he was going to.

I paused. "What is it?"

"I just—" He sighed. "You'd probably have said something if you had, but I have to ask: Did you see any sign of Dee when we were out by the palace?"

His anguish for his brother showed all across his face. He had loved ones in the Queen's grip too. I couldn't imagine it was any easier knowing one of them had put himself there purposefully.

"I'm sorry," I said. "I didn't. When we take the palace, the first thing we'll do is search for him, all right?"

"You don't need— I understand he's a traitor." He looked down at his hands. "I'm not asking you for anything. It's just hard for me not to wonder."

"Of course it is," I said. "And I *want* to find him, so we can hear his explanation for himself. He doesn't deserve whatever the Queen has in store for him—I'm sure of that."

Dum let out his breath. "Okay. Thank you."

He still looked pained. "*You* did everything you could to keep him safe," I said, remembering how he'd always looked out for his brother. "You know that, right?"

"Did I?" Dum said. "I've thought a lot about our last conversation, things I might have said differently or could have said but didn't… I should have found some way to convince him to stay with us. Or maybe I should have gone with him and we could have found another way that wouldn't have hurt the Spades, even if it was the death of both of us. He was ready to give up everything for family, and I wasn't."

"Hey," I said firmly, and waited until he raised his head. "You didn't know what he was going to do. And *you* did what you thought was best for everyone that matters to you. It was a horrible position to be in—it still is—but he made his own choices. Try to remember that and to keep hope."

Dum nodded, the tension in him relaxing only a little. I resisted the urge to hug myself as he went to talk with Doria about something.

My loved ones in the palace hadn't made any choice.

The only reason they were there was because of the Queen's vendetta against me and the war I was waging against her.

Theo emerged from the tower just then with an armful of supplies. He caught my eye with a tip of his head, and I waited for him while he distributed more tubes and thread and a substance Wonderlanders apparently used to make casts. Then he strode over to meet me.

With his head high and the sun glancing off his chestnut curls, he looked every bit the prince. Even heavy, my heart still fluttered seeing his commanding presence, even though technically I held more authority than he did now.

"How are you holding up?" he asked, coming to a stop a few feet away from me. That was the one area where he wasn't so assured anymore—navigating his closeness with me. He wouldn't have felt he needed to leave that much space before. I'd appreciated the consideration at first, but suddenly it made me weary.

We had so many enemies and troubles in front of us. Why let the past hurts linger on any more? I knew why he'd done what he had; I knew how honorable and devoted he was at heart despite it.

"Well enough," I said, which was the most I wanted to admit where the wounded Clubbers could hear me. "I just wanted to see how everyone here is holding up. I thought I owed them that."

"I'm sure your concern helped raise their spirits," Theo said with a smile.

Mallo passed us and paused to bob her head to me.

For the first time, even though her former leader was standing right next to me, her gaze fixed on me instead of Theo.

"I think we've taken care of all the injured as well as we can, Red Queen," she said. "What else can I do that would be useful?"

There was no irony or bitterness in her tone. She actually wanted my opinion. I guessed she was glad now that the Spades hadn't offered me up to the Queen of Hearts in sacrifice all those weeks ago. Part of me wanted to laugh, but all of me was glad to see I'd managed to make an impression on one of my harshest critics along with the Clubbers.

"Are there any other supplies we need gathered?" I asked Theo.

He shook his head. "I have that covered."

I turned back to Mallo. "We can't trust the Queen of Hearts to stick to the timeline she gave us. The more people we have patrolling the edge of the city, the better. Sound the warning if you see anything at all that worries you, okay?"

"Of course," she said, and darted off.

"Winning over hearts and minds," Theo said after she'd disappeared from view, sounding amused. He motioned for me to walk with him farther down the street, away from the resting patients. "You didn't need much time."

His praise brought a flush into my cheeks that was probably not very regal. "Apparently I was born for this. And it's not all that hard to look better than my counterpart, is it?" That being his mother. Maybe not the best point to raise.

Theo didn't look insulted. It wasn't as if he liked the Queen of Hearts' methods any more than I did.

"You sell yourself short," he said. "I know it's been hard. I know it must be even harder now, with the Knave's new plot. You've held your own better than most people would have. Born for it or not, this is you."

I swallowed thickly. "Thank you for helping me get my focus back during the battle. Seeing people from back home here—seeing how he was treating them—it was hard to think clearly."

"I only said what was true," Theo said simply. "I've been part of this struggle for ages longer than you have. I'll always speak my mind if I see a strategy I think we should use. And then you get to decide whether you listen to me, my queen." The corner of his lips curled slyly with that last comment.

We ambled around the corner onto a quieter street, and I stopped him with a hand on his arm. "Theo… You know I'm not at all angry with you anymore, don't you? I don't have any doubts about which side you're on. I don't have any doubts about whether you care about me. It's never going to be the same as when you were the White Knight and I was an Otherlander, lost and confused, but you don't have to hold yourself back with me. In case that wasn't clear."

Theo's smile softened. He stepped closer, setting his hands on my waist. "It is different now," he said, his voice low. "You *are* my queen. And I'm from the family that destroyed yours."

I made a dismissive sound. "At least one member of my family abandoned Wonderland instead of taking up the crown she was meant to. I'm pretty sure we're past judging each other by our ancestors. And I'm not just the queen. I'd better not ever be just the queen. I'm still the woman who was falling in love with you."

"Was?" Theo repeated lightly.

"I think we can say I'm finished falling."

He closed the last few inches between us and kissed me, one hand rising to trace his fingertips over my cheek. I leaned into him, wishing I could enjoy this connection for more than just a moment, knowing I couldn't.

Theo pulled back only slightly, his head still bowed. "I'm not perfect," he said. "I'm still her son, along with everything else I am. I think I'll have to grapple with the impulses of that heritage as long as I live. But after today… I have no fears at all that I can't overcome them. The rest of me is stronger."

"I know," I said. "You wouldn't be here at all if that wasn't true. Did you only just figure that out?"

His lips twitched with another smile. "I suppose it's taken me a little while to find my feet again. A prince never shows his weaknesses, you know. It simply isn't done."

I wrinkled my nose at that comment and gave him another quick kiss on the mouth. "Maybe not, but Theo had better know he can." I glanced down the street. "Where are we heading? I've got an awful lot of plans to make." The weight of the Queen's timeline and the threat that came with it pressed back down on me.

"I asked Hatter and Chess to meet us at the hat shop,"

Theo said. "I thought maybe, in light of the stakes, you'd prefer to talk things through first with those of us you know best rather than a whole crowd of Spades. Although if you'd prefer more or less or to be left alone to think it through, just say the word."

"No," I said, wrapping my hand around his. "Talking it through with you three sounds just right. I think it's going to take a lot of talking."

Anxiety crept back through my body as we made our way through the streets. It loosened a little when we stepped into the shop to the sight of the other two men I loved. Chess was perched on the edge of the counter, his legs dangling, and Hatter leaned against the glass display case next to him. He nudged today's bowler hat up over his spiky blond hair as he straightened up to greet us.

"So," he said. "We have quite the conundrum. I'm sorry, Lyssa."

The apology sounded like more than just an expression of sympathy. I blinked at him. "It's not your fault."

He grimaced. "It might be, in part. I noticed when we took this place back from the guards that Alicia's sketch of her house—your house—was missing. It never occurred to me the guards would have taken it, but… That has to be how they got to your mother and your friend. Whoever went through the looking-glass used it to focus on their destination and arrive there."

And Mom and Melody—and the mover—had still been at the house in the aftermath of my disappearance. It might have been only hours for them since I'd leapt back into Wonderland.

"It doesn't matter," I said. "You couldn't have predicted the Knave would use it that way. What matters is he's got them now, and I don't know what to do about it."

"What have you been thinking, lovely?" Chess said. "Ramble on all you want. I find I often make my way to an answer if I just keep talking toward it."

I wasn't sure any of my thoughts so far would get us anywhere. "I don't know. I just feel torn." I raked my fingers through my hair. "We can't surrender. The Queen of Hearts will slaughter me and all the Spades and who knows how many of the Clubbers—and I'm not naïve enough to think she'd even spare Mom or Melody once she's gotten her way. But I can't just march right back to the palace and risk her killing them to punish me. They never asked to be part of this. They *shouldn't* be part of this. It's my world, but it isn't theirs."

"I wouldn't put it past her to order them killed as promised," Theo said. "Not at all. But I will say that she's clearly scared of you. If she'd truly felt she had the upper hand, she'd have demanded your surrender immediately. But then you could have called her bluff, and if she'd killed them right away, she'd have lost her only bargaining chip. She didn't believe her guards could hold our forces back if we'd taken up the charge with full commitment again."

"So she left me to stew on it," I said.

"And she bought herself more time to rally her own defenses," Hatter said. "No doubt she's got another cartload of pearl-heads on the way."

"Then if we're going to strike again, we should strike

as soon as we can, before she has much chance to think up other ways to screw us over." I let out my breath. "But we can't get any prisoners out of the palace without storming it and forcing her hand in the first place. It doesn't matter how scared she is—I still have to make sure Mom and Melody get out of this."

Theo set his hand on my shoulder. "We've only just started talking. Between the four of us, and the minds of all the Spades and the city folk if we need to turn to them, we'll find an answer. That's what being a leader is—finding an answer that satisfies every side of the equation. The land itself is on your side. I know you can find your way through."

Hatter's eyes gleamed bright as he took my other hand in his. "And we have advantages the Queen of Hearts will never even think of," he said. "She approaches every problem in the same old standard ways. Make threats, try to bully everyone into submission. We're ready to do anything. All we have to do is find the right wild, mad plan, and she'll never know what hit her."

Chess scooted closer along the counter and bent over to brush a kiss to the top of my head. "And no matter what comes, you *do* have all of us. The Queen of Hearts orders everyone from a distance because she rules with fear. You've already got all the respect and love you need to put you on that throne. I'll think with you in whatever which way we need to until the right idea sparks."

My throat tightened with all the faith and affection surrounding me. I gripped Hatter's hand harder, leaned into Theo's touch, and squeezed Chess's knee as I glanced around at all of them. Even with the massive threat looming over me, it felt important to take a moment to say this one thing to the three so different but all so important men who owned my heart.

"I'm going to want you all to stay with me, you know. If—no, *when*—I take that throne. I don't know if any queen of Wonderland has had three partners before, but I don't really care what's normal. I want all of you by my side. We'll make Wonderland wondrous again together."

"Lyssa…" Hatter kissed my cheek, his voice abruptly choked. Chess embraced me from behind. Theo just beamed at me. That was all I needed to know they wanted to be with me as much as I wanted them.

Maybe they would have said more, except right then the door burst open to reveal a panting Kip.

"One of the jabberwocks came back," he said. "We need our queen before it charbroils the whole street."

CHAPTER TWENTY-FIVE

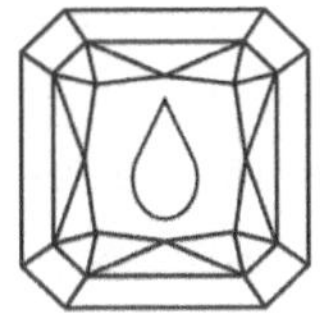

Lyssa

The jabberwock's burbling moans carried several blocks from the edge of the city where it had started its rampage. I picked up my pace to a run, sliding my scepter from its carry bag as my feet smacked the cobblestones. Kip sped up too, waving his arm to show me the right direction. My three lovers loped along just behind me.

An all-too familiar sickly sweet scent tickled my nose. I hesitated, my fingers tensing around the scepter's staff.

"Did the guards dump more roses here?" I asked.

Kip shook his head, wrinkling his nose. "There was an old batch in an alley out here we managed to miss. The drug is mostly faded by now, but some of the residents are still pretty dazed. We figure the smell is what drew the jabberwock. It's the palace folk they're really not happy with. Wish this one had taken its anger out on the guards instead."

No kidding. As we dashed closer, the faint prickle of smoke reached my nose as well. If the jabberwocks I'd encouraged to come to the city had hurt anyone else here… Guilt twisted my gut.

We came around a bend to the scattered buildings along the edge of the city. The jabberwock fluttered its frail, useless wings and let out a belch that sent flames licking over the side of the nearest house. Its head wove from side to side on its feathered, serpentine neck, and its clawed feet clattered against the group. I could tell at a glance it wasn't angry so much as distressed. Although an unhappy jabberwock didn't look very different from a raging one.

The Spades and a few of the Clubbers were hustling residents out of their houses and away down the street. Some of the locals, like Kip had suggested, swayed on their feet, their expressions dazed with growing confusion. This was not a sight I'd have wanted anyone to wake up from a drug-haze to.

My nerves shivered when the jabberwock swung its maw toward us with a rasp of its jagged teeth, but I clenched my jaw and strode into the middle of the street. Figures amid the trees caught my eyes with a stutter of my pulse. A couple of the drug-dazed Clubbers had wandered into the forest instead of deeper into the city. One stumbled over a branch just a few feet from the jabberwock's lashing tail. Its head snapped in their direction at the sound.

"Jabberwock!" I called out quickly, raising the scepter in the air. The tingle of its calming, clarifying energy washed over me and flowed out toward the massive creature with the ruby's crimson glow.

At my voice, the jabberwock turned back to face me. As the glow touched it, its body stilled, its gaze focusing completely on me. It let out another moan, but this one sounded more questioning than distraught.

One of the Clubbers behind it scrambled onward through the forest on unsteady feet. The one closer to us had stopped. The woman rubbed her eyes as if she'd just woken from a sound sleep. Her gaze settled on me, her eyes abruptly sharp with attention. Then she registered the jabberwock and leapt backwards with a squeak of shock. Despite being startled, she managed to keep her balance.

I glanced from her to the jabberwock. How had she come out of her daze?

A suspicion crept up through my mind. The scepter's energy might have washed over her too as I'd sent it toward the jabberwock. Had it cleared the drug's effects from her mind, just like it'd cleared the jabberwock's frantic impulses?

If I'd known that was possible, our job recovering the city would have been a whole lot simpler. Of course, maybe I'd have worn out the scepter's magic if I'd tried to bring the entire population out of their daze in the course of a day.

Right now, I had to deal with the jabberwock first. Keeping the scepter held up between us, I took a step closer to the creature. It bowed its head to meet me.

"Hey," I said in a soothing voice. "There's no danger here. There's nothing to fight. But it's good that you came back to us. We can still use your protection from the ones in the red-and-pink uniforms—the Queen of Hearts' men. Will you help us again?"

The jabberwock let out a sound that was closest to a sigh and nudged its muzzle against my extended hand. A smile touched my lips. It wanted to serve this land, to free it, just as much as I did. The creatures just needed a push in the right direction and guiding words to keep them on track.

"Will you call the other ones back before we march on the palace again?" Theo asked from where he'd stopped a little behind me.

I patted the jabberwock's nose and pointed along the line of the forest. "Go to the road and keep watch there. You know how to warn me."

As the creature lumbered off, I turned back to my companions. Chess was grinning, Hatter's eyes gleaming with a mix of awe and worry for me. Theo studied me, waiting for my answer.

"If we come up with a plan where I'm sure I can keep control of them, I will," I said. "They've been valuable allies. It wasn't their fault that they got confused during the battle. *I* was confused."

The woman who'd come out of her drugged state eased tentatively toward the buildings now that the jabberwock had left. "Is it safe?" she said, sounding totally alert.

"It should be," I said, and remembered the possibility that had occurred to me earlier. "Where are the rest of the Clubbers who are still recovering from the drug?" I asked Kip. "I want to see them—I think I might be able to help."

"The others were just taking them a couple of streets over," he said. "We figured staying out in the fresh air was the best thing if they're going to come out of it soon."

"Let's see if I can bring them out of it right now."

I brandished my scepter, and he led the way. Theo fell into step next to me. "What are you thinking?" he said.

"The scepter calms creatures down and brings them to me by clearing all the distractions out of their minds," I said. "The same way it can push back literal darkness. I think it accidentally had the same effect on one of the Clubbers who was still under the drug's influence. I'd like to see if I can do it again."

And if I could… The start of another idea trembled eagerly at the back of my mind.

Like Kip had said, the other Spades had ushered the drugged city people to a nearby street. They drifted over the cobblestones looking aimless and anxious at the same time. I adjusted my fingers around my scepter and held it out again, picturing the drug's tendrils retreating from all those minds.

"People of Wonderland," I said steadily but gently. "Remember what matters to you. Remember yourselves. Come through the fog and back to me."

The ruby's glow grew, filling my eyes and spilling out across the street. My breath caught with the energy streaming through that light. Gasps and startled cries sounded all down the street.

When the light faded, I peered, blinking, at the Clubbers it had touched. They were staring around, bewildered but present, like the woman I'd woken up by the jabberwock. A rush of triumph filled my chest. As the

Spades started answering their barrage of questions, I spun around to face the three men who'd followed me this far.

"Is there somewhere we could get to quickly where we could ambush just a few guards?"

Chess's eyebrows leapt up. "And where will you go with them after you get them?"

Theo considered my scepter, his gaze going thoughtful. When he spoke up, I knew he'd guessed my intention. "Is there any particular kind of guard you want to ambush?"

I dropped my voice, not wanting to get any hopes up outside our small circle in case this gambit didn't work. "I want to see what this scepter's magic can do for a pearl-head."

Hatter stared at me for a second. "You think—" He shook his head. "No. Their minds are gone. There's no one there to save."

"Maybe not, but we won't know that for sure until we try. Do you have any idea how pearling even works?"

"There's some kind of magic to it, but no, I've got no idea how it all comes together," he admitted.

"Then there's a chance I can help them," I said. "And even if I can't bring back any of the people they used to be... at least I can try to wipe the Queen of Hearts' influence from their minds. Free them from serving her."

Theo nodded. "It's worth a try. It could make a huge difference in our plans. Come on. I think I know a spot where they'll be stationed. We don't want to lose much time to this."

The Queen's deadline was hanging over all our heads, but mine especially, if I wanted to make sure my mother and my best friend kept *their* heads. I dragged in a breath. "You show me the way. Chess, why don't you come too in case we need help grabbing the one I'm going to try to wake up? Hatter, can you see if we can equip the people still willing to fight for us with some better armor in the meantime? You've got to have some good helmet techniques up your sleeve at least."

Hatter's mouth quirked upward. "I might have an idea or two. Don't get up to anything too exciting without me."

"I'll be right back." I stepped in to give him a quick kiss as if to make those words a promise.

Chess set off with a bounce in his step as if he was eager to get back into action. "Where are we off to, Whi —ah, Theo?"

"Through the forest," Theo said with a sweeping motion. "I know some of the favorite posts outside the palace grounds."

We stayed quiet as we moved between the trees. When we got close to the spot Theo expected to find guards on the look-out, he sent Chess ahead invisibly to scope out the lay of the land. Chess returned after a few minutes with a smirk.

"Three of them," he murmured to us. "One a pearl-head. What are we going to do with the other two while our queen is working her magic on him?"

Theo smiled. "I'm sure between the two of us we can come up with something."

"Don't hurt them any more than you need to," I reminded them. "We're trying to set the opposite example from the current rule."

Chess saluted me, and Theo pulled a length of metallic rope from his pocket. The two of them set off ahead of me. I trailed along behind, waiting for my turn to play a part. Stealthy attacks didn't seem to correspond with any of my queenly powers. I guessed it'd be a little much if I had the magic to handle every situation in the world.

Was it possible my scepter might bring back the people who'd lost their heads and then been pearled? Hope fluttered through my heart. If I could manage that, then all the innocent people the Queen had ordered taken and killed for her use—I could restore them to the friends and family they'd been stolen from. I could give them their lives back.

Theo and Chess sprang forward. There was a thump and a grunt, followed by a brief rustling. When I reached the guard post, two men who looked fully conscious sat against a tree trunk, gagged and wrists bound, another loop of rope around their chests tying them in to the tree. Other than a red mark on the verge of a bruise on one's forehead, they didn't appear to have suffered much damage.

Chess was holding the arms of the pearl-headed guard, his hand clamped over the man's mouth. From the puff of the young guy's cheeks, he was trying to yell anyway. His gaze floated dimly over us, his body jerking with a repetitive attempt to dislodge his captor.

My throat constricted. He barely understood what was happening, clearly—he was simply following the orders the Queen had given him as well as he could. No thought seemed to pass behind those glazed eyes. He might as well have been an actual pearl for all the independent consciousness he showed.

There was no point in prolonging his distress. We led him several paces away where the other guards couldn't observe us. Then I drew out my scepter and held the ruby level with his eyes. All the longing in me to undo the damage the Queen had done to him radiated through me into the warm wood in my hand. The ruby lit up with its soft glow.

"What the Queen of Hearts said, it can leave your mind," I said. "You don't need to follow her orders or those of her men. You can be who you were before. Follow who you want to follow. Everything they told you, everything they commanded you to do, let it fall away."

The pearl-headed man's body gradually relaxed. Chess eased up his hold, and the guy stood there without any resistance. He pursed his lips but didn't speak when Chess removed his hand. His eyes still looked glazed, but not quite as blankly as before. Or maybe that was just my wishful thinking.

"Hey," I said, lowering the scepter to my side. "Do you know who you are? What's your name?"

The man's eyelids twitched. He focused on me as if he were seeing me from a great distance away. "Name," he repeated slowly. "I— Who are you?"

"I'm the Red Queen," I said. "The rightful ruler of Wonderland."

His face brightened. "*You* are the one I should listen to. I hear it—I feel it."

He still sounded pretty vague. My stomach tightened. "I'm not going to order you to do anything. I just wanted you to be free. The Queen of Hearts was treating you like a slave. Do you remember anything from before? You probably lived in the city once…" I didn't know whether he was one of the recent people she'd snatched or someone who'd served her for a while.

His head drifted from one side to the other. "I saw a yellow house," he said dreamily. "I liked it. And there was… chocolate?" A pleased chuckle escaped his lips.

Theo and Chess exchanged a glance. My heart sank. Maybe there were a few fragments of the man this guy used to be that had survived the pearling process, but no more than that.

I wasn't bringing anyone back, not really.

But I'd still broken him from his subservience to the Queen. He was no longer her slave. And if I could do that with him…

"Come on," I said, giving him a gentle nudge. "Let's get you someplace safer."

"You accomplished the most important part," Theo said as we started walking. "He *is* free."

"And I can free the others. A lot of the Queen's army is made of pearl-heads now." How far could the scepter's glow reach? I guessed I was going to find out. "That'll make the battle easier, but it doesn't solve all of our problems."

"No," Theo said. "But it's given me an idea. And seeing you with the jabberwock gave me another one. Let's see if I can't invent our way to victory one last time."

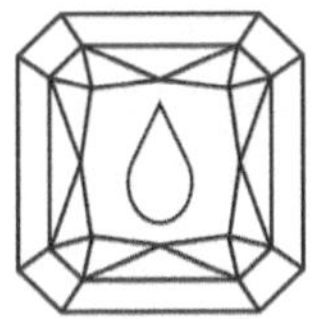

CHAPTER TWENTY-SIX

Hatter

"It doesn't seem quite right that you all have turned out to be more mad than I ever was," I said, eyeing the beast that Theo had just presented me with on the outskirts of the city.

Jabberwocks weren't the most reassuring sight on the best of days. The creature's red and gold feathers ruffled as it shifted its considerable weight, its searing violet eyes watching me from far over my head. I caught a whiff of its sour, meaty breath. But the worst part about the sight in front of me was the broad, metal-framed strips of fabric that Theo had slid over the creature's stumpy natural wings and strapped around its broad chest. It flapped them tentatively as I watched.

"The line between brilliance and madness is rather thin, in my experience," Theo said with a crooked smile. "*It* doesn't seem to mind."

"Do the wings actually work?" I asked, even though I

found it hard to believe we'd be standing here discussing this in the first place if he hadn't tested and confirmed as much already. "Can the beast fly?"

"We took a few trial runs over the mushroom stands once it got dark," Theo said. "I'm not sure how long the contraptions will last, but we don't need it to fly a marathon. Maybe ten minutes to fly to and around the palace, a matter of seconds to pull off the rescue—I expect it to go off without a hitch."

"Easy for you to say when you're not the one who'll be riding on it," I muttered. I would have asked why me, but I already knew that too. I was Hatter of the nimble fingers. If anyone was going to snatch Lyssa's loved ones to safety in time, it was me.

I just hadn't been counting on doing it from the back of a monster that had only just discovered proper flight.

"There are additional straps attached to the ones holding the artificial wings in place." Theo pointed. "You can wrap them around your legs to keep you secure, so you won't have to worry about falling when you let go with your hands. The loose straps at the back are for your passengers. Lyssa has told the jabberwock to listen to you. The rest of the plan is as we discussed with the group."

I crossed my arms over my chest and eyed the creature. "You're going to let me be the boss, huh?" I said to it. "Even without a fancy scepter? Let's see that head of yours down here where I can look at you face to face, then."

Even though I'd seen how well Lyssa could persuade the creatures, my pulse leapt with a hint of surprise when the jabberwock lowered its snout to my level. It cocked its head to one side and clicked its jagged teeth together with a sound that wasn't exactly reassuring.

"Good… boy," I said, and patted it on the muzzle the way I'd seen Lyssa do. "We've got an important job to do for our queen. We'll make sure we pull it off, you hear?"

The jabberwock emitted a huff that suggested it thought *I* was a lot more likely to screw this mission up than it was and hunkered down on its belly, ready for me to clamber on.

We had to get going soon. The sliver of a moon was high in the night sky, the air cooling around us. Only two hours remained before the Queen of Hearts' deadline.

If we couldn't pull this attempt off, we weren't going to get another chance.

"We should be ready to move out in ten minutes," Theo said. "If you're ready."

I made myself nod. I'd be ready. This was what Lyssa needed from me. And maybe it wasn't all that much madder than some of my exploits way back when.

"I suppose this is payback for turning my back on you and the Spades for the last twelve years," I said, raising an eyebrow at Theo.

He gave me that crooked smile again. I trusted it more than the smooth, confident one he'd always put on in his role as the White Knight. A princely smile, it'd been—I must have sensed it even if I hadn't known enough to consciously recognize what it meant.

"You're the best man for the job, Hatter," he said. "And even if I did think from time to time that you'd made the wrong decision by backing away from the

Spades… that wasn't really my call to make. I didn't understand the position you were in."

I wasn't sure what to make of that admission. "And you do now?"

Theo glanced toward the city. "Until recently, I never had anyone that mattered to me as much as Wonderland did. I couldn't imagine putting anything else first." His gaze slid back to me. "Now I know what it's like to want to protect someone with all of your being. I'm not going to tell you that being a great father was less important than being a great Spade."

There was no denying the earnestness in his words. If I'd had any lingering doubts about his intentions toward Lyssa, they disintegrated in that instant.

I tipped my head in acknowledgment. "And sometimes, on the other hand, what or who you care about means you end up taking some crazy risks trying to make things better for them. It's easier for me to see now why you felt so much urgency about setting Wonderland right."

"Yes. I suppose we both know a lot more than we did back then."

The jabberwock shifted its weight impatiently. I looked up at it, and my throat constricted. "If this goes wrong somehow, you'll watch out for Doria? I know she doesn't need someone at her heels every second, but just, in general…"

"Of course," Theo said, sounding honestly startled. "You don't even have to ask that."

I exhaled. "Okay. Good."

He clapped me on the back and wished me luck

before he left, and that felt just about right. I patted the jabberwock's neck and pondered whether I wanted to get settled on its back just yet or to wait until the last minute when the signal came. I hadn't quite decided when the rasp of footsteps sounded on the cobblestones.

Lyssa emerged from one of the side streets, sword at her hip and scepter at her back, the rubies on her armored vest gleaming as bright as her blue eyes. So much power emanated from her stride that my heart skipped a beat, watching her approach. I tugged at my hat with a fidgety twitch of my fingers.

"Shouldn't you be off preparing for your part in this grand battle?" I said lightly.

"I think we're as prepared as anyone could be," Lyssa said. "You didn't know exactly what you were signing up for. Are you okay with this?" She nodded to the jabberwock.

Did she really think I was going to say no at this late hour? The idea seemed absurd, and yet at the same time I was sure she'd accept it if I did. I forced a smile.

"I've got to remind everyone why I'm Mad Hatter, don't I?"

I obviously hadn't completely erased my nerves from my voice. Lyssa peered at me in the dim glow that seeped from the lamps on the streets behind her. "All you have to do is scatter the guards around the hostages and get the three of them onto the jabberwock, and then get the hell out of there. We'll take care of the rest. I'll have your back."

Those last words reminded me of Chess's comments. My smile relaxed a little. "And I'll have yours."

She stepped closer, her hand coming up to curl around my tie the way she'd grasped it the first time she'd kissed me, the way that made my heart thump harder in an instant. "I also remembered that the last time I kissed you for good luck, things turned out pretty much perfectly. Let's see if we can pull that off again."

I didn't need more invitation than that. I slipped my arm around her and tugged her to me, and for a few seconds everything was her fresh sweet smell and the hint of the tea we'd drunk during that last meeting, sharp and hot on her lips. Hearts take me, I'd ride a hundred jabberwocks if I got moments like this in between.

She pulled back reluctantly. "I'd better get back. I'll see you after it's over."

"Let's make that a promise," I said.

When she'd jogged back to where the rest of our sort-of army was preparing, I finally gathered my courage and scrambled up to my perch between the jabberwock's extended wings. The straps Theo had pointed out weren't hard to fix in place. I secured my legs, trying not to think of the possible negative consequences of being strapped to a deadly fire-breathing monster.

"Fucking wow," a voice murmured as I finished up. Doria eased out of the shadows where she must have been lurking. Her eyes were round as she took in me and the beast I was perched on. "I thought they were kidding. You're really topping your old exploits, aren't you, Pops."

My fingers tightened around the feathers between my mount's shoulders. "I wouldn't get too close, Mouse."

She let out a faint laugh. "I'm good here. I just wanted to see... And I figured someone should tell you to be careful. Since that strategy always worked so well with me."

I couldn't contain a laugh of my own. "So it did. Worried about your old man, are you?"

She crossed her skinny arms over her chest, hugging herself. "I'm allowed to, right? It can go both ways."

How long had she been watching—and listening? Had she heard my comment to Theo about watching out for her?

"Doria," I started.

"I'm going to do that," she said before I could go on, with a familiar defiant raise of her chin. "I'm going to worry about you too. And… maybe sometimes it's nice to know you're around to worry about me, even if it bugs me in the moment. Okay?"

I wished I wasn't up here in this ridiculous saddle so I could have hugged her if she'd let me. I had to settle for smiling with all the fatherly fondness I had in me. "I'll remind you that you said that the next time you complain."

She wrinkled her nose at me, but she was smiling too.

The first chime rang out. Doria glanced toward the city where the others had assembled and back at me. "I'll see you out there. Good luck!"

"To you too," I called after her as she darted away. *I'll only take as much as you can spare.* Then I tapped the jabberwock's shoulder, and it pushed onto its feet. "Almost our time."

It answered with a little snort and a puff of smoke.

The second chime sounded a minute later. Lyssa had instructed the jabberwock well. It didn't even wait for a signal from me, just leapt into the air with a flap of its new artificial wings. I could have sworn from the glimpse of its face I got as it shot a quick look toward the city that it was grinning.

The cool wind warbled against the taut material of the wings and licked over my clothes. My fingers tightened around the feathers along the creature's shoulders as we rose up toward the sky. The lights of the city and the palace up ahead fell away beneath us. My pulse raced, but as much from exhilaration as nerves.

This was… actually pretty amazing.

The jabberwock soared forward, its body hitching slightly with each flap. After the first couple minutes, I adjusted to the rhythm enough to release my death grip on its feathery shoulders.

We left the city behind, making straight for the glittering lanterns that dotted the royal gardens. Lights glowed from several of the palace windows and along the parapet over its main door. I could already make out dozens of guards patrolling the grounds, as aware as we were that the deadline was fast approaching.

Beneath me, Lyssa would be making her way up the road with Theo and Chess and a handful of other Spades. Dum was leading the rest of our force, including Doria, through the forest, stealing the guards' tactic from this morning. Lyssa would present herself supposedly for surrender but would demand to see that her loved ones were still alive before she came through the gate.

I wouldn't be able to hear any of that conversation, as far up as we needed to stay to avoid the lights catching on the jabberwock's form, but the moment the three

Otherlanders stepped out of the palace, we'd have to move in an instant.

The road between the city and the palace was so shadowed I couldn't even track Lyssa's progress that way. The jabberwock wheeled high above the palace, its wings holding steady as Theo had promised. What did it make of this, deep in that strange monster brain of its?

"Good work," I said, giving its neck an encouraging rub like I might have a horse. Then more lights flared on below around the gate.

As we circled back that way, figures darted between the gate and the palace. The lights along the wall glinted starkly in Lyssa's white blond hair where she stood on the road just outside. My lungs constricted. If they laid one harsh hand on my lover, my queen…

The main doors to the palace were opening. This was our moment. I leaned forward, peering down as the jabberwock swept in a tighter circle.

The Knave strode out, flicking a hand over the striped fur of his face. Several guards joined him, the three Otherlanders held between them. They strode forward and halted where Lyssa would have been able to make them out from the now-open gate, but not close enough that she could have hoped to reach them.

They weren't prepared for me.

"Now!" I said with a nudge of my fingers.

The jabberwock dove. The wind shrieked past my ears and whisked away my hat, but I didn't have time to miss it. We were hurtling toward the ground, so fast I left my stomach behind. For an instant I thought we might smash right into the hedges.

The jabberwock banked at the last second. Its feet slammed into the ground just a foot from the nearest Otherlander, crushing at least one guard under it, kicking others to the side, spewing a burst of flame at a couple more.

"Here, here," I shouted, grasping the older woman's elbow, the younger's wrist, heaving them and the man onto the jabberwock's back and fastening the straps around them so quickly my arms ached with the effort. The man almost fell when the jabberwock lurched around to belch more fire at the Knave, but I snapped the buckle in place just in time.

"Go!" I cried, tapping the creature's shoulders. As it shoved off the ground, a shriek rang out above us. My head jerked up.

The Queen had come out onto the parapet over the palace's front door. Her face blanched white with rage at the sight of her bargaining chips being swept away from her.

Seeing her, it occurred to me with a thump of my pulse that I could end this right now. My hand darted to the straps holding my legs.

The jabberwock knew where to go with its precious cargo. As it soared upward, I could spring from its back onto the parapet, stab the Queen of Hearts through the heart she barely knew how to use with one of the hatpins up my sleeve, like I had the old Knave before, and there'd be no one to stand between Lyssa and her throne. The guards she must have nearby would kill me for it in turn, but wouldn't that sacrifice be worth it?

Except I couldn't guarantee killing the Queen would

stop the guards swarming the gardens, not in the crucial early moments when the most blood would be shed anyway. I couldn't even guarantee that I'd land my leap in time and close enough to end the Queen's life before her guards took mine.

And I promised Lyssa I'd see her again, after.

Get the hell out of there, she'd said. *We'll handle the rest.* I'd had her back, and now she had mine, like Chess had said. Lyssa had her own plan, a plan that didn't involve my death if she could help it, and that was the plan she'd want me to follow.

She'd want me to trust her that she could bring down the Queen without me throwing my life away. She'd want me to be by her side when the battle was over.

Damn it, I wanted that too. I wanted to be there to worry about Doria and banter with Chess and love my rising queen.

My hand stilled on the strap. The jabberwock soared up, past the palace, into the night sky. A pang filled my chest, but I welcomed the sensation, the strange sense of having lost and gained something at the same time.

Perhaps this was what love was meant to be, really. Not holding the one you loved back from the fray or throwing yourself in front of them, but facing it together, side by side, with all the faith you had.

CHAPTER TWENTY-SEVEN

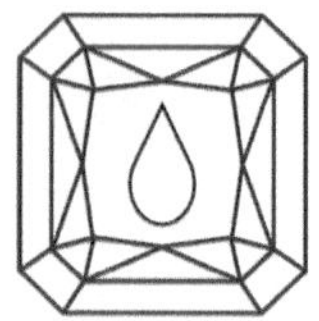

Lyssa

The jabberwock's bright feathers flashed against the night, lit up by the palace's lanterns. The smoke of its fiery attack tainted the thick scent of the garden's roses. As the creature rose up, Hatter's form showed as a dark silhouette between its crafted wings with three figures clinging on just behind him.

That was all I needed to see. I yanked my sword from its scabbard and swung it toward the gate.

"Now!"

The Spades and Clubbers who'd been gathering behind the treed slope beside the road broke from that shelter and rushed down to join me with a volley of cries. I charged ahead toward the gate with Theo and Chess at my side. The guards who'd eased it open so I could see the Knave's hostages leapt forward to shove it closed again, but I slashed out with my sword before they'd heaved it more than a couple of steps.

The blade's power thrummed through the air and smacked into the gate and the guards. The door careened open, the men in their pleated uniforms toppling in its wake. I barreled onward with the thumping of hundreds of determined feet behind me—and the burbling moan of the other jabberwocks I'd summoned, now loping over from where they'd been waiting by the city.

The guards from all across the palace grounds raced to meet us. I stopped with a hitch of breath and thrust my scepter out in front of me. My gaze caught dozens of glazed eyes and blank faces beneath those helms. I focused on them, on the need to wash away the Hearts' horrible influence.

"I am the Red Queen," I called out with all the force of my lungs. "The guardian and ruler of Wonderland. I dismiss every order you've been given from the tyrant who stole my throne. May your heads clear and your minds go free. Get yourselves away from here, to the ends of the garden, to as much safety as you can find!"

A pulse of energy rolled off the scepter. The ruddy glow flowed over the horde of guards descending on us. Within the space of a breath, many of them stumbled and lurched to the side. They wavered on their feet for a second before my last command sunk in. Their heart-shaped helms tumbled off their heads as they dashed out of the fray.

When we'd discussed this plan earlier, Theo had suggested that I could ask the pearl-headed guards to fight for me instead of the false queen who'd made them. Maybe that would have made this battle a little easier. But most of those people had never asked to serve the Queen of Hearts; had given their lives to her cruelty only to be battered with blades all over again. I wasn't going to use them the same callous way she had.

I did not intend to build my reign on a foundation of suffering.

I shoved my scepter back into its bag and tightened my grip on my sword as I hurried onward. The city people who'd joined our cause flooded into the gardens around me, everyone with some kind of weapon in their hands. The Spades wove along the edges of the crowd, tossing smoke bombs and skitter cubes to disorient the guards that were closing in. The jabberwocks dove into the mass of uniformed figures with slashes of their claws and gnashing teeth.

Theo, Chess, and Dum moved to flank me as we pushed down the center of the path. Some of the guards skirted the wider fray to come down the middle of it at us. I knocked them back with the power of my sword. Dum sprang ahead to kick the ones who'd toppled to the side with his elastic legs. Theo and Chess fended off the few who sprang closer, Theo with the sword he'd found for himself and Chess with his fists flashing in and out of sight.

Despite the cool night air, sweat was trickling down my back by the time the palace doors came into sight through the chaos. I readied my sword and fixed my gaze on the dozen or so guards assembled in front of the entrance.

"I don't want to hurt anyone. I'm just here to take back what was stolen from my family. Go, and I won't have to go through you."

The furor of the battle and the powers they'd already seen me demonstrate must have finally overcome their fear of the Queen of Hearts. Half of them scattered. The others charged at us, weapons drawn. I propelled them backward with a slice of my blade. Its power rattled the hinges and sent the door bursting open.

Theo stepped into the lead, pointing the way with his sword. "This hall will get us to the Queen's chambers fastest," he said. The rest of us hustled after him, leaving the worst of the fray behind.

We dashed down the hall, dispatching a few more guards who rushed at us along the way. Theo gestured us up a staircase.

Just as we reached the top, the Knave marched out to meet us. His tiger lips were curled in a sneer that showed his vicious teeth, and he was shoving Dee in front of him, his dagger pressed against the young man's throat.

The once-cheerful twin's red hair lay lank on his head. His face sported a black eye and a split lip. Whether the Queen had ever planned to keep up her end of the bargain or had decided their deal was forfeit when the Spades had escaped the tunnels, I didn't know, but it looked like he'd spent the last two days in the dungeons.

"There are no jabberwocks to swoop down in here," the Knave snarled, looking at Dum. "How much is your brother worth to you?"

He hadn't even gotten his final words out when Dum was springing at him with all the force of his sprightly legs. Theo gave a shout of warning, too late. Another guard had been waiting in the shadows. He leapt out in front of the Knave and stabbed his sword into Dum's gut.

A cry broke from my lips. As Dum's body slumped on the floor, the pool of blood spreading beneath his belly stark red against the mauve carpet, more guards threw themselves at us. And Dee threw himself against the Knave's hold.

He slammed his fist, driven by his springy arm, into the Knave's hand. The dagger still raked across his throat, drawing a gush of blood, but the wound wasn't deep enough to stop Dee. The Knave stumbled backward, and Dee hurtled toward his brother, pummeling every guard in the way.

"No," he rasped out. "Brother, stay with me, dammit." The last word came out with a choked sob. He gripped his brother's shoulders, but Dum's head only lolled against the ground.

My heart wrenched. Dum had loved his brother so much, even after that traitorous turn. He'd given up everything for him after all.

With my teeth gritted, I lashed out at the rest of the guards. The sword's magic slammed them back into the wall. Theo flung himself ahead of me, his face tight with anguish, his sword singing in the air. He rammed it straight into the Knave's heart.

The Knave barely managed to spit out one last gasp of a snarl before his body crumpled. Theo yanked out his sword, looking no more satisfied for the kill. The Prince of Hearts wasn't one for revenge. But nothing we did was going to bring back the young man he'd promised to protect from childhood.

We didn't even have a moment to grieve the loss. Every minute that passed before I ended this war, more of my people were dying out there while the guards fought on.

I had to get to the Queen.

We left Dee hunched over his brother's body and hustled down the hall. I knew we were almost at the Queen's quarters when the rose smell thickened again. Theo's shoulders stiffened, but his steps didn't falter.

"Out of the way!" I shouted when the door came into view up ahead, more guards clustered around it. "I'd rather go around you than through you. It's your choice."

I brandished my sword. A few of the guard's expressions wavered, and they broke from the bunch. The others braced themselves, knuckles whitening where they clutched their weapons. My stomach clenched, but my resolve didn't shake. I swung the sword's sharp magic into them.

The door flew open, the guards doubling over around it, the ones who'd been right in front tumbling through. Chess darted ahead to shove and yank them out of my path. More guards charged toward us as we hurried through the interconnected rooms with all their ornate furniture and paintings, but I dispatched them with a few swipes of my sword. The thump of my pulse filled my body.

I was here. I was so close I could feel it, taste it. This was the palace I should have grown up in, the home that had always belonged to me even while I struggled to find my place in the Otherland, not knowing Wonderland even existed.

Chess battered through one more squad of guards, blinking invisible and then visible again when they'd fallen. We strode through one last doorway, and I found myself face to face with the Queen of Hearts.

I'd never seen her this close before. She perched on a throne carved from the same red-brown cherry wood as the staff of the scepter at my back, but fitted with the gold plates Theo had mentioned to me, as if she'd bound the royal seat itself. Magic rippled through the air around her, stirring the copper coils of her hair and the ruffles of her expansive pink dress. Her eyes sparked with their eerie sheen.

But now, for the first time, I noticed the lines around those eyes that make-up couldn't completely conceal. The veins that stood out on her hands where they clutched the arms of the throne.

She'd held onto her illegitimate rule for a long time. And now that time was over.

"Don't take one more step!" she snapped at us as I stepped forward. My feet halted. Theo tipped his head. I reached to my belt to press the switch on the device my Inventor had made just for me, to set off the chain reaction he'd planned before he'd even known if he'd make it out of this palace alive or if I'd make it back to Wonderland.

A sharp hiss cut through the air, and the gold plates burst from the sides and back of the throne. The Queen screeched, lunging forward, and the seat seemed to wallop her at the same time. She staggered rather than flying at us and fell to her knees.

I was already sprinting forward. I bounded right over her and dropped onto the throne. As if drawn by the power humming through the wood, one of my hands rose to set the sword against the right arm and the other reached to place the scepter against the left.

The rubies blazed on those artifacts, all across my armored vest, and on the ring beneath it too, if I was going by the blast of heat that washed over my chest. In that instant, I felt all of Wonderland stretching out around me through the base of the throne. I saw the train streaking around the Checkerboard Plains and heard the breeze whispering through the Topsy Turvy wood, smelled the scones baking in the city and tasted the salt of the sea. The sensations soaked into my skin and quivered around me with a wash of warmth that made me gasp with joy.

I was home. I was exactly where I belonged, in a way I'd never experienced before this moment.

With all those impressions colliding around and inside me, I could hardly focus on what was happening right in front of me in the room. The Queen of Hearts threw herself to her feet and spun on me with a screech. But before she could lunge at me, Theo caught her, clamping her elbows to her sides with his strong arms.

"No, Mother," he said, his voice low and firm. "It's over. The time of the Hearts is done. This rule was never meant to be ours at all."

He glanced at Chess, who lifted the crown from the former queen's head. Chess flashed a brief grin at me. "I think we'll find or make a new one for our rightful queen."

"No," the Queen of Hearts protested, squirming against Theo's hold. "It was mine. This was all *mine*." But the power that had once reverberated through her had faded the moment I'd claimed my throne. Even the sheen in her eyes had faded, leaving them an ordinary light brown.

Theo sat his mother back on the ground, keeping one hand on her shoulder to restrain her, and fished a web of dark strands from the pouch he'd been carrying. Chess knelt down to hold her still as Theo set the contraption over the Queen of Hearts' head. He caught my eye, and I lifted my scepter again, ready for when he gave the cue.

He pressed a button at the base of the web, and a faint hum carried through the room. "Mother," he said, his voice even softer now. "I want you to forget all the reasons you think you have to hate and fear. Forget your greed for the throne."

"Let it all go," I murmured, my throat tight and my fingers gripping the scepter's staff. "Let it fade away."

The scepter's glow spread out to mingle with the device's hum. The sound rose, the air vibrating against my skin. Theo stared down at his mother, his eyes worried but his expression determined.

The glow contracted back into the ruby. The hum died off as well. The Queen of Hearts slumped where she sat, the tension seeping from her stout body. She lifted her head. One of her stiff curls fell loose across her forehead. Her gaze fixed on Theo, her brow furrowing.

"Jack?" she said hesitantly. "What am I doing here?"

Theo's mouth formed a tight smile. "You're setting things right, Mother. Come with me. We're going to end a war."

The throne called to me to stay, but I'd be back soon. I pushed myself off of it, taking up my sword as well as my scepter. The power that had flowed into me kept tingling through my nerves as we made our way out of the royal chambers, along the hall, and to the parapet where the Queen had watched the beginnings of the battle before it had started to turn against her. A battle that would now be finally done.

We stepped out into the cool night. Clangs and shouts clashed in the gardens below. "Stop!" I shouted at the top of my lungs. "The fighting ends now! The throne is mine. The Hearts have fallen."

"Tell them," Theo said to his mother, gripping her arm.

The guards had fallen back at the sight of their former queen, who stood shaken and crown-less before them. She blinked, her chin trembling before she found the words.

"There's nothing to fight for," she said. "The throne isn't mine. I give it up."

"And the Red Queen claims what was rightfully hers!" Chess called out.

The Spades and Clubbers whooped, excited laughter spilling through the gardens. The palace guards dropped their weapons. I gazed out over them in my first act as Wonderland's official queen and felt the breeze wash over me like a wave of peace spreading across the land all around me.

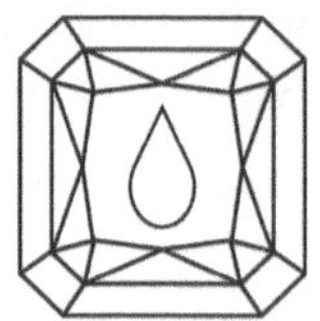

CHAPTER TWENTY-EIGHT

One month later

Lyssa

"Do you really have to go already?" Melody asked as the waitress cleared our lunch dishes from the café table. My best friend gave me a pleading look that was offset by her wry smile.

There was something comforting about the muted colors and the soft melody of normal Otherland music in the room around me, but coming to this world already felt like taking a trip, not coming home.

"A queen's work is never done," I said with a grin. "But I promise I'll do my best to make it for your big fashion show next week. We're still studying the whole mirror connection thing to figure out how to predict the passing of time."

"Well, until you do have it figured out, I'm happy to stay on call for spontaneous meals whenever you happen to drop in." Melody shook her head, still smiling. "I just tell myself that you've relocated to some other actual country. That's a whole lot easier to wrap my head around. The less said about that crazy place you're actually going back to, the better."

I laughed as we stood up. All three of the Otherlanders the Knave had held hostage had been pretty shaken up by the experience, to say the least, but Melody had bounced back the fastest. We had an unspoken deal that I didn't talk too much about the weirdness of my new life and she wouldn't hassle me about how much danger I'd put myself in, and we'd continue on like friends who just didn't live as close to one another anymore.

"Have you heard anything else from your mom?" Melody asked.

I grimaced as I pushed past the café door into the parking lot. "Her last few texts were still in full freak-out mode. I'm sticking with the whole no-contact thing until she can talk to me without having a breakdown." The last time I'd seen Mom—as well as the last time I'd talked to her, a week after that visit—she'd sobbed and cajoled and demanded that I go back to a hospital or at least come "home" so she'd know I was okay. The way she was acting, she needed help a whole lot more than I did.

The same old sense of duty had prickled over me. But I had other people counting on me now—and I shouldn't have had to be the one to support Mom back when I was a kid either. At a certain point, enough was enough.

I'd told her I loved her, that I was happy, and that I couldn't keep talking to her until she could accept those facts without constant reassurance. I'd also nudged her to get in touch with the therapist she'd seen a few times. If she could turn to a counselor instead of to me with all her worries, maybe we could have a better relationship down the road.

"I'm sorry," Melody said. "Even if I kind of get where she's coming from."

"It's only been a few weeks," I said. "I think she'll come around with enough time."

What the moving guy had made of the whole experience, I wasn't totally sure. He'd stammered something about needing to get home the second I'd brought them all back through to my house and practically torn a hole in the driveway getting out of there.

When we stopped at our cars, which were parked side-by-side, Melody touched my arm. "You know, even if I kind of get where your mom is coming from, I'm really happy for you at the same time, Lyss. There's something about you… Like you're lit up from the inside in a way you weren't before. Maybe I don't understand this whole situation, but I can tell you're doing the right thing for you. That's the best I could ask for, for my best friend."

Affection for her swelled in my throat. I gave her a hug, and she squeezed me back tightly.

"I'll give you a call as soon as I make it here again," I said.

"I'll be looking forward to it," Melody said. "Bring me a couple more of those Wonderland dresses if you can spare them, all right? I got some great inspiration from the first one."

I gave her a thumbs up and got into my car.

My spirits lifted as I drove through the dreary weather

toward Aunt Alicia's old house—my house now, not that I spent much time in it these days. Mrs. Plisby, the woman I'd hired to take care of the place during my absences, was out in the front yard pulling up weeds. I waved to her before heading inside. I paid her well enough that she didn't ask any questions about where I disappeared to during those absences.

All the furniture Mom and Melody had ordered packed up was now back in place, other than a little rearranging to suit my tastes. The mirror to Wonderland stood in the master bedroom, freshly polished. Even now, a giddy sensation raced over my skin as I stepped close to it and watched my reflection fade away. I touched the glass and reached through it to the surface on the other side.

After some trial and error, I'd found that I could direct my journey through the Otherland side looking-glass just like I could when I traveled from the Wonderland side. No more pond dunkings every time I slipped through. With a whisk of wind and a whoosh of darkness, I popped out into the entrance hall off my royal chambers.

A lot of the grandeur the Queen of Hearts had decorated her rooms with had been stripped away. I'd discovered the cherry wood floor under the thick carpeting and stripped the gold-gilded paper from the walls. The plaster was now painted a subdued moss-green that happened to be one of my favorite shades. On it I'd hung not fancy oils but sketches and paintings the city folk had made in celebration of their newfound freedom.

Out in the rest of the palace, people were still at work removing the unwanted traces of the Hearts' rule.

Afternoon sunlight streamed through windows no longer choked by thick velvet curtains. The smell of fresh paint tinged the air. The workers smiled and waved at me from where they were swiping their brushes over the wall farther down.

I hadn't checked on two of the former royals in residence today. I stopped by a second-floor room and knocked on the door. Mirabel's voice rang out on the other side. "Do come again soon!"

She was looking mainly backwards today, it sounded like. I eased open the door to find her sitting on one of the sofas we'd moved to this set of rooms from her Tower apartment. In the last few weeks, she'd decided to put aside her knitting to give embroidery a try. Beside her, the former Queen of Hearts was stitching away at her own strip of cloth.

The older woman looked up at me and offered a faint smile. She always gave the impression that she didn't entirely remember me but suspected that she was supposed to. Whatever the combined effects of Theo's memory gadget and my scepter had accomplished, it'd both wiped the violence from the tyrant's mind and left her a little vacant. But Mirabel seemed to find her mother's company pleasant enough in her new state. It was easier keeping an eye on her here in the palace than off where the rest of her children might nudge her in less positive directions.

Like every day, I asked, "How are you doing?" and "Is there anything you need?" Today Mirabel asked if she could have some silver thread sent up, but otherwise she showed nothing but contentment. I didn't ask her to try to pry into the future or dredge up the past. We'd left her head aching with enough of those requests in the past.

Besides, everything around me told me the future was bright.

As I came past the grand staircase into the wide front hall, I caught sight of Doria slipping away into one of the side rooms with Kip and Mallo, all of them laughing. A figure shifted in the shadows beside the staircase—Dee, watching them go, his expression so fraught it sent a twinge through my heart.

He'd apologized profusely for his betrayal, and his guilt over his brother's death hung over him like a cloud. I wasn't sure any of the Spades would ever feel comfortable treating him like a real friend again, though. As someone who'd once sacrificed a lot trying to save her mother from going under, I wasn't going to keep kicking him while he was down, but I wasn't sure when I'd be ready to give him much responsibility either.

He hadn't even managed to save his mother. We'd found her body in a pile of what Carpenter had called "discards" out at the Oyster Cove, her reformed head stalled in mid-growth. Apparently they'd lost nearly a quarter of the new pearl-heads thanks to the hasty adjustments to speed up the process. I couldn't imagine how painful that loss must be for Dee on top of the other.

"I can take a little comfort knowing the Queen of Hearts couldn't force Mom into being her slave," he'd said when I'd delivered the news. We'd held a memorial for her and all the other fallen city folk not long after the battle.

I followed the railing around to the door that led to the parapet. From that high vantage point, I could see across the palace grounds all the way to the little town the Diamonds and the remains of the Hearts family were building for themselves on the opposite side of the club from the main city. We'd never found any definite proof that the Duchess and her allies had meant to betray us, and I'd wanted to give everyone a blank slate for the beginning of my rule.

They *did* have to build the homes they wanted for themselves, though, since they preferred not to mingle too much with the city folk, and I wasn't keeping them in the palace.

The rough scrape of stone sliding against stone reached my ears from their construction site. Caterpillar's hulking, segmented form came into view briefly between the trees, lugging a slab the size of a boulder. He'd decided to look to them for new career possibilities now that I'd relieved him of his club.

"I think we need new management all around," I'd told him, remembering the way he'd leered at me when he'd thought I was just a Dreamer who'd stumbled into Wonderland. Rabbit hadn't been able to hide his giddiness when I'd handed him the keys.

Closer by, Unicorn had just finished a run around the lawn we'd set down where the mass of rose bushes used to be. Chess ambled over with a remark I could tell was bantering from his tone even if I couldn't make out most of the words, and Unicorn chuckled in response.

The bright feathers of the royal jabberwocks gleamed as they meandered between the freshly planted flowerbeds —every sort of flower Wonderland had to offer, other than roses. One of the creatures sprawled on its side, soaking up the sun. Since the Hearts had fallen, all the aggression had seeped out of their temperaments. They acted like overgrown feathery puppies most of the time. But if a bunch of Diamonds, say, got it into their heads to storm the palace, then the teeth and the fire would come out.

The main gate opened, and Theo strode into the garden with a couple of the Spades he'd been making the rounds with. A queen needed a royal guard of some sort, and I'd asked the former White Knight to take charge of that area of my rule. No more oddly shaped helms or pleated uniforms, though. He'd gone back to his preferred white dress shirts and gray slacks. They did suit him, after all.

I left the parapet and headed down to meet him. As I came out into the courtyard beyond the front doors, Hatter approached a couple of women sitting on a granite bench at the edge of the garden path. He held out a hat with a tuft of jabberwock feathers to the younger one.

"Fully customized to your requests," he said with a tip of his own hat. He'd restarted his business out of one of the rooms in the palace, and in the celebratory mood after our victory, there'd been plenty of call for eye-catching hats among the Clubbers.

"It's gorgeous," the woman said, setting it on her braided hair. "Thank you so much." She turned to show it to her companion. The older woman considered it with clear but wandering eyes. She was a pearl-head—maybe the woman's mother.

"Very nice," she said in a quiet voice. None of the pearl-heads I'd freed from the Queen of Hearts' commands had really recovered, but they had some sort of lives still. People had reported a few memories and little signs of their loved ones' original personalities surfacing. Maybe over time they'd become more themselves.

Theo reached the courtyard as I came down the steps outside the palace. He gave me his assured smile and dipped into a bow as he kissed my hand. "How was your visit, my queen?"

"It was good," I said. "But I'm always glad to come back home. Have there been any problems today?"

"Nothing major," he said. "A minor dispute between a couple of the city folk, a complaint from one of the Diamonds." He arched his eyebrow wryly with the latter comment. "All of it easily taken care of."

"It's a good thing I've got you to be where I can't be."

"You've certainly been covering a lot of ground yourself. Every time I see you you're either coming or going. Where are you off to now?"

There were plenty more things on my to-do list. We'd started Wonderland on the path back to joy, and the atmosphere here already felt so much lighter, but we still had a lot of distance to cover. The thought of all the responsibilities on my extensive list rose up in my head.

Having Theo's warm eyes on me reminded me that my royal blood wasn't the only connection that had kept me here. I *had* been running around a lot in the last few weeks. As his fingers twined with mine, a tingle raced up my arm. It had been days since I'd taken the time to fuel that other, more private connection. None of the items on my to-do list were so urgent I couldn't put them off for a little while.

I didn't ever want to get too busy for, er, getting busy.

"There's actually a matter in the palace you could assist me with," I said with a sly smile, squeezing his hand. "If you have a moment."

"Anything for my queen," Theo replied, his voice dipping low, full of promise.

Chess had turned from his chat with Unicorn to look our way. I made a quick beckoning gesture as I caught his eye, and he bounded over with a grin. Hatter was just heading back into the palace at the same time we reached the doors. I grasped the lapel of his suit jacket—deep green, today—with a playful tug.

"I require the use of your nimble fingers," I said with a twitch of my eyebrows.

He took the three of us in, and amusement and hunger lit together in his eyes. He tipped his hand to me. "As you wish, Your Highness."

I did have some sense of propriety. I didn't touch more than Theo's hand or Hatter's jacket as we walked—fairly quickly—through the halls to the Queen's chambers. Somehow the heat between us flickered higher all the same, fueled by anticipation.

Theo's thumb traced over my knuckles, sparking a tingle of desire. Chess teased his fingers down my back as I opened the door. It was all I could do to push past that door and make sure it'd shut behind us before I pulled my three lovers to me.

Theo's mouth crashed into mine. Hatter kissed the side of my neck. Chess eased the straps of my dress down, nibbling my shoulder in the first one's wake. I gave myself over to the rising passion, kissing Theo back hard, knocking Hatter's hat aside as my fingers tangled with his spiky hair, whimpering when Chess's mouth dipped lower to the swell of my breast.

We didn't always come together at the same time. It was nice to have just one or two men to focus on now and then. But there was nothing more delicious than the rush of having all three of them around me.

I tore my mouth from Theo's and yanked Hatter's lips to mine. My other hand fumbled with Chess's shirt. He tossed it to the side and jerked the zipper of my dress to send it pooling at my feet. Theo sucked in a breath and set to work lapping my nipples into peaks with his tongue. Pleasure shivered through my chest.

Hatter wrenched off his jacket at my tug. His hot mouth trailed to my earlobe, and Chess captured my lips. Hatter dipped his hand between my legs as Theo continued working over my breasts, and need flooded every part of me. My hips arched into Hatter's touch. My core was aching to be filled.

We'd barely made it two feet from the door. I spun myself and Theo around, shoving him up against a mahogany end table. He grinned, yanking down my panties as I loosened his pants. I freed his cock and stroked the silky skin over that rigid length, but I was too hungry for much teasing.

Theo must have felt the same way. With a shift of his arm, he hefted me up to straddle him, braced against the side table. "Whatever my queen desires," he said, his dark brown eyes glinting as he gazed at me.

I slid down onto his cock with a gasp that turned into a satisfied moan. Theo's breath hitched. He thrust up into me, gripping my side to hold me in place, bringing his lips to my throat.

I turned my head, my skin blazing everywhere Theo pressed his mouth. "Hatter," I said breathlessly.

He didn't need more encouragement than that. I'd chosen this position for a reason. Faster than should have been humanly possible, the swiftest man I knew slipped into the royal bathroom and returned with the oil I'd obtained an ample supply of. He kissed my back, and Chess reclaimed my lips.

Hatter slicked the oil over my other opening. His fingers circled and slid into my ass with the same slow, building rhythm as Theo pumped up into me. I shuddered with longing. The muscles relaxed to give way. Then the head of Hatter's cock slid into me, filling me doubly.

I clung to Theo's half-open shirt, to Chess's arm as he tweaked my breast. A cry tumbled out of me. I loved this, but every time that sensation of total fullness somehow shocked me.

Bliss rang through my nerves. I bucked against Theo, Hatter matching my pace with his own thrusts. Chess stroked down my side and up Theo's.

My third lover needed attention too. I groped at his pants, and he dropped them for me with a smirk. His expression melted into a dreamy smile when my fingers closed around his straining cock.

Chess leaned closer, pumping into my grasp, as Theo and Hatter pounded into me in time. Their hands gripped my thighs, my waist; the jerk of their hips as they filled me sent me higher and higher. As pleasure swelled from my core all through my body, for a moment before I reached my peak, I felt raised up between the three of them, lifted to great heights by their love and their desire.

I soared on and on, riding that ecstasy until it burst inside me like a firecracker. My muscles tightened with the surge of bliss, and Hatter groaned. He came with a stuttered motion, and then Theo made a choked sound and followed him over. Chess pressed his face against mine as I pumped him faster, and found his release with a hot spurt over my arm.

I came back to earth cradled between the three of them, my skin damp with sweat I didn't remember forming, giddiness racing through me. For a few minutes, we just basked in the afterglow with soft lingering kisses. Then reality started to seep back in with its reminders of all my queenly duties.

I eased off Theo and found my footing on the floor. "I guess I should get back to my royal work. I was going to check on the reconstruction of those buildings the jabberwocks burned—and I've been meaning to get out to the Topsy Turvy Woods sometime—and—"

Theo cut me off with a laugh and another kiss. "My queen," he said, his voice bright with fondness, "all of that can wait a little longer."

"We had a little talk," Chess said, walking his fingers up my side. "Made some plans for our queen who's full of plans."

"What plans?" I said, glancing around.

Hatter smiled and trailed his thumb along my jaw in a gentle caress. "You, looking-glass girl, have a bad habit of putting all your energy into taking care of everyone around you and none into taking care of yourself. Consider this an intervention. If you're not going to take care of you, then that's obviously our job."

"Come here," Theo said, guiding me deeper into my chambers to my bedroom. He nudged me onto the airy surface of the feather duvet.

Hatter vanished. Chess sat down on the bed next to me and set his broad hands on my shoulders. "If anyone can teach you how to relax, it should be me," he practically purred. His thumbs dug into the tense muscles along my spine. A different sort of pleasure radiated out from those pressure points. I sighed, letting myself sink into the massage.

"Okay, I can spare a few minutes for this."

He chuckled and kissed the spot just behind my ear as his hands continued their kneading. "We have music ready too," he said. "When you're loosened up, you can let loose on a dance floor all your own, if you'd like, like old times."

Hatter ducked into the room a moment later. I recognized the smell that came with him before I'd even gotten a look at the plate in his hands.

"Vanilla-cranberry-pine scones!" I said with delight I couldn't restrain. Various chefs and bakers had been volunteering their services in the palace, but nothing I'd tasted yet compared to my very first favorite food in Wonderland.

Hatter offered one to me with a twinkle in his eyes. As the sweet buttery dough melted in my mouth, Theo bent down beside the bed.

"I had a little Inventor inspiration," he said. "If you

want the full experience, we'll have to adjourn to the Tower one of these days, but for now…"

Something under the bed clicked. With a faint hum, the frame lifted off the floor. It hovered there, drifting gently to the side. A giggle tumbled from my lips. We were flying on it as if it were weightless, like in Theo's anti-gravity room.

Hatter and Theo scrambled up onto the bed. I sank into the warmth of my lovers, pleased from head to toe.

No matter what awaited us, I believed I could safely say that Wonderland was in very good hands—and so was I.

ABOUT THE AUTHOR

Eva Chase lives in Canada with her family. She loves stories both swoony and supernatural, and strong women and the men who appreciate them. Along with the Looking-Glass Curse trilogy, she is the author of the Their Dark Valkyrie series, the Witch's Consorts series, the Dragon Shifter's Mates series, the Demons of Fame Romance series, the Legends Reborn trilogy, and the Alpha Project Psychic Romance series.

Connect with Eva online:
www.evachase.com
eva@evachase.com